They Came

Beyond Deja Vu

They Came

Beyond Deja Vu

- A Novel -

by Walter Zajac

For Elisabeth, Andrew

Very special thank you to:
Andrew Kent, Annie Jo, Venita Ramirez, Joseph
DeBeasi, Craig McKay

Chapter One

He loved his dark red metal sedan, which was the favorite of his four toys. He lifted it up so that the tip of his nose was directly on one of the soft black tires. He held it there, absorbing the clean, sweet, yet pungent smell of the rubber. Adoringly, he ran his index finger up along the glistening silver chrome of the front bumper, then over to the driver's door which he opened slowly, seeing himself get inside.

He was laying on his stomach on the floor in the hallway, guiding the car intently along the worn grooves of the old wood slat floor near the door of Apartment 1B. He vividly imagined feeling the softness of the dark red seat underneath his butt, and the cold hardness of the red steering wheel as it obligingly responded to him spinning it sharply to the right.

On his left, the door to the cellar was open the slightest bit, and he noticed the musty odors of raw onions and potatoes, and the dirty sooty stench of coal, which sat in the various big bins in the dusty darkness at the bottom of the stairs. Cold stale air came up from the blackness swirling around his legs and into his short lederhosen, causing thousands of hard little goose bumps to rise on his soft skin. He shivered.

Whiffs of hot buttery boiled potatoes, creamy sauerkraut, and frying pork schnitzel suddenly came into his awareness. His stomach growled from hunger. Mama opened the door to Apartment 1A behind him.

He turned around and his heart raced as he felt the love in her beautiful soft brown eyes.

"Wolfi, dinner will be ready in ten minutes!" she whispered, pointing a greasy metal spatula at him.

He gave her a quick warm smile, nodded his head "yes," and continued his trip in his car. The rubber tires gave a nice smooth ride.

"Wolfgang!!"

It came from the blackness of the cellar. A harsh foreboding whisper that invaded his being.

"Wolfgang!!"

A gripping chill suddenly gushed up from his groin to the back of his neck! He shuddered.

"Wolfgang!!".

His chest was exploding. He was dizzy, about to throw up. Now the smells from 1A made him gag.

"Wolfgang!!".

His hand jerked upward. The red sedan crashed loudly onto the floor and spun around twice on its back.

"Wolfgang!!" This time it was a man's intense voice. Wolfi's whole body buzzed with deep chilling vibrations.

He tried to stand up. Wolfi's legs would not budge! Neither would his arms!

His mouth gaped open as he tried to scream. No sound came out!

"Wolfgang!!!" The voice was louder now! Powerful! Horrifying!

Summoning all his strength and courage, he again tried desperately to stand up. Nothing! He was paralyzed!

Suddenly two invisible hands grabbed him by the waist!! He looked down - his feet no longer touched the floor! The cellar door creaked slowly open with a ratcheting loud moan.

All the air gushed out of his lungs! Painful intense spasms of fear shot up his back to the top of his head and back down to his groin. In the darkness at the bottom of the stairs he glimpsed the vague outline of a man dressed from head to toe in black!

Now powerful waves of sickening electric buzzing energy were slowly and assertively floating Wolfgang down the stairs towards this terror!!

He tried desperately to scream again. Nothing!!

Then, summoning all the power he could muster, with the entirety of his being, Wolfi finally forced out a horrifying piercing scream!!!

"No!! No!! No!!"

* * *

"Wolfgang!!"

"Wolfgang!! Wake up... Hey!!! You're dreaming, sweetie". Mama shook him very gently, and picked him up to hold him close.

"Mama," he mumbled, giving her a look of deep relief.

"A man!! All black!! In the cellar!! I was scared, Mama!!" He could barely get the words out between loud sobs. His pulse was drumming ferociously inside his ears.

"You had a nightmare, sweetie. You're safe now. Come," she said soothingly. She squeezed him tight and rocked a bit on her feet. "We'll go get some hot milk."

With one hand she tossed a couple pieces of black coal into the old black free-standing stove which warmed the whole apartment. She poured some milk from a glass bottle into a saucepan, which made a metallic clunk sound as she set it on the hot stove top.

Mama plopped down heavily into one of the chairs at the dining table, her arms around Wolfgang as he sat on her lap facing her. She kissed both his cheeks tenderly a few times and stroked the back of his head. Her voice was silky and gentle.

"I love you, sweetie. Mama's here, baby. Mama's here."

The sweet smell of her lilac perfume filled his nose. In a soothing beautiful tone which reminded Wolfgang of angels, Mama began to sing to him.

"Wolfi, wise and powerful, will always find his way."

Softly but intensely, she sang the melody with burning love.

"Wolfi, wise and powerful, will always find his way."

Wolfgang took a deep breath and sighed, his body beginning to relax.

Mama continued singing. Her angelic passion declared to him that she meant every word. Wolfgang felt safe now. He felt loved, and he felt safe.

Soon his body sank limply into her chest and his eyes drooped shut.

* * *

"Wolfgang... Wolfi... Wake up... Wolfi... Hey you!!" Manfred was shaking Wolfgang roughly and impatiently.

"Breakfast is almost ready. Go to the toilet now. Come on!", demanded his cousin. Manfred was sixteen, more than ten years older than Wolfgang who saw him as his hero.

Struggling, Wolfgang poked his tired feet out from the warmth of the featherbed cover. He shivered as they touched the cold hardwood floor. The smells of boiling eggs and burning toast filled his nostrils. His empty tummy growled and vibrated his aching bladder uncomfortably as he ran to the toilet.

When Wolfi sat down at the table, Manfred shoved a faded white plate of burnt toast and a peeled soft-boiled egg towards his little cousin.

"Today's your train ride," said Manfred, trying to show enthusiasm.

"Yayyyy!!!" Wolfgang could hardly contain himself. "I get to ride a train all by myself!! I'm a big boy!"

"Yep. Big boy," Manfred said under his breath. He quickly glanced elsewhere each time Wolfgang looked in his eyes. "Eat your toast, big boy, or you'll be hungry on the train."

Wolfgang downed the egg quickly. The toast made a crunching sound as his teeth chomped into it. Suddenly there were four aggressive bangs on the apartment door! Both of them jumped in shock!

"She's really early!" Manfred was clearly annoyed.

"Hurry! Go put on your lederhosen, your white shirt, and your shoes!" he said to Wolfgang, pushing him towards the bedroom. Booming knocks reverberated through the whole apartment again, this time five.

Manfred walked to the door and opened it hesitantly.

A very large woman darkened the entire doorway.

"Guten Morgen," she said in a deep hostile tone. Good morning. "Frau Limburger, Youth Sector," she added, offering her hand for him to shake. "Where's the boy?"

"He's getting dressed," Manfred responded defensively.

The woman let out an impatient sigh and looked at her watch. She glared at Manfred as if she suspected him of something. Manfred scowled back at her for a few tense moments, then gladly walked away to see if Wolfgang was ready.

"Wolfi, it's time," he called urgently down the hall.

When he came out of the bedroom Wolfgang was unable to hide the amazement in his eyes as he took in the entirety of this giant female creature who had taken possession of the whole hallway.

"Limburger, Youth Sector," she barked stiffly and held out her hand. Wolfgang just looked at her, unable to find an appropriate response, repulsed at the thought of shaking her hand because she stunk! She actually smelled like Limburger cheese, the stinkiest of all the stinky cheeses, as if she was making an effort to live up to her name. Or, maybe it was just that she smelled like a fart.

Wolfgang stepped back a few paces. He did not like her at all. His nose was very sensitive and stinky people made him gag. She stared at him silently with cold black beady eyes, breathing hard. The red cross on her white nurse's cap and her tent-like white dress, made her appear to him like a huge white package of stinky cheese from Switzerland. He forgot momentarily that the Swiss flag actually had a red background with a white cross.

Manfred came back down the hallway carrying a raggedy small brown suitcase.

"Shall we go?" he said, making a statement rather than asking a question. He shut the apartment door firmly without locking it. They walked down the short main hall and out the front door of the building.

It was a sunny summer day in the village of Hirschberg. The sun's rays warmed Wolfi's chest and his face. Suddenly he felt the warmth of Mama's love in his heart. Wolfi was always groggy for a long time when he first woke up, and it just now occurred to him that Mama had said she would take him to the train station.

Where's Mama?!! The thought made him shiver.

The Youth Sector cheese woman grabbed Wolfgang's hand tightly as they neared the street, even though no cars were driving by. There were almost never any cars on the streets because very few people owned autos after the war. Wolfgang pulled his hand out of her grip and moved a few steps away from her as they kept walking. He wrinkled his nose at her disgusting fart smell. She promptly seized his hand again as if he was a prisoner. Wolfgang quickly got away once more. Manfred came closer and Wolfi clutched his hand eagerly. Stink woman gave in, knowing she wouldn't have a chance against the love between the boys.

The big red city bus came heaving around the corner, pulling a separate bus trailer behind. The conductor in his tattered navy blue uniform, came down the steps and out the double doors of the bus trailer. He walked authoritatively to the forward part of the bus.

"*Guten Morgen,*" he sang in a detached but commanding tone while ushering everyone into the front door. Good morning.

Wolfgang's favorite was the front seat across the isle from the driver, where he got a great view of the driver powerfully wrestling that huge black steering wheel in order to turn the massive bus around the corner! As Wolfi plunked himself down happily into that seat, the large stinky creature brutally and painfully seized his upper arm, jerking him towards the back of the bus. He stumbled as he tripped over his own foot. Tears filled his eyes and his arm stung with pain, but his fear of stink woman caused him to remain silent.

After the bus lumbered the short distance from Hirschberg into Mannheim, they saw the familiar ruins of bombed-out buildings block after block. Most of this part of the city looked this way. Some of the buildings were completely demolished, flattened, where only a huge heap of rubble indicated a building once stood there. Often there were only two adjoining jagged grey walls still standing. Glimpses of blue sky beyond, or a brief view of the bombed out structures next door, appeared through their glassless window frames. Occasionally the bus passed a deep black crater that had been created by exploding bombs.

"That one was a school," Manfred muttered in a voice choked with pain and anger, pointing at the shell of what used to be a big building on the left. "The day after there were five piles of dead bodies about twenty bodies high, lining the street in front of the school. So many buildings in the city had piles of bodies outside. I still smell it! The decomposing bloody bodies gave off a horrifying sickening rotten smell."

Wolfgang smelled it faintly too, right now. He gagged. The dirt had been so saturated with bodily fluids, burnt flesh, guts, blood, concrete dust, and charred wood, that the stench still lingered in the air, even eleven years after the war had ended!

"Mannheim and every city in Germany was eighty or ninety percent leveled, destroyed, flattened by the fucking American and British bombers, including my family's apartment!!" Manfred continued, with an intense angry sneer on his face. "Those assholes shot my dad in Italy, and their fucking bombs killed my mom in the raids here over Mannheim. I hate them!!"

Manfred wiped a tear from his cheek, hoping no one on the bus had seen it. He missed his mom horrendously and it showed through his frequent explosive anger, but he rarely talked about her. "Women, children, civilians, everybody and everything was a target for those assholes - even hospitals and churches." He wiped his face again quickly.

"It's 1956, eleven fucking years later, and we still have vast areas to rebuild! 180,000 people, over two thirds of the population of Mannheim, died in American bombing raids. Every city in Germany lost half or more of the people living in it! Women and children!! My mom!!!" His body shivered in anger and he scowled, wiping a bit of spit from his chin.

Manfred was five years old during the last year of the war, and it was clear that he remembered the horror and pain of it in vivid detail. His father had been Mama's brother. When the air raid sirens had blared that night, Manfred's mother and he hurried down to the cellar of their building. Manfred's mother then went back to the top floor to help old Frau Brandt down the stairs. Just then a massive bomb exploded and leveled the whole building, killing both ladies instantly. The rescue workers found thirty survivors and Manfred under the rubble which covered the cellar. He was coated with dust from head to toe and screaming hysterically.

After Manfred came to live with Wolfi's family, he spent long periods of time in the cellar, afraid to be upstairs. Whenever the Americans and British bombed the city again, Manfred stood on a box by one of the high basement windows of their Hirschberg apartment, looking down the hill at Mannheim as it was being destroyed. Trembling, tears in his eyes, scared to death, he had watched cascades of powerful bombs raining fiercely down on the city. Bright blinding explosions caused the basement windows to rattle violently, and the thunderous boom of each blast reverberated against his face and body.

In spite of frequent bombing raids, they still had to go into the city to shop, see the dentist, visit friends and relatives, and that's when he saw the mounds of rotting bloody bodies.

"I hate them!! Americans!! Shitty *Ahmeeeeeese*!!" Manfred prolonged the word as he hissed angrily. "Shitty *Amis*!!" he hissed again.

Every time that Manfred told these stories, Wolfi really hated the *Amis* too!

* * *

The train whistle screamed piercingly and Wolfi jumped in shock!! The monstrous black locomotive seemed to be in a rage as it pulled into the station. Its shiny black, silver and red pistons, and twenty gleaming powerful red steel wheels came to a jerking stop only five yards from where Wolfgang was standing! Suddenly the locomotive released a huge blasting *Boooooooooosh!!!!* Massive clouds of dense white steam gushed out from every point on the locomotive, enveloping Wolfgang completely. He shrieked in terror and ran several steps back, certain that he would get scalded. He didn't. No one else panicked.

Eight massive passenger cars came lunging forward one by one, each of them slamming violently into the heavy steel hitches of the car in front of it as slack was taken up between the couplers. Bam!! Bam!! Bam!! Bam!!... Wolfgang jumped in fear from the fast series of ear-splitting metallic booms, expecting the cars to be destroyed by the ones pummeling into them from behind. Sixteen double doors then banged open simultaneously, accompanied by sixteen simultaneous blaring gusts of exploding air! *Beeeeeeeeesh!!* Wolfi jumped again.

Then what seemed like hundreds of people stepped off the train cars onto the station platform, many of them running through the thick clouds of white steam.

Wolfgang almost lost his balance as people's baggage, purses, arms, and legs brushed against him.

Wolfi's nose was saturated with odors of black coal, dark smoke blasting out the top of the locomotive, engine oil, and damp steam, blending in with the vast array of fragrances from people's perfumes and pungent body odor, the mouth-watering smell of sausages roasting on the vendor's cart nearby, the aroma of freshly-baked cake and just-brewed coffee from the Bahnhof coffee shop. Wolfgang was joyously lost in all the fascinating smells, and mesmerized by the breathtaking magical sights and sounds all around him.

Suddenly a hand seized him aggressively on the neck, pulling him further away from the locomotive. "*What are you doing?!!*" the fart lady demanded fiercely. "*Get back!!*"

Her fingernails dug into his skin, causing stinging scratches as Wolfi tore himself away from her. He ran the few steps over to Manfred, who put one arm around him and patted the top of his head with his other hand. Manfred stared blankly at the train car while Wolfgang leaned into the safety of his big cousin's embrace.

"Hey!! Where's Mama?! She said she'd be here to see me off!" Wolfgang gulped and stuttered as he whined. Manfred continued staring silently ahead.

"Where's Mama?!!" Wolfgang repeated with emphasis. He shivered and goose bumps covered his skin.

Expressionless, Manfred peered briefly down at him and then looked away. He remained silent for quite some time before he finally spoke.

"She's not coming. Not feeling well," Manfred finally offered in a half-hearted weak voice, still staring at the shiny dark green rail car. "You should just enjoy your train ride."

Wolfi's heart throbbed in his chest and a tight knot seized his throat. *Is Mama mad at me? She didn't even say goodbye!*

"Come, we have to board," announced Limburger gruffly from behind Manfred. The locomotive shrieked another piercing loud whistle, as if it agreed with her. Cheese woman turned and started walking down the platform towards the end of the train, emphatically pointing her fat pale hand in that direction. Her large round bottom swaying broadly from side to side as she waddled away, like the butts of the elephants in the circus.

By the first set of doors on car number 4, Manfred stopped, faced Wolfi and knelt down. He stroked the back of Wolfgang's head once, and gave him a lingering affectionate hug, holding him very close. Wolfgang was pensively watching the conductor's round puffy cheeks as he blew his shrill whistle and ushered people towards the doors. The man strutted authoritatively in his all-black uniform while holding his quivering double chin high. His head slid forward and back again with each step he took, like the rooster that lives behind the apartments.

"Be good, have fun, Wolfi. I'll miss you." Manfred's voice cracked with emotion. A few tears ran down his face. He hugged Wolfgang tightly one more time and kissed his cheek. "I'll miss you, Wolfi."

Mama. Is she mad at me? Wolfi's heart ached.

Then in his mind he heard her beautiful soft angelic voice singing to him. He was soothed just a little bit.

"Wolfi, wise and powerful, will always find his way."
"Wolfi, wise and powerful, will always find his way."

* * *

Bam!!

Wolfgang jumped in his seat, as the sliding glass door to their compartment crashed loudly against the wall. The rooster-head conductor had shoved it open savagely.

"Anyone new here?!" he demanded loudly. "Tickets, please!" His head slid forward and back just like it did when he was walking, as he looked inquisitively at the older couple now sitting in the seats facing Wolfgang.

Wolfi's attention was diverted to the red sedan on the two-lane highway which paralleled the train tracks. The auto was driving in the same direction and at the same speed as the train, so it was always in the same place right next to their train car. He thought somehow he should be able to walk right over and get into it!

Wolfi waved a couple times to the dark-haired little girl in the back seat of the car. She grinned widely and waved back, then tapped her mom on the shoulder and pointed excitedly to Wolfi on the train. Her mom waved too, and then so did her dad who tipped his feathered dark green hat as well!

He was having a marvelous time! This was very fun! Wolfi was so glad he got to go on a train ride! He glanced briefly over at Limburger. Her fat bottom lip was drooping open and her chubby eyelids were shut. Wolfi was happy she was sleeping.

Wolfgang became absorbed in the hypnotic rhythm of the train's wheels as they raced along the tracks. Clickety clickety clickety clickety... It sounded to him like the booming drums of a big marching band, and he bounced along with them in his seat. His eyes absorbed the grand views of half-timbered houses and barnyards in passing villages, the lush green forests and meadows in the rolling hills, and he found animal shapes in the soft puffy white clouds scattered across the bright blue sky.

Bam!!

The sliding glass compartment door crashed open again, and the conductor bellowed "South Marburg, next stop!"

Limburger snorted loudly, startled out of her drooling sleep.

"*Dankeschön.* Thank you," she mumbled in a deep voice. She stood up, grabbed Wolfgang's arm gruffly, and pulled him away from the window. "We're getting off here," she commanded.

Limburger dragged him forcefully down the narrow hall of the rail car. They both lost their balance when the train came to a jerking stop.

Beeeeeeeeesh!!!! All the train's double doors exploded open simultaneously! The rail car steps were made of open metal grates and Wolfi could see right through them to the concrete platform. He stood rigidly, afraid to move. Limburger clenched Wolfgang's hand like a vice grip and jerked him violently towards the ground as she was already bounding clumsily down the steps. Wolfi almost fell on his face.

She continued to clutch Wolfgang's hand painfully during a frigid short conversation with the unshaven skinny old man sitting behind the ticket window. Wolfgang heard the man say something about "up the hill".

"How are we getting home?!" Wolfgang asked her anxiously as they started walking. He glared intently at her profile.

"We're not going home, we're going someplace else now," she snapped. Her iron grip caused a sharp pain to shoot up his elbow to his shoulder.

Limburger walked even quicker now and kept pulling him aggressively to keep up. He was becoming frightened. A stinging chill surged through his groin.

The neighborhood street turned into a dirt road which led up a steep hill, winding back and forth through multiple switchback turns. Wolfgang soon became exhausted and his legs were shaking. His heart thrashed ferociously from physical strain and fear.

Where are we going?!!

When they reached the top of the hill, Wolfgang ripped his hand out of her steel grasp and abruptly stopped walking. He crossed his arms defiantly and glowered down at the dirt.

"*I want to go home!!*" he screamed, trying his best to command her with rage. A stabbing pain streaked down through his tummy to his groin. His body buzzed and felt very heavy.

"*I have to go home!!!*" he screeched again, adeptly dodging cheese woman's attempt to grab him.

"*I have to go home, I have to go home!!!*

The ground shook with a strong boom as Limburger lunged at him with her stomping fat leg! She seized his hand again and clamped down mercilessly! The brutal pain brought tears to his eyes and he whimpered.

"We're going someplace else now!" she snapped once more. Her voice was savagely cold and empty.

Wolfi's mind raced wildly as it searched for possible explanations. *When are we going home??* His arms and legs felt monstrously heavy.

"Mama!!!" he muttered between gasping breaths, not quite loud enough for Limburger to hear him.

"Mama!!! What's happening?!" he whispered in a horror-filled fragile voice.

"Mama!!!"

He remembered Mama's warm loving hugs, and thought he could smell her delicious lilac perfume. Then he heard her soft angelic voice singing to him.

"Wolfi, wise and powerful, will always find his way."

"Wolfi, wise and powerful, will always find his way."

* * *

Wolfgang marveled at how incredibly huge this massive oak tree was! It must have been forty yards high and thirty yards across! The breeze caused its thousands of leaves to sing in an immense chorus of intensely passionate airy whispers. He had never seen anything alive that was so gigantic, nor heard such an enchanting sound. Wolfgang felt energized by the oak tree's immense power. It felt like a beautiful comforting old friend. *This must be God's tree!* he thought to himself.

Fart woman was still charging through the countryside, actually allowing him to walk freely now, but he practically had to run to keep up. His hands throbbed and stung from her previous clenches, he was totally out of breath, completely exhausted. The weather-worn ruts of the dusty old road snaked their way past God's tree and a meadow, then wound downhill through a forest.

"Here," she said suddenly, her voice moving upward in pitch as if she was asking. Then she turned onto another long dirt road.

In the distance Wolfgang heard voices, children laughing, and a girl screaming in delight.

"Ah, yes," declared Limburger.

Gradually the voices got louder, and after a while she turned again to walk up an embankment which was covered with the green and faded-yellow colors of hundreds of stubby chamomile plants. Their sweet fresh scent filled the air.

Further up the hill on a grassy knoll to the right, at least 30 kids were riding and frolicking on the most humongous seesaw that he had ever imagined!! It was a giant log that was almost 2 feet thick, 20 yards long, with a 2-yard high fulcrum at the center. Fifteen kids sitting in a long row on one end screamed in unison and bounced precariously up into the air as that part of the log rose up 3 yards toward the sky! At the same time the other end of the colossal tree trunk pummeled down so hard against the grass that the ground shook!

"Bwah!" exclaimed Wolfi loudly, his eyes fixated on the seesaw. He stumbled into Limburger and tripped on her foot, gagging as her stench filled his lungs again. She grunted angrily and shoved him in the direction of an old wooden building on the left whose sides were plastered with tattered grey wooden shingles that desperately needed paint. They walked through the chipped and faded dark green double doors.

"We are here to see Frau Sandmann," fart woman announced impatiently to the girl at the end of the hall.

"*Jawohl.* Yes, ma'am, this way," responded the mild-mannered girl in a soft voice. She led them silently up a worn creaky staircase to an office overlooking the grassy knoll and seesaw. She motioned for them to sit down in two chairs that were sandwiched between a couple of tall lush-green plants. The chairs faced an ancient shabby brown desk that was cluttered with piles of documents and notebooks.

"She'll be right with you," said the girl, and quietly walked away.

Soon they heard quick footsteps bounding up the staircase and a short stocky woman in a modest grey and green pattern dress entered the room. She held out her hand to Limburger and said, "Sandmann. Headmistress."

"Limburger. Youth Sector," replied Cheese Woman as she stood up to shake the petite Headmistress's hand. "Good day, Frau Sandmann".

"*Guten Tag*, Frau Limburger. How was your journey?" asked Frau Sandmann politely, wincing a bit as she noticed the large white-clad woman's foul odor.

Limburger nodded her head and grunted. "Good."

"Ah, this must be Wolfgang." Frau Sandmann turned to face him. "Welcome, Wolfgang."

How does she know my name?! Wolfi thought, very distressed.

"I want to go home now!!!" he yelled in a commanding loud voice as he suddenly bolted to a standing position.

Frau Sandmann looked him up and down sternly for a few tense moments. Her short quickly exhaled breaths were the only thing that broke the silence. The brash authority in her dilated fierce green eyes subdued him for now. Quietly she focused on reading and then signing the documents which Limburger had just handed her. She gave some of the papers back to Limburger and the two women exchanged some words in half-whispered voices.

Limburger's white-draped elephant butt then waddled towards the door. When she got there she turned politely saying, *"Auf Wiedersehen"* to the Headmistress, and threw an insincere "goodbye, Wolfgang" in his direction.

"I want to go home now!!! *My Mama's waiting for me! I have to go home!!!"* Desperately, he screamed at Frau Sandmann, his voice shaking. His heart raced wildly. *Nothing makes sense today!!!* He absolutely hated Limburger stink lady, but suddenly as she walked out he wondered if she was his best chance of getting home again!

"I want to go home!!!" he demanded once more in a rage.

Frau Sandmann came over to the corner of the desk where he was defiantly posturing. She knelt down and lightly caressed his upper arms in silence for a few moments. Warmly but somberly, she gazed into his eyes. Wolfgang trembled, his torso and legs shook visibly. Tears ran down both cheeks.

"Wolfgang, sweetheart...," she paused to gather her thoughts and find the right words.

"Wolfgang, sweetheart... you're not going home".

Wolfi's stomach plummeted down to his feet.

What??!!!

His chin quivered. He shuddered.

What??!!!

"Your Mama has asked that you live here with us," she continued. "Your Mama is very, very sick, and you won't be going home any more."

Wolfgang glared at her in total disbelief.

What??!!!

What??!!!

A biting chill overwhelmed his entire body, his knees buckled, and he stumbled forward into the Headmistress's big droopy bosoms. His heart was exploding!! *This is insane!!!*

"I want to go home now!!!" his voice cracked as he screamed the words at the top of his lungs!!

Hysterical, he lunged towards the office door to run after Limburger and get back home!! Frau Sandmann was way too quick for him, jumping up to catch him easily in an iron grip with both her hands.

"I *have...* to go... *home!!!*" he was barely able to force the words out between sobs.

Wolfi hopped up and down maniacally in Sandmann's grasp, screaming and wailing!!

"Calm down now, Wolfgang!" Frau Sandmann tried her best to use a soothing calm voice. Wolfi continued his insane bawling and screaming. She attempted to hug him, assertively pulling his head into her supple chest. Wolfgang refused to be embraced and jerked away immediately, but her strength and vast experience had him quickly locked in her vice grip again.

Frau Sandmann almost whispered now, "I think that you could really use a nap. You're tired from your long..."

"No!! I have to go home!! I have to go home!!" Wolfgang was screaming again, desperately wanting to take his power back!

Frau Sandmann walked to the door and called down the stairs, "Julia! Will you come up here please?"

"*Jawohl,* Frau Sandmann," called a 12-year-old girl's voice faintly from below.

Wolfi heard the muffled sounds of dishes being stacked and clanging silverware. The delicious aromas of hot pork and sauerkraut wafted into his nose as the girl's light footsteps up the stairs got increasingly louder.

As the girl entered the office she looked warmly at Wolfgang and smiled. It was the one who had led them upstairs.

"Julia, Wolfgang's going to take a nap. Please take him to one of the beds in the storeroom," ordered Frau Sandmann.

"*Jawohl,* Frau Sandmann. Yes, ma'am," she replied softly.

* * *

There were no windows in the room. Just inside the door cardboard boxes and wooden crates were stacked in sloppy piles, and quite a few worn dusty chairs looked as if they had been thrown into the room. Laundry was hanging on three lines that stretched wall-to-wall at the far end. Julia guided him gently toward one of the two single beds by the clothes lines.

She knelt down next to the bed and looked warmly into his eyes. Tenderly, she put her hands on both sides of Wolfi's head and pulled him towards her, kissing his forehead and both his cheeks lightly.

"I know", she said softly, and then held him close for a few moments. Wolfi fell gratefully into her embrace.

Julia turned down the featherbed cover, then unbuttoned the straps of his Lederhosen and pulled the pants down. Her touch felt full of love and kindness to Wolfi.

"Get in," she said, holding up the top end of the cover. Wolfgang climbed hesitantly into the bed. Julia sat down next to him and gave him a long hug. He snorted and began to cry again, as his arms latched on to her and squeezed her with desperation. She planted a few more affectionate kisses on his cheek. Her skin and soft sandy-blond hair smelled like fresh air and fragrant sweet wildflowers.

Julia began to sit up. Wolfgang frantically grabbed her blouse and almost ripped it.

"Don't go!!" pleaded Wolfgang. *"I don't want to be alone!!"*

"Hey!! Wolfgang. Stop!" Julia pulled his hand off her blouse. "If I stay, Frau Sandman will be mad! I have to go back to class!"

Julia lovingly laid her hand on his chest for a minute to pacify him, and slowly stood up. "Go to sleep!" she whispered softly in his direction, just before she opened the door.

Wolfi heard her spin the light switch over and the room went black. There was a faint clunk as she closed the door behind her. Wolfi smelled her lingering sweet freshness on his cheek. He shivered.

Some light from the hallway was shining through under the door. Now he noticed dozens of arms and legs hanging menacingly all around him on the laundry lines.

He gripped the covers fiercely with both hands as he pulled them over his head and whimpered. The saliva in his mouth tasted distorted and somehow electric. He gagged as he noticed the musty semi-sweet odor of the laundry blending with the moldy stench of this room. He heard his pulsating heart pounding against his eardrums in a hypnotic tribal rhythm. He saw himself standing in a freezing white nothingness. Utterly alone. Abandoned. The bitter wind howled. He shivered.

He poked his face out from under the covers. There! In the darkness, one set of hanging arms moved!!

Mama!!!

Severe chills ran up and down his spine and his entire body was now buzzing with terror!

The floor made a cracking sound! Wolfi screamed and gasped for air!

Panicked, he held his breath and feverishly listened for sounds in the darkness. The ominous tribal drumming of his pulse against both eardrums was the only thing he heard now.

"Mama!" he cried anemically.

What is happening to me?!!

He was unimaginably exhausted. His eyes drooped shut. Immediately he burst them back to a wide-open position and stiffened his body.

But, soon he was flying playfully among the clouds.

Chapter Two

"Wolfgang!!".

It came from the blackness of the cellar. The voice was adamant, invasive, a dark harsh foreboding hiss.

"Wolfgang!!"

A gripping chill suddenly gushed up from his groin to the top of his head.

"Wolfgang!!".

Wolfi was dizzy. The aromas of food coming from 1A made him gag.

"Wolfgang!!".

His hand jerked upward. His red sedan crashed loudly onto the floor and spun around twice on its back.

"Wolfgang!!" This time it was a man's intense voice. Wolfi's body buzzed with deep chilling vibrations.

He tried to stand up. Wolfi's legs would not budge! Neither would his arms!

His mouth gaped open as he tried to scream. No sound came out!

"Wolfgang!!!" The voice was louder now! Powerful! Terrifying!

Summoning all his strength and courage, he again tried desperately to stand up. Nothing! He was paralyzed!

Then two invisible hands grabbed him by the waist!! His feet no longer touched the floor! The cellar door let out a ratcheting loud moan as it slowly creaked open by itself.

All the air gushed out of his lungs! Painful intense spasms of fear shot up his back to the top of his head and back down to his groin. In the darkness at the bottom of the stairs he saw the vague outline of a man who from head to toe was dressed in black!

Powerful waves of electric buzzing energy were assertively yet slowly levitating Wolfgang down the stairs towards this horror!!

Again, he tried desperately to scream. Nothing!!

By now he was halfway down the stairs! His heart thundered explosively in his chest. He gagged violently. His body was dripping with sweat, trembling savagely.

Then the nightmarish black form reached his arms out to Wolfi!!!

"Wolfgang!!"

It was a piercing hoarse whisper.

Summoning all the power he could muster, with the entirety of his being, Wolfi finally forced out a horrifying piercing scream!!!

"No!! No!! No!!"

* * *

Wolfgang heard a voice in the distance, "*Hallo! Hallo,* boy!"

Suddenly he noticed someone was touching his arm! He popped one eye open and saw the face of a brown-haired boy peering down at him intently!

"Ahhhh!!" Wolfgang screamed in shock!

Wolfi jerked up into a sitting position. In a quivering voice he demanded, "Where am I?!"

"Bliss Cottage!" the brown-haired boy answered energetically.

Wolfi rubbed his eyes with his fists as if he were turning round faucet knobs. Now he saw the laundry hanging over the bed and remembered Frau Sandmann's voice telling him he could not go home! His stomach sank to his knees again and his heart hammered anguished blows against his rib cage.

"What's Bliss Cottage?" he blurted out after a few moments. He was totally bewildered, still half asleep, staring down at the featherbed cover.

"Bliss Cottage Orphanage," the boy answered. His bushy brown hair flipped forward as he nodded his head for emphasis.

Wolfi didn't understand.

"Mama!!"

Wolfgang's heart was racing and he choked as he whispered to himself, hoping the boy hadn't noticed. Goose bumps covered his body now.

Barely audible over the howling of the freezing wind in his mind, echoes of erie voices whispered his frenzied thoughts.

Cottage - Bliss - Seesaw - Forest - Hansel and Gretel - Witch!!

"Get dressed!" urged the brown-haired boy, smacking Wolfgang's arm.

Dazed, Wolfi stood up and slowly pulled on his Lederhosen. He tried his best to remember if he had seen a cottage anywhere outside. *What's a bliss cottage?*

Wolfi really hated looking stupid in front of others, but he had to know what that other word meant, the word he'd never heard before. Wolfgang eyed the boy carefully for a moment. He appeared to be about Wolfi's age and seemed nice enough.

Wolfgang shivered, and then quietly and timidly asked.

"What's orphanage?"

The boy's jaw dropped and his eyes shot out a look of disbelief. *"You don't know what an orphanage is?!"* he snorted disdainfully.

He repeated it two more times with a twisted sneer on his face.

Wolfi felt really very stupid now, and his face turned beet red.

"Don't forget your shoes," said the boy. Very impatiently he was watching Wolfgang's every move. Wolfgang couldn't look him in the eyes.

"Frau Sandmann wants to see you," said the brown-haired boy as he guided him along the upstairs hallway.

Wolfgang's heart jumped. Sandmann! She was scary!

The boy knocked timidly on the wooden frame of her open office door. There was no response, so he motioned for them to wait obediently right outside the door. Wolfgang marveled again as he glimpsed the giant log seesaw through the office window.

"Oh, Wolfgang!" Frau Sandmann said absentmindedly when her stomping feet reached the top of the staircase. Her eyes were focused on something sitting on her desk as she walked briskly past the boys.

"Benjamin, here, will take you over to the boys' dorm area. You and he are to wait there until the other boys and counselors come back from their walk." Her high heel shoes scuffled loudly against the wood floor as she rushed past them again to call loudly down the stairs.

"Frau Reichert! Frau Reichert!! I need your assistance up here with some documents."

Wolfgang stared at the accordion-like wrinkles on the side of Sandmann's neck as she contorted it trying to see around the corner downstairs.

"I have to go home," he managed to get out in a shaky tone.

Brown-haired Benjamin yanked firmly on Wolfgang's white shirt sleeve. He motioned very nervously towards the bottom of the stairs with his face, and held the side of his index finger up against his lips.

There was no answer from downstairs. Sandmann abruptly blasted like a river boat's fog horn, *"Frau Reichert!!!"*

Wolfi jumped in fear, shocked by how loud she was!

Benjamin jerked Wolfgang's arm again, harder than before. They both lost their balance and almost tripped down the stairs!

"Careful, boys," warned Frau Sandmann, then spun around and scuffled loudly back into her office without looking at them.

"You don't want to get in trouble!!" Benjamin whispered with grave intensity. His hand trembled a little as he pointed down the stairs.

When they approached the other ugly gray building further up the hill, Benjamin offered bluntly, "This is the boy's building, and the other one is the girl's building. The dining room and the classrooms are in the girl's building. So is Frau Sandmann. She's a girl."

"Come on!" said Benjamin as he bounded up the staircase to the second floor, stopping about half-way.

Inside the building, it smelled like fresh paint, and that funky stench of kids; whiffs of urine and poop, traces of vomit, drool, stinky feet, a faint bouquet of soap, and a touch of the sweet fruity fragrance of bubble gum.

Wolfgang was so weak with fear he could barely move his heavy legs. He did not want to go up those stairs and further into the fearsome unknown!! He was dizzy. He held tightly on to the handrail so as not to fall.

"Come on, boy!" said Benjamin again, quite impatiently, and then disappeared around a corner upstairs.

Wolfgang wrinkled his nose at the disgusting smells in here. Clumsily, one agonizing step at a time, he conquered the staircase all the way to the top.

Suddenly, Benjamin came running around the corner, his feet stomping thunderously!

"Ahhh!!!" shrieked Wolfgang, startled out of his daze. His body jerked in shock. His face turned white.

"Are you a fraidycat?!" taunted Benjamin with two cocky twists of his hips.

Wolfgang winced with pain. He said nothing.

He followed Benjamin through a doorway which opened to a big room that held about twenty beds lined up in two rows against the walls.

Just inside the door were two large, freshly painted yellow and red wooden boxes that were brimming over with toys.

"Come on! Let's play!" Benjamin said, pointing at them enthusiastically. He hopped twice and then slid along the hardwood floor on his knees towards one of the boxes.

Wolfgang had never seen so many toys at once! He could hardly believe his eyes, but he was not smiling. Benjamin was hastily pulling multi-colored toys out of one of the boxes. Wolfgang knelt hesitantly down in front of the other box.

"Whose are these?!" asked Wolfgang. He wondered how anybody could own so many toys!

"They're ours! All of ours. You can play with any of them!" answered Benjamin with both delight and impatience. "The American soldiers gave them to us."

American soldiers! A shivering tremor ran through Wolfgang's body! He thought of Manfred's stories of American bombs and piles of dead bodies!

"Are there soldiers here?!" he asked, his eyes wide with fear.

"No, stupid!! They're not here! They're at their soldier places!!" answered Benjamin, clearly agitated by Wolfi's ignorance.

Wolfgang stared into the box. His mind reeled from confusion. He was terrified.

What kind of a place is this?!!

Why do they keep children here?!!

Why do the horrifying American soldiers come here?!! When are they coming again?!!

His legs gave way and he collapsed into a sitting position against one of the boxes. His hands trembled. Stabbing pains shot through his heart. Beads of sweat tickled him as they ran down his lower back.

Wolfgang's incoherent gaze landed on a large red metal firetruck. He rolled it once along the floor between his legs and stopped. He felt paralyzed.

Mama!?

Why am I here?!

Why??! Why am I here?!!

He was exhausted. His eyes drooped slowly shut.

* * *

Whaaam!!

Wolfgang's head jerked forward as he felt a stinging powerful slap on the back of his neck! Then, instantly, the metal fire truck was ripped out of his hands, badly scraping the skin on two of his fingers.

"Hey, boy, that's mine!!" yelled a slender but tough-looking kid with jet-black hair. He quickly walked off with the truck, arrogantly doing a little winner's dance as he moved.

Electric jolts that felt like piercing knives shot up into Wolfi's head, the skin on the back of his neck sizzled and stung from being slapped, his badly scratched fingers burned with pain. But, more than anything else, his heart ached!! Tears rolled down his cheeks. His chin quivered uncontrollably.

Still in a sleepy stupor, Wolfi was just now noticing that the floor had been shaking and booming stomping noises were all around him! A large number of boys were thrashing wildly around the corner and into the room, yelling and aggressively shoving each other! Wolfgang pulled his legs up into a fetal position and slid back against the toy box.

"Frank!!!" yelled an attractive young woman with sandy blond hair from the doorway. "Frank, come back here, now!!" she belted out.

"What did I just see you do?!" she yelled at the top of her lungs and swiftly raced after him. Brutally she grabbed him by the straps of his Lederhosen! His shirt made a ripping sound as he tried belligerently to escape her grip.

"We have told you hundreds of times that those toys belong to all of you!! *That fire truck does NOT belong to you!!" she* screamed as loudly and authoritatively as she could! "Now, you apologize to this boy. *Right now!!"* she demanded.

The lady tore the firetruck out of Frank's hands, seized him irately by the arm and brutally dragged him back to where Wolfgang was sitting. She put the firetruck down next to Wolfgang's leg and said, "There!"

Wolfi's face was bright red from embarrassment and anger. He was still sobbing and snorting. He glared angrily at Frank.

"Frank!?" the blond lady demanded, still looking for an apology.

After some long drawn-out moments of staring at the floor, Frank quietly and very insincerely said "sorry". Just as the lady turned her gaze toward

Wolfgang, Frank jerked himself free of her grip and ran off to the other end of the big room.

"Are you Wolfgang?" The lady bent down on her knees and gently touched his shoulder. The sweet light smell of carnations drifted into his nose from her chest. He felt the warmth coming from her body.

"Yes?" he responded meekly and very uncertain.

How does this lady know my name already, just like Sandmann?? Again a freezing electric chill ran up his back.

She moved closer to him on her knees and tenderly wrapped her arms around his torso. Her soft warm carnation cheek against his and her loving embrace caused him to promptly burst into loud sobs once more.

"You're gonna be just fine," she said soothingly, lightly stroking his back and patting his hip. "It's all right."

"I wanna go home!!" pleaded Wolfgang in a terrified raspy whisper. His spastically contorting lips made it hard to form the words. Tears were streaming down his face. His heart hammered against his rib cage.

"I'm sorry, sweetheart, but you're gonna be living here now," the lady said in a soft and kind voice. "Frau Sandmann says your mother is really very sick, and you can't go home,"

"She's not sick!! I was with her last night! She wasn't sick!! Mama's waiting for me!! I have to go home!!" His words came out in a high-speed desperate torrent.

"You can't go home, sweetie, I'm very sorry," the lady answered with genuine compassion while caressing his cheek. She shook her head slowly from side to side as if doing so would help him understand what she meant.

Suddenly it occurred to him that this place is called cottage and it's in a meadow in the forest! *Hansel and Gretel!! The evil witch lives in a cottage in a meadow in the forest! And, she eats children!!! Frau Sandmann, is she the witch?!!!* Wolfi gagged twice. Sweat blanketed his forehead.

"You don't have to worry, you're safe." It was as if this lady knew his thoughts. Gently she brushed Wolfgang's blond bangs away from his blue eyes and wiped his wet cheeks. "I'm going to be with you, Wolfgang, I will take good care of you. You're safe here. My name is Fräulein Edel."

She warmly kissed his cheek and squeezed his head affectionately between her hands. "Come on, let's meet the other boys, shall we?" Fräulein Edel proposed with a forced awkward smile.

Wolfgang rubbed his eyes and wiped his nose on his sleeve. "But, soon I can go home?!"

"What the hell is going on here?!!" boomed a powerful man's voice from the doorway. The floor seemed to explode under each of his feet as he thundered into the room! "Frank!! Stop hitting him! Robert! Put that gun down, you're gonna hurt somebody! All of you!! Quiet!!"

"Quiet!!" The man was roaring now, a bit crazed. *"I need you boys to behave!!"* He lunged forward and briskly took the toy gun away from Robert. "Do you understand?!" he said to the whole group while pointing the gun their way.

"Yes, Herr Schmidt," murmured a few of the boys half-heartedly and then went on giggling, poking and teasing each other.

He glanced at Wolfgang, then at Fräulein Edel, pointed vaguely in Wolfgang's direction, and said tersely, "Is this the new boy, uh... Wolfgang?"

He knows my name too?! Why do they keep children here?!!

Wolfgang shivered as he looked into the man's eyes. He noticed a large brown lumpy mole in the middle of his pale right cheek. In the center of the mole a thick black hair had grown so long that it curled back toward his face. Dense curly black hair covered his head like a poodle.

"Hello Wolfgang, I'm Herr Schmidt," he said with a faint stiff smile. He extended his hand for Wolfgang to shake.

Wolfgang wondered if he ever clipped the mole hair.

"Why don't you come meet the other boys." Herr Schmidt lifted Wolfgang up to a standing position.

"I was going to introduce him," offered Fräulein Edel.

"Yes, good."'

Fräulein Edel loudly clapped her hands together a few times, and then almost yelled, "Boys, listen please." Gradually the ruckus subsided.

"This is Wolfgang and he's new today," she announced. "Wolfgang, I'll let you learn everyone's name as you play with them. You'd never remember them all now."

Some of the boys glared at him briefly, the others didn't even acknowledge he was there. They hated new kids! It was hard enough to get affection and attention from the few adults at this place.

"Wolfgang," said Herr Schmidt, "play with the boys until we go down to eat supper."

Schmidt walked over to Fräulein Edel, whispered something into her ear, and wrapped his arm affectionately around her waist. She tilted her head close to his and smiled self-consciously as she looked into his eyes and at his pink lips. Wolfi saw Schmidt's hand squeeze her butt cheek as they walked out the door together.

Leaning with his back against the wall by the toy boxes, Wolfgang stood shaking, silent, terrified, insanely and excruciatingly alone. His heart was seething with the horrific agony of being abandoned and his gut was filled with intense rage! Tears zig-zagged down his cheeks.

"Ah, look at the little cry baby!" someone growled. It was Frank. He moved in closely and started jabbing Wolfi repeatedly with his fists on the shoulders and chest. Frank shoved his face within an inch of Wolfgang's face, and spit as he jeered indignantly, "Are you crying for your mommy?! Poor little baby. He's crying for his mommy. Look at the little baby!"

Frank had him cornered. Wolfgang could not escape. Quickly Frank's fist jabs turned into violent painful punches!

A rush of adrenaline-fueled rage surged through Wolfi! Powerfully he thrust his arms upward to clear away Frank's punching fist! Frank jumped back abruptly, clearly caught off guard by Wolfgang's fury.

"Hey!! He hit me!" Frank shrieked.

"Frank!! You leave Wolfgang *alone!!*" Fräulein Edel bellowed as she poked her head around the corner of the doorway. She glared at him authoritatively for a few moments. His reputation obviously preceded him.

"You hit me, and I get into trouble?!" Frank whispered viciously. Wolfgang jerked his head to one side as Frank's spitting lips almost touched his nose.

"We'll see about that. I'll get you. You wait. *I'll get you!"* Frank punched him angrily in the chest one more time and then threw the firetruck into a toy box.

"Supper!! Line up!!" shouted Herr Schmidt, clapping his hands forcefully as he stomped back into the room.

Twenty boys' racing feet wildly pummeled the floor with loud booms as they tossed their toys back into the wooden boxes and ran to form a line near the door.

* * *

Fräulein Edel showed Wolfgang to a chair at a table for six, and then walked to the other side of the large dining hall. Benjamin and Frank and two other boys were already sitting here. The sixth chair stayed empty.

Frank grabbed Benjamin by the arm, pulled him close, and whispered something in his ear. They giggled and both stared at Wolfgang. A lightning bolt of intense pain shot through Wolfi's heart.

Wolfi watched intently as a number of women and girls came through the kitchen doors with serving bowls of food for each of the 24 tables. It smelled strange to Wolfgang, not like food he was used to. But his tummy growled from hunger.

A pretty girl of six or seven gently placed a big steaming bowl of white rice on the table. Her soft light blond hair fell forward over her face as she put the rice down. She straightened up and stared curiously into Wolfgang's blue eyes for a moment, a shy smile on her lips, and then giggled and skipped away. Wolfgang's heart smiled and his face tingled! His eyes followed her every step until she disappeared behind the kitchen door. An older girl brought slices of farmer's rye bread, another one delivered creamed cucumber salad, and a pimply-faced teenager set a pitcher of milk on the table very carefully.

Wolfgang suddenly jumped in his seat as the chair next to him moved, its feet making a loud trumpeting noise on the wood floor! A very odd-looking woman clumsily plopped her butt down into it. Wolfi scanned the paleness of this creature's very narrow pockmarked face, the red veins in the whites of her bulging black eyes, and her large crooked thin nose. Her black hair was greasy and frizzy. A jagged wart reigned over the left side of her enormous oily snout.

She looks just like a witch!! His heart was pounding heavily again. *Is SHE the witch?!! What is this place?!!* A stinging freezing chill invaded his groin, his chest, and his head.

"Good evening, boys," said the witch creature while staring across the room. Her chair made two more trumpeting noises as she shifted her weight to pull it close. No one responded to her greeting.

The witch woman began tapping her fingers on the scruffy wooden table, and awkwardly shot quick nervous glances around the dining hall. The other boys continued to giggle and fidget, sometimes pointing at Wolfgang.

Wolfgang's mouth was watering. *Why isn't she serving the food?* His stomached growled angrily.

"Quiet, please!!!!" Frau Sandmann stood up and clapped her hands loudly on the other side of the dining hall.

"Children! Be quiet now!" she bellowed again, still clapping. Gradually the blanket of noise in the room subsided.

The moment Sandmann had finished saying grace and sat down, an explosive wall of sound filled the air again.

"So. We'll serve the newcomer first," said the witch lady, as she dumped a scoop of the hot rice onto Wolfgang's plate. Her thin lips formed a faint smile revealing crooked yellow teeth that were coated with a pasty white film. A little saliva bubble formed between her upper lip and her teeth in one corner of her mouth. She was scary and repulsive! Wolfi gagged.

Hungrily he picked up his fork and tasted the rice.

Yech! Cinnamon!! Salty, no sugar!! That was like nothing he's ever eaten and it tasted horrible!! The witch and the other boys were devouring it. Wolfi gagged again.

"Oh, I feel so bad!" witch woman blared out suddenly, with a yodel in her voice. "I'm sorry, Wolfgang, I didn't introduce myself to you. My name is Frau Reichert."

This witch knew his name already, too! Wolfi's chin quivered and his heart raced again. *What kind of a place is this?!!* The witch looked past him off into the distance as she spoke.

"This is Frank, and this is Benjamin, Werner, and Robert," she said pointing vaguely towards them. Wolfi quickly wiped a tear from his cheek hoping they hadn't noticed it. The boys continued shoveling big bites of food into their mouths without looking up.

The creamed cucumber salad tasted quite good and he began thrusting large bites vigorously into his mouth.

"Don't do that!" said Frau Reichert in an agitated tone. Wolfgang glanced up and saw that she was looking at him. He didn't understand.

"Don't do that! Don't hit your teeth with your fork! It gives me chills!" she said forcefully.

Wolfi had no idea that he was hitting his teeth with his fork. *Damn!!* (That's what Papa would say) *I hate this ugly woman!!*

He took a few more bites.

"I said do *not* do that!" This time she yelled. Her frightening face was red.

Wolfgang had no idea that he had done it again! He'd never thought about how his fork was put into his mouth.

"Eat your rice! You haven't touched it!" she commanded.

Wolfgang managed a slight nod, but was unable to speak. *I hate this place!!* Another tear rolled down his face.

Mama!! What is this place?!

Wolfi stared at his plate. He pictured himself hugging Mama's waist as she fixed supper and basked in her powerful love for a while.

"Frau Reichert, what's wrong here?" Frau Sandmann boomed as she approached the table authoritatively.

Wolfgang jumped, startled out of his daydream. He noticed that the other chairs were empty now and so was most of the dining hall.

"Wolfgang won't eat his rice."

"Wolfgang!" said Sandmann stooping forward to put her face close to his. She continued in a stern demanding voice, "Everyone here is expected to eat everything on his plate, so that they remain healthy. With the little money we can bring in, we do our best to feed you and keep you children healthy and alive. Your job is to eat the food and be grateful! Do you understand?!"

His eyes fixed on the table top, Wolfgang nodded his head slightly and shivered, tears rolling down his face. His heart ached.

"Now," she said looking briefly at the floor, then glaring at him, "I'm going to make an exception because you're new and you've had a hard day. But from now on you have to eat everything on your plate, always! Do you understand?!"

His head twitched slightly sideways as he tried weakly to nod yes.

"Now, run outside and go play with the other children."

* * *

He snorted inward deeply through his nose to clear it of mucus, wiped the tears off his face with his shirt sleeves, and walked slowly up the grassy hill.

At the top he found a place to stand near the middle of the giant log seesaw. His eyes and nostrils flared open as he took in the massive dimensions of this thing! Suddenly the ground under his feet shook with a large boom as one end of the enormous log slammed thunderously down against the grass!

The fifteen kids sitting on the end that was up in the air seemed to be touching the clouds! A few were actually running from side to side to put more weight on whichever end that was up, so that it would crash back down even harder! Each time it smashed into the ground again the butts of the fifteen kids sitting on the other end bounced so high into the air that it looked like they would fall off and get injured for sure! Wolfi was mesmerized by the frightening movements of this monster.

He felt someone staring from his right, and glanced over to see the soft pretty face and wavy blond hair of the shy girl who had brought the disgusting rice to his table. She was smiling at him from a couple yards away. She saw him looking in her direction, then tried to brush off the brown stain on the front of her white blouse, and adjusted the waistband of her faded red skirt. When she looked up again Wolfi connected with her sparkling jade green eyes and felt warm tingles in his tummy and groin! His heart beat faster!

He smiled back at her hesitantly, looked down at the grass for a few moments, and then again into her eyes. She continued to gaze at him warmly but silently. Usually he absolutely hated it when someone stared, but her presence, her attention, felt marvelous! She can stare.

"Hey, Wolfgang," called another girl's voice from behind him. The shy girl suddenly turned and walked away in silence.

Wolfi spun around. It was Julia! She was grinning and waving! Julia came up to him and put her hand on his shoulder affectionately. He felt the warmth of her soul through her skin and a brief moment of happiness rushed into his heart.

"Hello, Wolfgang," she said in that sweet voice which had comforted him in the store room. "Are you having fun?"

Wolfgang managed only a slight nod of his head as he looked into her affectionate blue eyes. He was distracted by the glowing warmth inside his tummy which also radiated in the air between him and her. She returned his gaze warmly for a few moments and he finally smiled.

"Robert, be careful, you're gonna fall off running like that!" Julia suddenly yelled towards the seesaw. "All you boys are crazy! I can't believe how you..."

Wolfi no longer heard her words. He was still staring, completely spellbound by the magic of her. She noticed his adoring gaze and wrapped her hand around his. The sensuous warmth of it was fabulous! His head rested lightly against her bicep for a moment.

A breeze swept towards him from behind her and her alluring wildflower scent filled his being. His cheek felt the tender kisses she had planted on it in the storage room. A euphoric lightness swirled in his tummy and groin. The material between two buttons on her blouse had separated a bit and most of a small naked breast greeted his eyes. His heart thumped with delight! Wolfi wondered if the skin on her chest was as soft as her hands were. He thought of Aunt Sasha's daughter, Elke, his best friend who lived upstairs back home and how much they both loved playing doctor in the cellar. He peered down at Julia's thighs and wondered if she would like that too.

"Do you want to get on?" he heard her say. Immediately he took his eyes off her thighs!

"No!! No!!" Wolfgang said emphatically, shaking his head and looking sheepishly at the ground. His face was bright red.

"Too scary, huh?" said Julia. Now he realized she was talking about the seesaw.

Wolfgang nodded and looked up into her shining blue eyes. Butterflies danced in his tummy and he smiled at her self-consciously.

"Well, I'm gonna go play. You have fun watching," she said, and skipped away over the grass.

The hand she had been holding now felt very cold. His heart ached.

Chapter Three

"Wolfgang, come with me," said Fräulein Edel when he reached the top of the stairs. She took his hand gently and walked a few steps to a baby's crib just inside the door of the big dormitory room. She got down on one knee and began unbuttoning his shirt. Wolfgang was shocked when he looked over and saw his own blue striped pajamas laying in the crib!

I'm actually spending the night here?! The reality of that had not occurred to him until this moment. His heart pounded wildly as he remembered that the stinky cheese lady had been carrying a small brown suitcase. Then he spotted it, sitting on the floor. His tummy sank to his knees.

"Am I sleeping in this?" Wolfgang pointed to the crib. He was pouting. His chin quivered.

"Yes," answered Fräulein Edel in a matter-of-fact tone, "I know you're a big boy, but it's the only empty bed we have for a while."

"*I don't wanna sleep in a baby's crib!! I'm turning six years old very soon!!*" he bellowed furiously! Wolfi's knees trembled and he began to cry again. Fräulein Edel stroked his arms for a moment, then quietly continued undressing him until he was naked.

Frank came trotting by just then and taunted, "Look at the little cry baby who has to sleep in a crib!"

Wolfgang's face turned bright red again. He felt extremely vulnerable standing there naked, he was angry, and he really hated Frank!! Then he realized that Frank was also naked and so were most of the other boys, some of whom were stomping across the hall and into the big washroom. There was frantic commotion and reverberating racket everywhere.

Fräulein Edel walked him over to the urinals, showed him where to pee and then she hurried off to check on another boy. He felt the brittle coldness of the concrete floor on his bare feet, and he looked down to make sure he hadn't stepped in anything wet. He shivered. It reeked of pee and poop and soap in here. He stood there for quite some time before he could relax enough to actually urinate in the midst of all the chaos.

When he was done Fräulein Edel came over, picked him up and placed him into one end of a very long white sink which had eight rusty faucets along its length. Wolfgang panicked that he might fall out of the sink and onto the hard concrete floor! He clamped down hard on her forearms and his fingernails dug deeply into her skin.

"Owww!!" she protested loudly, and quickly removed his hands. She turned on the tarnished faucet next to him, adjusted the temperature as the water flowed over her hand, and then scooted him under it. She picked up a bar of soap and a washcloth and began washing him off. The soap smelled a bit like Mama's lilac perfume.

Mama!! Where are you?! Why am I here?! A stabbing jolt of pain exploded in his chest just below his rib cage.

Herr Schmidt was hastily bathing a red-headed boy near the other end of the sink. The washroom was filled to the brim with piercing reverberating noises, as boys were screaming, running, giggling, shouting, and shoving each other. Some of them were brushing their teeth at another long sink. Frank was sitting on one of the toilets pooping, while poking and grabbing anyone who came within reach.

"Settle down!!" blared Herr Schmidt to no one in particular, his voice echoing slightly. The havoc continued unchanged.

When she had finished washing him, Fräulein Edel put her hands under his arms and lifted him to a standing position in the sink. Wolfgang hit his head on the hard edge of the white metal lamp that hung over the sink. He jerked back sharply, his foot slipped, and he began to fall backwards towards the concrete floor! He screamed! Fräulein Edel grabbed him immediately, pulled his dripping wet body tightly against her chest, and slowly guided his feet down to the floor. He felt the heat of her body radiate against his bare skin. She smelled like carnations and even her scent seemed to caress him. His body tingled.

She grabbed a white towel, knelt down and began drying him off. Her blouse was very wet where she had just now held him and Wolfi could see the pink skin and brownish erect nipples of both her breasts showing through the material.

She got a quick glimpse of her own wet nipples as she noticed him staring at her chest. She shook her head in mock disapproval and then smiled at him. Her torso was pivoting side to side as she vigorously rubbed the towel through his hair, which caused her breasts to do a wet wild dance for Wolfi. His excitement caused him to shiver.

"Oh, you're shaking. You poor thing. Here..." she said, and she wrapped the towel around his back and shoulders.

Fräulein Edel put his pajamas on him and lifted him into the crib.

Wolfi lay there motionless and silent, staring at the white sheet that covered the thin lumpy mattress. He felt feeble from exhaustion, completely disoriented. He was insanely lonely and unbelievably scared! And he was angry, ashamed to be in a baby's crib!

He looked past his feet through the low window. Beyond the valley and the distant forest he saw the last slice of the pink and orange sun slipping below the horizon. Puffy white, purple, and orange clouds were scattered around the sky. Above a few stars twinkled brightly in the dark sky between the clouds. They seemed to be greeting him.

In his mind, he flew out the window and made a wide arc over to a plush white and purple cloud. He felt its velvety cool mist against his face and hands. It seemed to caress him with love, with God's love. He thought of how he loved flying to the clouds with Mama. He heard her giggle.

Mama!!!

* * *

Suddenly the crib was shaking and rattling furiously!! His body was bouncing as if there was an earthquake!!

"Now, I'm gonna get you!!" snarled a boy's voice hatefully! It was Frank! He was climbing up the side of the crib and had one leg already over the top!!

Wolfgang choked and snorted, gasping for air!! His body froze momentarily from terror!!

Frank lunged down hard onto his chest, forcing nearly all the air out of Wolfgang's lungs! He smashed his ass down aggressively on Wolfi's stomach, pinned Wolfgang's arms and hands under his shins, and then dug his knees into Wolfgang's shoulders, rocking back and forth violently! Wolfgang tried fiercely to get him off but Frank did not budge! Wolfi was way too weak from exhaustion.

Frank's knees dug down ferociously into Wolfi's shoulders causing acute stabbing pain!!

"I didn't do anything to you!!!" Wolfi protested feverishly and began to sob.

"Aw, look at the little cry-baby! I told you I was gonna get you, you little shit! You little asshole, who got me in trouble!" said Frank in a vicious growl, spitting as he fumed, with his nose now pressed against Wolfgang's. "I hate you, you little asshole! Nobody messes with me!!"

Unbearable bolts of pain shot through Wolfgang's shoulders as Frank leaned forward with his boney knees stabbing into them, painfully stretching and pinching the skin too. Now in a rage, Wolfgang summoned all the strength he could and tried to throw Frank off him once more!! Frank's body barely shifted.

That made Frank even more angry, and he began to slap Wolfgang's face as hard as he could with both hands! His arms extending way up on either side, Frank blasted each palm down into Wolfgang's face and ears!!

Wolfi's ears stung like they were on fire!! His lips made wet flapping sounds like a horse as he tried again to force Frank off of him! Frank locked both arms and shoulders securely up under the top railings of the crib and forced himself downward. The instant Wolfgang couldn't resist any more, Frank clenched his fists and began punching him in the face with all of his infuriated might!! Horribly intense pain exploded throughout Wolfi's face, ears, and shoulders!!

The smell of poop from between Frank's legs nauseated Wolfgang. Frank formed a ball of spit with his lips and let it drop down onto Wolfgang's cheek! Then two more balls!! Wolfgang rolled his head furiously from side to side trying to avoid his slobber!

Insanely enraged, Wolfgang finally let out a piercing bloodcurdling scream!!!

Fräulein Edel suddenly pounced into the room from the washroom!

"*Frank!!*" she shrieked!

Brutally, she wrenched Frank up out of the crib!

"*Frank, you leave him alone!!!*" Fräulein Edel screamed at him in her loudest deepest authoritative voice. "I'm so damned tired of you bullying everybody!!! I want you to leave everyone alone!! *Do you understand me?!!!*"

She clamped a hand like a vice grip onto one of his arms and began smacking him violently on the butt with her other one! Frank tried unsuccessfully to pull away. Dark crimson splotches developed on Fräulein Edel's creamy face, and she was breathing hard as she bombarded his rear end with vengeful justice!

Frank then grabbed three fingers of her vice-grip hand and bent them backwards! The pain caused her grasp to weaken and he got away! He raced to his bed and immediately dove under the covers.

Wolfgang gagged as he furiously wiped the spit off his face with his pajama sleeve. He started crying and wailing traumatically at the top of his lungs!! Everything on his body stung agonizingly, painful chills shot up and down his spine. He was shivering, shaking severely.

Wolfi heard some of the other boys laughing. He felt completely humiliated!

Suddenly he screamed with explosive rage and savagely slammed both his fists down into the mattress! One fist cracked loudly as it hit the wood frame on one edge of the mattress! He howled with pain and held it to his chest!

"Let me see you. Are you all right?" said Fräulein Edel as she put her hand on his shoulder and rolled him over. His face was bright red and drenched with tears. Clear thick mucus ran down from his nostril past one corner of his mouth.

"Oh, sweetie! I'm sorry!" she said, inspecting his hand and face closely. "Well, at least you're not bleeding. You must be all right." She pulled the comforter up to his chest. Affectionately she rubbed his tummy with one hand while she stroked his cheek with the back of her other. Wolfi's heart felt like it was going to explode in agony! He turned his back to her and curled up into a fetal position.

Fräulein Edel patted him on the back warmly a few times and then turned around.

"Alright, boys! Under the covers!" she called out into the room. "Goodnight. We'll be right outside until you fall asleep". She flipped off the light switch and walked out the door.

Out in the hallway one could hear Herr Schmidt laughing and whispering excitedly, "Just look at them, will you?! Still soaking wet. I'm sure they're calling out to me!"

"Stop it! Shhhhhhh!" hissed Fräulein Edel's voice playfully. She giggled and insisted again, "Stop it!! You can't touch them here! Not now!"

Then Wolfi heard their footsteps hurrying down the stairs.

* * *

In the darkness Wolfi turned over quickly to face the direction of Frank's bed. He couldn't see a thing. He snorted, and then immediately stifled his sobs so he could listen!

Is that footsteps?!! His heart was galloping!

Someone whispered in the shadows. He held his breath for a few moments, but quickly had to resume his terrified heavy breathing.

Mama!!

Why am I here?!!

He felt unimaginably alone, completely powerless, scared to death, insanely violated, and unbearably vulnerable. His heart continued to pound wildly and his soul hurt like he had never ever imagined it could!! His body jerked and bounced as he lay there shivering uncontrollably. Everything, inside and out, was aching, stinging, and throbbing with agonizing searing pain like he had never known!!

What is this place?!! Why am I here?!!

Mama!!

The floor made a sudden cracking noise!! Wolfi jerked up to a sitting position! His heart pounded so thunderously in his chest that he wasn't sure if he could hear anything else!! His eyes searched the blackness intensely!

There had been a continual loud ringing in both his ears ever since Frank's fists hammered them so brutally. Now it dawned on him that the ringing might be preventing him from hearing Frank sneak up! Physical waves of terror slammed into his body as if the room was caving in on him!

Someone whispered in the pitch black distance.

Stop ringing!!!

Is someone coming?!

He was sure his heart was going to splatter blood everywhere as it throbbed wildly in his chest and head! *Thump-ubb!! Thump-ubb!! Thump-ubb!!*

A high-pitched terrorized whimper quietly escaped between his wet chapped lips, and two heaving sobs spurted out before he was able to suppress his crying.

What was that?!!!

Someone's knee cracking?!

"Don't do it!!" whispered someone.

Suddenly the crib was shaking violently again!! Its rickety old wood frame and rusty metal braces were clattering, jerking and bouncing heavily against the floor and the wall!!!

"*Ahhhhhhhhhhhhh!!!!!*" shrieked Wolfgang!! This time immediately and with a powerful animal roar!!

"*Ahhhhhhhhhhhhh!!!*" he screamed once more, in a primal rage!!

Herr Schmidt virtually flew up the stairs and pounced powerfully through the door, furiously jabbing the light switch on!

"*Fraaaaank!!!*" he roared, as he saw him sprinting away from the crib. Schmidt charged after him and ripped his pajama pants as he grabbed him barbarically. With one arm he put Frank into a tight headlock and the other jerked Frank's pants down to his ankles! Then he began whacking Frank's bare ass fiercely with his open hand!!

Over and over he walloped Frank's naked bottom, with enormous wrath! With each savage smack on Frank's buttocks, he bellowed one syllable: "*I... have... had... e... nough... of... you... you... lit... tle... ass... hole...*" He repeated it numerous times, each syllable accompanied by a furious bash of his hand on the little asshole's rear end!!

Frank screamed with each savage syllabic whack!! He sobbed and choked hysterically! But no matter how ferociously he struggled, Frank was unable to get out of Schmidt's enraged iron grip! Schmidt continued delivering blow after blow!

Hit him!! Hit him harder!!! Smack him!! Wolfgang cheered in vengeful silence!

By now Schmidt's hand was stinging painfully. Without bothering to pull Frank's pants back up, he picked him up brutally and threw him onto the bed!

Frank's body crashed down onto the mattress with a huge boom!

Schmidt stomped toward the door, then turned and punched his fist and index finger through the air towards Frank.

"You behave, you little son of a *bitch*!!" Both his heels rose off the floor as he roared the word *bitch!*

The entire second floor of the building thundered under his feet as Herr Schmidt stomped out the door! Fräulein Edel aggressively slammed the light switch off while strutting out close behind him.

They were gone.

* * *

"Wolfi, wise and powerful, will always find his way."
Wolfi, wise and powerful, will always find his way."

He heard Mama's soft angel voice singing in his heart as he lay on his back in the crib. It soothed him, but only for a moment.

Wait!

Wait!!

Mama must have known where the train was going!!
She must have known!!

Suddenly, a horrifying thought shot more waves of cold crippling terror through his body!!

Did I do something wrong?!!
Am I being punished?!!

"Whhhhhhhhhhhh!!!!" Wolfgang sucked a long hysterical breath into his lungs and his heart leaped into his throat!

Because I liked it when Aunt Sasha played naked with me?! And when Aunt Monika did too?!!

Am I in trouble?!!

Eerie hissing sounds filled his ears. A freezing wind wailed as it blew through his soul and he shuddered.

Oh my god!!! Oh my god!!!

Did she send me to the man in black?!!

He gagged and had to concentrate intensely to avoid vomiting! The sickening potpourri of poop, urine, stinky feet, modeling clay, fresh paint, and mold nauseated him.

The minutes passed by unbearably slowly as he lay there wide awake with his heart racing. Wolfgang's exhausted body was now limp. His eyelids began drooping shut. As he slowly turned over on his side, one eye blinked momentarily open. Something was there!

By the window!!

The man in black!! Is it??!!

With a jolt he sat up to look! A hideous green face was jetting towards him through the air from his right!! He jerked backwards against the crib wall trying to escape. But then it shot right through Wolfgang's chest and disappeared with an airy whoosh!

Then another face!! A monstrous red one came racing towards him!! Wolfgang tried multiple times to duck, but the red face also passed completely through him with a blast of air!

Wolfi looked at the window again.

Oh my god!!! It's him!

The man in black!! Oh my god!!!

He was gazing at Wolfgang with fierce intensity while floating mysteriously back and forth to either side of the window! Still hovering, the freakish black figure turned, grabbed the lower part of the window with both hands, slid it upwards in slow motion and opened it all the way!

Somehow the twinkling stars and the night sky reached into the room and touched him, as if they were beckoning him!

Now, the man in black was gliding towards the crib!!!

Wolfgang was paralyzed! Everything buzzed and sparked profusely with electricity. His body felt incredibly dense, massively thick and heavy, yet somehow like he was floating in the air. His heart was racing insanely!! There was no escape!!!

The man in black then stopped and motioned for Wolfgang to follow him to the window!!!

Wolfgang quivered and shuddered!! He tried to scream! No sound came out of his mouth!

Still unable to move his body, Wolfi suddenly began to float in the air too!!

Wolfi was being pulled right to the man in black!!

Again he tried to scream!! Nothing came out!

All of a sudden Wolfgang shot straight through the open window!! Immediately he felt enveloped by the warm loving tenderness of black space as he soared through it now. The brilliant stars shimmered and sparkled magically inside his being! Each one seemed to actually radiate affection! Planets in dazzling arrays of colors seemed to welcome him with tenderness as he streaked past them.

Wolfi felt light.
He felt love.
He was not alone.

* * *

The perfume filled Wolfi's nostrils and his body with a heavenly glow. The aroma was mystifying and it seemed to be alive! It was a sensuous musty yet light blend of roses, lilacs, and baby's breath (the flower!). He loved inhaling it deeply and often. It actually seemed to make his heart sing when he smelled it!

"Is it dark chocolate cake under the frosting?" she asked her mom. Mom nodded her head yes. The frosting was dark blue and so was the very rich cake under it. After her mom cut a piece for her, the girl stuck her fork in it and put a big blue bite into her mouth. She sighed and closed her eyes for a moment to fully savor it. Her soft dark blue lips formed a heart-felt smile. She opened her tender indigo eyes again and they sparkled with delight! The back and sides of the collar on her light blue blouse were turned up which then framed and accentuated her gorgeous blueish-white face.

"Soooooooo good!!" she moaned as if in a trance.

"Happy birthday, baby," said her dad. He cupped the girl's soft oval-shaped face affectionately with one hand. "You're the love of my life! That day eighteen years ago when you arrived on this planet was the happiest day of my life!"

Her mom silently poured a cup of dark blue coffee from a navy blue coffee pot. She winced uncomfortably.

"You're the nicest daughter a mom could want, Maria. People very obviously find your beauty and charm irresistible." Her mom's voice cracked just a bit with sarcasm, as she took a quick huffy breath in through her nose and pretended to flick something off her royal blue blouse.

Dad was fondly rubbing Maria's thigh and gave her a quick kiss on the cheek. Maria glowed and blushed. She gently put her hand on top of his.

"Thank you, mommy! I love you!" Maria said genuinely, but still looking into dad's eyes. She let out a passionate little-girl giggle and a beautiful smile radiated from her blue lips. Wolfgang's heart melted!

"I have a big surprise for you, baby!" beamed dad, pulling his hand off her thigh, "A big surprise!!" He was grinning from ear to ear. "I have to work today. I'm actually leaving soon, and since you're now officially eighteen years old..."

"Oh, wow, really?!! *You mean it?!!* I can do it?!!" Maria interrupted him before he could finish. She screamed, jumped up and down wildly a few times, and then slapped dad's thighs with fierce intensity. Dad flinched from the sting.

"I can do it?!!! For real?!!! Oh, my god, thank you, daddy!!" She threw her arms around him and kissed him numerous times on his cheeks, forehead, and on his nose too! Dad was grinning from ear to ear as he folded his arms uncomfortably over his light blue denim shirt.

"You're giving me chills, baby!" he snickered. "Well, it's legal now, and I know how long you've wanted to!"

Outside, Maria watched as dad walked around the long flatbed trailer, carefully inspecting and testing all the chains, straps and bindings. They were securing twelve huge spools of blueish-grey steel cable. Each one was marked with a gross weight of 4,341 pounds.

"It's a heavy load today," said dad as he continued his inspection. "Twelve of these add up to over 52,000 pounds."

The spools were lined up one behind the other sitting on their dark blue rims so that they formed what looked like 12 massive railroad car wheel-and-axle sets rolling in the same direction.

"Dad, is that ok?" Maria asked him, pointing at how the spools were arranged like train wheels on a track. "Wow, if you had to brake hard or had an accident and if any of the spools got loose, they could easily roll forward into the truck cab and crush us. Is this really a safe load, daddy?"

"Yep," yelled dad from the back end of the trailer as he kicked a tire to check its air pressure. "We've got heavy blocks underneath the round parts. They load them that way because they can get four more onto the flatbed in this formation, so it saves shipping costs."

"I don't know, daddy. It seems really dangerous. It scares me. Should I really go with?" she asked him with a lot of hesitation in her voice.

"Up to you, baby. You know that I want you to come." Dad was on the other side of the dark blue rig now opening the door. He grabbed the high grip bar, put his right foot into the steel stirrup behind the front tire, and then climbed towards the left up into the driver's seat of the jumbo eighteen wheeler's cab.

"Should I?" Maria nervously called up to him through the open passenger's door. She put one foot into the stirrup but kept her other foot on the ground.

Suddenly Wolfgang heard many voices yelling out passionately, "No!! Don't go!! No!!"

Maria put her hand on the grip bar and began to climb in.

Again, Wolfgang heard a chorus of voices shouting, "No!! No!!".

She gave no indication that she heard them! Suddenly Wolfgang felt very afraid for her!

"They know something!! Don't go!!" he bellowed out, not able to contain himself.

"What the hell! It's my birthday, let's have an adventure!" Maria was clearly oblivious to all the yelling as she bounced quickly up into the passenger's seat. Grinning broadly, she shrieked, *"Where?!"*

"Up north about two hours, then back home," Dad beamed as he hit the starter button and the powerful motor roared to life. He was visibly thrilled to have her come! "Should take about five hours with unloading."

Maria let out another infectious happy shriek! Wolfgang felt her beautiful little-girl passion, and somehow he loved her with all his heart! She touched his soul. He felt ecstasy and lightness from her being!

Roses, lilacs, and baby's breath filled Wolfi's nose and lungs again. Maria's magical love mysteriously pervaded that scent with intoxicating passion and made him feel like he was floating!

On the road whiffs of diesel exhaust occasionally caressed their noses as the huge engine thundered in their ears and vibrated under their butts like a massage chair. Two feet of snow blanketed the countryside here, but the highway was mostly bare and dry. She and dad silently absorbed the beauty of the blueish-white rolling hills, forests, and fields as they cruised along.

"It's snowing!" Maria suddenly cried with excitement, pointing at the blue-grey cloudy horizon. "It's snowing!"

"Not good, actually," said dad in a loud and very concerned voice. He backed off the gas pedal a bit and peered at the blueish-white gauges in the blue dashboard. "It's 24° Fahrenheit. That means yesterday's snow melt has turned into ice. Not good! Not good at all. And, we're not even halfway there!"

White snow swirled and danced across the dark blue pavement for the next twenty minutes. It was mostly small light flakes and was not accumulating any depth. Dad relaxed just a bit and rambled on at a brisk 55 MPH.

"Gotta stay on schedule," he said focusing intently on the highway ahead.

"Here's another really great golden oldie!" sparkled the radio DJ in his deep electronically-compressed voice.

Maria cranked the volume way up. It was one of her favorite old pop songs!

When the chorus came around they were both singing so loud they were yelling, while pointing at each other, and grinning from ear to ear! "I... want you more today than ever before..."

"What a great song!" he shouted at her in order to be heard over the booming big speakers and the roar of the engine.

"I know, dad! You met mom the first time at their concert!." Her face glowed with delight as she yelled back at him.

"Fell in love the moment I saw her!" he bellowed over the music with a smirk on his face. "I could not resist wanting to fondle and kiss those cute dimpled cheeks!"

Dad, you're a dork! She thought it but she didn't say it.

Maria smiled lovingly at him as his hands commanded the steering wheel and his butt danced to the music. All of his wet smoke-stained teeth were revealed as he let out a big laugh just like an uninhibited teenager. The chorus of the song came around again and both of them sang at the top of their lungs once more!

"I... want you more today than ever before..."

Without any warning, the truck suddenly swerved to the right, then spun quickly left!! Now they were sliding sideways toward the concrete columns that supported a freeway overpass!!

"ICE!!!! SHIIIIIIIIIT!!!" Dad slammed both hands hard against the steering wheel! His body tensed up like a rock! *"SHIT!!!"* he bellowed again.

Maria exploded into a terrified piercing scream!! The band was still rocking their asses off on the radio!

"Shit!!!" Dad's knuckles were blueish-white as he desperately tried to conquer the dark blue steering wheel and gain control of the truck!

He screamed again fiercely. *"Shiiiiiiiiiit!!!!"*

* * *

Water whooshed powerfully out of the long shaft above the huge old waterwheel. As they rolled under the shaft at the top, one after the other of its many wooden box receptacles became completely filled with water. The weight of the water caused the wheel to turn slowly to the right. Glistening sunlight reflected magically off the bouncing waves of water inside each receptacle, dancing wildly in all directions.

The loud creaking, groaning and cracking sounds from the turning wooden wheel made it seem like it was alive, as if it was a massive powerful beast. Over the loud whooshing and plopping water sounds of the wheel, Wolfi could hear cuckoo birds calling in the trees and brown tree pipits chirping their melodic birdsongs. Somewhere behind him a crow cawed three times.

A warm gentle breeze brought the clean smell of fresh water into Wolfgang's nose and lungs. Glistening wet drops of water spray accumulated on his cheeks and forehead as he leaned on the old wooden railing which guarded the pond around the ancient mill's waterwheel. He felt amazing power and strength coming from the wheel and the falling water, yet it also seemed sensuous and soft, inviting and nurturing. And, it was definitely very magical! He was mesmerized, and somehow the power of the waterwheel soothed his aching heart just a little.

Oh, how he would love to share this moment with Mama like they've always done! Now tears filled his eyes and his tummy ached as he realized again how incredibly much he missed her.

Mama! Why am I here?!

She leaned in and put her elbows on the railing to Wolfgang's right. The blond girl's hair smelled sweet and fresh, like daisies. Her upper arm and shoulder rubbed against him and her hip pressed against his. His heart began beating noticeably faster as he felt the warmth of her body. Because she was leaning way out towards the water, he could see only the back of her head. He stared intently at her wavy light-blond hair which flowed just past her shoulders onto the back of her white blouse. He was just a bit stunned by the surprise of her arrival and by the fact that her body was leaning into his.

When she turned her head slightly in his direction he realized that it was the shy rice-bowl girl who had stared at him yesterday at the giant seesaw. Her presence, her being, radiated breathtaking delight towards him!

"Heidi, we will be at the other pond."

Wolfi turned around and was confronted by the long thin warty nose of the witch lady! A chill ran up his spine!

"*Jahwohl*, Frau Reichert," answered the shy girl softly.

Heidi. I like that name, thought Wolfgang.

Silently, they both continued gazing at the beauty and power of the waterwheel. Heidi leaned in closer to him. Wolfi felt a strange magnetic pull of energy from her, as he became aware of the warmth of her soul and the softness of her small feminine body through her clothes. Wolfi's heart smiled joyfully in silence for quite some time, accentuated by the sweet fresh aroma of daisies radiating from her. He was floating.

After a while Heidi wiped the coat of sparkling wet mist from her cheeks, dried both her hands on her ragged red skirt, and grinned at him playfully! Then abruptly she grabbed Wolfgang's hand, turned him around, and pulled him with her as they ran off!

"Swans!!" was the only word that came out of her mouth.

Several large geese honked indignantly and wildly flapped their wings as they scrambled to get out of Heidi and Wolfgang's way. Racing, she dragged Wolfi over the lush green grass towards another pond which he could see was crowded with blue-green brightly colored ducks and more grayish-white geese. Dark brown turds in the shape of mini Vienna sausages were scattered everywhere. The kids were careful to avoid squishing them as they ran.

Heidi finally stopped abruptly at the railing by the edge of this pond, which caused Wolfi to almost trip and fall! Excitedly, she pointed at three beautiful large white creatures which were majestically and silently gliding through the water.

"Swans!!" she gushed gleefully!

"Bwaaahh!!" exclaimed Wolfgang, clearly thrilled.

The swans were exquisite, elegantly beautiful, and their graceful dance-like movements conveyed a sense of serene wisdom and intense power. They were benevolent queens gliding resplendently and authoritatively above all the racket and annoying hectic energy of the honking geese and quacking diving ducks!

Wolfi felt the adoration coming from Heidi's warm soft hand resting on his naked forearm. She tilted her head close to his as they leaned against the dark wood railing and admired the swans. The wind blew strands of her silky blond hair into his face.

Daisies, he thought, as her scent reached his nostrils. Wolfgang's heart was beating faster again and he smiled just a little. The way she felt so very good to him reminded him of Mama.

"Wolfi, wise and powerful, will always find his way..."

"Wolfi, wise and powerful, will always find his way..."

For the moment he felt a bit of peace, hearing Mama's soft loving voice singing to him in his head.

"Ahhhhhhhhhhhhhh!!!!" It was a piercing scream from behind him!!

Wolfgang's ribs were suddenly slammed into the fence by the body of another boy!! Five other kids screamed and laughed and pointed! The uncoordinated boy quickly picked himself up off the ground and ran off in shame.

Heidi raced off without a word.

Wolfi's ribs and torso stung with pain, and now his heart was burning once more from loneliness.

Emptiness. Freezing void.

He was pummeled with the thought that he did not know anybody or anything in this world of strangers and bliss cottages and swans. Tears streamed down his cheeks.

He was incredibly alone.

Exhausted.

Mama...

* * *

"Boys, form a single line! It's a new day, let's see if you can behave today!" barked Herr Schmidt as the girls and boys were gathering in front of the orphanage.

The morning sun bathed the bluebells by the side of the dirt road with a golden mystical glow. To Wolfi they seemed to actually send out heavenly vibrations from their powder blue blossoms which were shaped like miniature bells. His heart felt lighter as he heard the sweet-flavored high-pitched mysterious "ding, ding" of their bells in his mind. The vibrations tingled his tummy.

"Magical! They're ringing!" whispered an impassioned soft sweet voice just to his right.

Wolfgang's heart danced in his chest as he glanced over and saw Heidi admiring the bluebells too! He smiled with his whole body as she turned and his eyes connected with her beguiling jade green eyes. His heart felt mystical affection radiating from her soul and from her heart when she grinned back at him.

"Good morning," she said in a shy quiet voice and moved a few steps closer to him.

Wolfi continued smiling, staring silently into her eyes. He reached out and lightly touched her bare forearm in greeting. The warmth and euphoric energy coming from her skin felt wonderfully inviting to his senses, and the experience was heightened by the aroma of daisies wafting from her. Somehow it felt like they had been friends for years.

"Alright, girls and boys, let's walk, two abreast, stay close together and on the right side of the road!" Herr Schmidt trumpeted.

The five to nine-year-old girls and boys paired up and all thirty six of them began to shuffle, skip and dance down the dirt road as Fräulein Edel walked along guarding the rear.

Wolfi's cheeks, his chest, and his bare knees were bathed by the warmth of the sun as he and Heidi walked next to each other near the back of the line. The morning air smelled fresh, clean, and vibrant. Frank and a few of the boys near the front were cackling and screaming like intoxicated old witches, whispering secrets in each other's ears. Heidi grabbed Wolfgang's hand and pointed with her other hand at the hundreds more bluebells that were growing where they walked.

"Ding, ding... ding, ding...!" she whispered to him as her fingers gracefully twirled upward to accentuate the bluebells' chiming.

He cherished the warm love he felt from Heidi's soft hand and her heart. He felt enamored looking into her beautiful face. And the divine vibrations of the bluebells in his ears, in his tummy, and in his heart, captivated him.

"They're gonna start shooting!!!" screamed Frank suddenly, and he began racing furiously down the road!

Most of the other kids chased excitedly after him, anxious to see what was happening in the field ahead! Heidi and Wolfgang continued walking normally, still holding hands, watching the others with curiosity.

"Tirer!!!" bellowed a man's voice way off in the distance.

Suddenly the air was filled with explosive deafening sounds of war!! Machine guns blasted ferocious long bursts of bullets!! Dozens of rifles exploded in furious volleys that blared from all directions!! Mortar rounds detonated and viscously pounded the air!!

Every one of the kids on the road were now screaming at the top of their lungs, running in various directions! Three tremendous anti-tank cannons near them each fired immense booming blasts towards the edge of the forest where eight massive AMX-50 tanks with their engines howling were maneuvering towards this direction!! Dense plumes of black diesel exhaust gushed savagely up into the air behind each tank. Thick gray smoke enveloped everything and everybody, reeking of the pungent sulfur-like smell of burning gun powder and of diesel fumes.

Wolfgang's face and body were pounded by monstrous shock waves of air as he stood in place temporarily immobilized from terror! Then four of the enormous tanks simultaneously shot thunderous ear-piercing blasts directly at Wolfi!!

Wolfi let out a shrill penetrating scream and immediately fell face-down to a fetal position in the dirt, with his arms over his head!

Fräulein Edel hurried over to Wolfi, softly stroked his back, and yelled at him in order to be heard over the enormous noise. "Wolfgang, it's alright, they are only shooting blanks! They're just pretending to have a war. Just practicing! The explosions are all blanks. You can stand up!"

She was trying her best to calm and soothe him, but the fact that she was yelling just upset him more. And he had absolutely no idea what blanks were! Nor did he have the slightest clue why these men and tanks would be shooting these horrifying blanks things at each other and at him!!

He thought about the piles of bloody dead bodies in his cousin's stories of the bombing raids on Mannheim! He screamed again! Now he was sobbing and his body trembled severely.

"STOP IT!!!" He roared as loud as he could, but no one heard him over the booming blasts of exploding tank shells.

Fraulein Edel continued to shout at him about blanks, and most of the other kids were still screaming and running around, but nobody else had fallen to the ground.

"Look at the crybaby!! What a baby!" Frank cackled obscenely and pointed at Wolfgang.

Several other boys and girls were also laughing at Wolfi's panicked ignorance. Fräulein Edel finally pulled him up to a standing position and wiped the tears from his face with her sleeve. He was still sobbing and shaking. Frank and the others seemed to enjoy his humiliation. Wolfi's heart sunk to his stomach. He felt agonizingly alone.

Now as he succeeded in tuning out the world in his mind, the explosions of war faded into distant muffled sounds. Then the thumping and pounding of his anguished heart dominated his awareness. Its hammering rang loudly in both ears, with a forceful rhythmic cadence, like hundreds of marching soldiers...

MA - ma, MA - ma, MA - ma, MA - ma...

* * *

Wolfgang's teeth had been chattering for quite some time, and he was face down in a fetal position on the mattress, with the featherbed cover pulled tightly over his head. A freezing chill had run up his spine. He always felt just a little bit safer here between the sheets, where he could fly to the world of white light and bask in peace and security for brief moments.

"I'm safe! I'm safe!" he had whispered frantically, trying to convince himself. He was panting hard, shivering, and his naked body was damp with sweat.

All of a sudden someone's hand was on his back! He jumped in fear and shrieked!

"Wolfgang!" It was a loud breathy whisper.

"Wolfgang!"

He stuck his nose hesitantly out from under the covers.

"Aunt Sasha!" He was very relieved to see her!

Her enchanting scent of chamomile soap filled his lungs as his eyes quickly scanned her soft wavy brown hair, tender brown eyes, and the cherry red lips that formed a warm smile on her beautiful face. He got up on his knees and threw his arms around her! His tummy and groin hummed!

"Move over," she whispered, and laid down on her back in the bed with him.

"Why am I here?" asked Wolfi, still half asleep.

"Your mama's not feeling well, and she brought you upstairs to stay with me again today. Remember?" replied Aunt Sasha.

Wolfi groaned briefly in acknowledgment, and then snuggled up to her, reveling in the warmth of her soft skin underneath her lacy nightgown. Aunt Sasha lived upstairs and she was Mama's best friend. She wasn't actually Wolfi's aunt, but just like Mama did, he really loved Aunt Sasha because she was so very nice to him!

"Did you have a nightmare again? The man in black?" Sasha asked him lovingly.

"Yes!!" he blurted out and whimpered a bit. "He almost grabbed me this time!! I screamed as loud as I possibly could, and then I flew back here!!"

"I heard you scream. You woke up," she offered.

"I flew back here!" he repeated with a tone of insistence.

"I'm sure that he'll never ever catch you, Wolfi!" Sasha said in a quiet reassuring voice. "Never!! Someday I know you'll understand why you keep dreaming of him. Then the dreams will stop."

"Wolfi, wise and powerful, will always find his way," she sang softly with all the love of her being. Sasha had heard Mama sing it to him many times in the last six years.

"Wolfi, wise and powerful, will always find his way."

Wolfgang felt just a bit better as she sang. He rested his cheek on her chest and felt the rigid nipple of her velvety warm breast underneath her nightgown. Gently, he laid his hand over her other one and sighed with happiness as he felt her love radiating into him through the softness.

Sasha let out a faint moan and held him closer.

Wolfi was always fascinated by how tall and hard her nipples became. Before long he began gently fondling the amazing height of one of them with his fingertips, while his teeth occasionally caressed the firmness of the other one through the satiny cloth which covered it.

Sasha groaned with pleasure and arched her back. Soon she grabbed both thin straps of her lacy white nightgown and pulled it down to reveal her supple naked breasts.

Wolfi's heart was dancing with delight! His groin buzzed with an intense euphoric feeling and he was hard, as he slurped her chamomile-scented sumptuous beauty into his mouth.

After a while Aunt Sasha put both her hands on his head and guided him down to where she had pulled up her garment. With an innocent little squeal he nestled his cheek on the nakedness where her thighs met, moving his head back and forth a few times until he found the most comfortable spot.

It was his favorite place to fall asleep, a place where he experienced breathtaking love coming from Sasha! He continued shifting his cheek every few moments for quite a while, searching for that ideal position where the hair didn't tickle his nose.

He felt Sasha arch her back just a bit from time to time and heard her moan. Eventually he was sleeping peacefully.

* * *

"Soldiers!!" There was intense fear in Heidi's voice as she shouted! Clenching Wolfgang's hand she jerked back aggressively so he would halt. "Look!! Stop!!"

A short distance ahead on the dirt road, facing the other way, were about one hundred green-clad soldiers!

Fräulein Edel was bringing up the rear of the line again and pushed firmly on Heidi and Wofli's backs. "Keep walking! We have to stay together!"

"I'm scared!" insisted Heidi.

Beads of sweat trickled down the small of Wolfgang's back and his mind was on high alert, as he expected thunderous explosions and war to break out at any moment like it did last week!

As they got close the kids stopped, stood anxiously in place, and stared. Some of them whispered nervously to each other. Nearly all of them were terrified of soldiers and no one dared to go any further now!

Several of the military men turned around to check out the children. A very thin Corporal with a perspiring splotchy red face pointed at them and snickered in a high-pitched voice , *"Regardez cette!"*

Wolfgang didn't understand.

"Compagnie garde à vous!!!" screamed one of the soldiers in the front of the large group.

Immediately two hundred dark green legs bolted to their assigned place in the formation, stiffened and slammed together with a great massive thumping that was so loud it actually shook the ground and moved the air! A dense cloud of beige-colored dust drifted slowly up from the dirt beneath the soldiers' feet and towards the field. Now every single man stood rock hard with their back to the kids, completely motionless, and silent.

The children were transfixed, petrified to make a move! No one said a word. A very long sixty seconds passed in absolute stillness. Wolfgang shivered as an overhead crow broke the silence with three caws.

"Compagnie marche!!!" came a sudden piercing scream from the one standing to the side at the front of the formation.

Instantly the ground trembled from the furious stomping of two hundred heavy feet as the formation began marching away!

"Un, deux, trois, quatre, un, deux, trois, quatre...," the screaming soldier chanted in a blaring monotone which was barely audible over the powerful rhythmic pounding of scores of boots!

"Fräulein Edel, I don't understand soldier words. They talk funny!" said Wolfgang once they were further away and the noise had died down.

"You idiot, they're not talking soldier words, they're talking French," yelled Frank and laughed at him.

Benjamin and Robert laughed too, and so did a few of the girls.

"What's French?" Wolfgang insisted, staring blankly over at the field.

"It's what French people speak, you stupid pig!" screeched Frank, and laughed again scornfully.

Wolfgang's heart stung and tears filled his eyes.

"Frank, that's enough!!" yelled Fräulein Edel.

"The soldiers are French, from France," she offered to Wolfgang. "The Americans, English, French, and the Russians won the war. Although Germany lost, we were so powerful that it took those four countries and even more to defeat us! When it was over nobody wanted Germany to become too strong again so they divided our country into four zones for their armies to occupy. We live in the French zone and all the soldiers here are from France."

"They eat snails!!" shouted Benjamin, twisting his face into the shape of a dried prune. He poked his finger down his throat as if to vomit. "Bowls full of snails!"

"Snails?!" questioned Heidi, "Snails?!! You mean the slimy things in the shells, ummmm, like that one?!" She pointed to one that was leaving a gooey wet trail in the dirt as it oozed its way across the road.

Wolfgang's stomach turned and he felt nauseous.

"How could anyone eat anything like that without puking?!!" he asked.

Fräulein Edel took a long deep breath. "Well, they're used to eating snails and they prepare them in a great-tasting butter and garlic..."

"Tanks!!! Tanks!!!" screamed both Benjamin and Frank in unison, and sprinted towards the intersection ahead!

"Tanks!!!"

The ground actually began to move back and forth under their feet now!! There was a massive deep rumbling sound coming from the earth! An enormous erie roaring from many powerful motors was gradually getting louder and vibrating against Wolfi's torso and face.

As the kids approached the intersection, they saw a huge billowing black and beige cloud down the road on the right. Some of the girls screamed and giggled nervously as they searched the cloud with their eyes! The ground shook ever more violently!

Suddenly a gigantic green AMX-50 tank burst out of the cloud with a monstrous roar!! Another massive tank thundered and bellowed right behind it, each one with dense black smoke surging fiercely up into the sky! Then another mammoth, and another one, and... There must have been thirty of them!

The kids were literally bouncing up and down from the movement of the earth as they stood in silence, stunned and terrified by the savage stampede of these titans!

The immense thick cloud of road dust and stinky black diesel smoke now enveloped everything. It stung their eyes, invaded their lungs, and most of the kids were coughing.

When the earth was once again calm and the smoke had cleared away, Fräulein Edel said, "Kids, follow me, I want to show you something very important!!"

Herr Schmidt and the kids followed her across the road and to the top of a grassy knoll. As she came to a place where the ground was bulging, she pointed silently to a crude cross made of tied-together twigs where a green soldier's helmet was hanging on one side. Everyone was captivated and they quickly gathered in a circle around her.

"There's a hole in it! Right through the steel helmet!" exclaimed Frank as he grabbed it. "He got one in the head! Bam!!!" Frank fell limply to the ground pretending to die.

A sharp jolt of pain shot through Wolfgang's own head as he felt what it must be like to have a screaming bullet smash into his brain.

Oh God, don't ever let that happen to me! he thought.

"This is a grave? A dead person is here?!" asked one of the younger girls, shivering just a bit.

"Yes," said Fräulein Edel. "This was a German soldier who was killed here during the war."

Everyone stared at the grave in silence for a few moments.

"This, boys and girls, is the truth of war, the reality of war, the seriousness of war, the consequence of war!" said Fräulein Edel in a somber soft voice. "This was probably a lovely young man who was in love with a sweet young woman and wanted nothing more than just to live a happy life!" Her lips contorted just a bit as if she was about to cry.

"Did the French soldiers kill him?" asked Robert.

"No, there were no French soldiers here at that time. The American soldiers were here then," answered Fräulein Edel.

Wolfgang's thoughts went once more to the piles of dead bloodied bodies, to all the people who were massacred by the American bombs at home in Mannheim! *Americans are killers!* he thought to himself.

Wolfi imagined what it's like to be this dead soldier. He felt the damp musty cold dirt and rocks pressing heavily against his body. He visualized knowing there will never be another chance to run and play, never another hug, no more love, no more happiness... Just darkness, cold...

"I never want to die!" he said quietly under his breath.

Chapter Four

"Wolfgang, he's here!" shouted Julia with excitement as she came clomping up the stairs.

Wolfgang hesitated nervously just inside the young boys' dorm, but when he saw Julia's beautiful blue eyes and her loving warm smile coming around the corner he was happy to see her. She threw her arms around him and gave him an adoring hug!

Wolfi felt her love rush through his body from head to toe as the luscious wildflower scent of her hair pervaded his lungs. He held her very tightly and wouldn't let go, just like he did that first day when she tucked him into bed in the storage room. Affectionately Julia put her hands on his trembling thighs and pushed him back firmly so she could look him in the eyes.

"You've been desperately hoping for this moment for about five weeks now and it's finally happening, Wolfi!! He's here!!" she said softly. "I know you want to see him! You know you want to see him!" She gave him another loving squeeze.

"Here!" Julia offered him her hand and he followed her dubiously down the stairs. As she held the heavy green door open to let him outside, he got a glimpse of him and Wolfi's heart sunk to his stomach!

"Papa!!" he shrieked! Wolfi's voice cracked as he hopped up and down.

Eagerly, he ran into Papa's arms! With a huge grin on his face he grabbed Papa's waist and hugged him passionately!

"Wolfgang!" Papa muttered. A single tear ran down his cheek and he quickly brushed it away with his gloved hand.

"Where's Mama?!" asked Wolfgang apprehensively.

Papa took a long deep breath. "We'll talk about it."

"Mama? Is she coming?!" Wolfi's voice quivered.

"We'll talk about it," Papa said again very quietly.

Wolfgang leaned his head into Papa's arm and briefly ran his fingers underneath the edge of the black armband on his grey suit jacket.

"Frau Sandmann told me that we could walk to where there's an old mill with a restaurant?" said Papa.

"Yes!! I want to show you the waterwheel!" exclaimed Wolfgang. He grabbed Papa's hand with excitement and began to pull him down the hill towards the road.

"Let's eat first, before the waterwheel. I'm hungry!" insisted Papa.

Wolfi had never been in this restaurant. It was relatively dark and a red candle was burning on every table. Wolfi's nose and lungs were permeated with a hundred fascinating smells! The air was thick with smoke from many cigarettes and cigars, with the odors of numerous kinds of sweet and musty perfumes, with the yeasty pungent scent of beer, with the delicious aromas of fried schnitzel, potato dumplings, sweet-and-sour red cabbage, creamy sauerkraut, scrumptious cakes, and freshly-brewed coffee!

All around him he heard the clanging of silverware against an abundance of dinner plates, the crashing sounds of dishes being piled into tall stacks, two women laughing hysterically, a man yelling in the kitchen, and the underlying deep hum of dozens of ongoing conversations.

Wolfgang quickly devoured his delectable red cabbage, potato dumplings, and Wienerschnitzel, while he told Papa tedious details about his life the past five weeks. Mostly Papa just looked inexpressively around the restaurant, barely acknowledging Wolfi who was spewing enthusiastically about his wonderful sweet friend Heidi, about his older friend Julia who gives such amazing hugs and says she loves him, about adventures with French soldiers who actually eat slimy snails, about the brilliant flashes from ferocious explosions in a pretend war that they had right there in the fields, how the massive tanks made the whole earth shake and his teeth chatter, and about the bullet hole in the steel helmet of the dead soldier.

After lunch Wolfgang dragged Papa joyfully outside to the waterwheel!

"It's magical! Look at it!!" he cried, brimming with excitement.

A crow cawed once and several tree pipits chirped melodically over the wooshing sound of rushing water, the fierce creaking groans, and the intense cracking noises coming from the waterwheel. The wheel was a living breathing beautiful massive beast to Wolfgang! He felt it's mystical power penetrate his chest and tingle all the way down to his toes as it revolved.

"Yes," Papa muttered dismissively, "magical". He wiped the spray off his forehead.

He doesn't feel the magic. Wolfi knew it in his heart.

An uncomfortable silence weighed heavily on them as they both stared at the waterwheel. After a few minutes, Wolfgang leaned his head against Papa again and wrapped his hands around his bicep. Subconsciously he playfully ran his fingers underneath the edge of the black armband once more.

"Don't do that!" barked Papa and smacked Wolfi's hand sternly.

Wolfgang jerked back.

"But it looks nice, I like it!" he protested in a faltering tone. The back of his hand stung.

"Don't you know what a black armband means, boy?!" asked Papa arrogantly and impatiently.

"No..." whispered Wolfi feebly looking up into Papa's face.

"Your Mama died four weeks ago!" Papa was expressionless as he gazed straight ahead.

Wolfgang ogled the waterwheel in immobilized silence for a long while.

"Mama?! Why didn't she come today?" he asked, feeling very disoriented. He was not able to process what he had just heard.

"Don't be stupid!" snapped Papa and scowled at him.

"But why didn't she come?!" Wolfi winced acutely as he felt his heart being pierced by hundreds of razor-edged daggers.

"Don't... be... stupid!" snarled Papa again in a higher-pitched voice. He grabbed Wolfi's hand angrily and began barreling towards Bliss Cottage.

Wolfi's legs now felt tremendously heavy and fatigued. Sharp pains shot through his fingers because

Papa was clenching his hand so vehemently while he dragged him down the road in a hurry. Wolfi was gasping for breath trying to keep up!

"Are we going home now?" Wolfi asked between gulps of air.

"Not today," answered Papa with no emotion and without breaking his stride. The two of them trudged on for a bit.

"Why not?!" Wolfi broke the silence, wheezing as he spoke.

"Can't today!" Papa scolded. "I'm working on getting permission. I'll come back for you in a few weeks. Besides, I'm on the bike today."

When they reached his fat motorcycle, Papa pulled his tattered black leather jacket out of one of the saddle bags and quickly put it on.

Tears began gushing down Wolfi's face as he stood watching. Agonizing pain possessed his heart!

I want to go home!!

Papa bent down. gave him a short hug, and patted his bottom once. "I'll be back," he mumbled and stood up.

Papa quickly threw his leg over the motorcycle's black seat, kicked the starter lever with a downward jerk, and then slammed the kickstand up against the engine with his other foot. He revved the motor a couple times, turned the front wheel once to the left and the right, and then glanced over at Wolfgang to wave goodbye.

Wolfi had fallen to his knees and was shaking and sobbing severely!

Agitated, Papa shut the engine off and set the motorbike back on its kickstand. Then he squatted down and silently held Wolfgang close. Wolfi screeched and shuddered uncontrollably in Papa's arms!

"Mama's... dead?!"

Wolfi's contorted mouth could barely pronounce the words in between desperate grieving howls.

"I'm sorry, boy," offered Papa matter-of-factly.

"Mama's dead?!"

* * *

"I'm ah... killer! I killed a bunch of 'em! You should be... afraida me!" the one-legged man had yelled as he waved his fist at the bartender. "Don't keep tellin' me... I gotta pay now! Gimme another beer... goddammit!!"

He had slammed his fist down on the bar, hunched his shoulders under his black leather overcoat, and snorted loudly. He was slurring his words badly and spitting as he shouted, "Did it... forma country. Whata hell didjoo do forya country?!"

"I served as a cook in the army and we worked our asses off all day seven days a week!" the bartender had replied, aggressively wiping the counter with a grey wet rag.

"Oh, ya poor boy! Slaved ina... hot kitchen, didja?" sneered the one-legged drunk. "Me?! Me?! They were tryin' ta kill me... all day seven days a week... blew off ma goddam leg! Germany owes me!! Goddammit!! Gimme another beer!!" The cripple screamed his last sentence at the top of his lungs while flailing his arms awkwardly, lost his balance, and started to fall backwards. The stump that used to be his right leg hit the underside of the bar with a heavy thud and broke his fall.

"Look!! The bartender barked emphatically. "I'm sorry that you lost your leg, but you've had enough to drink, way too much to drink, and you have to pay your bill! Pay it now and leave!!"

Wolfgang sat up straight in his chair and looked anxiously at Papa! He put down the tiny glass of beer that Papa had poured him and pulled his hand away from the Spanish peanuts.

Papa wrapped his arm around the back of Wolfi's chair in a protective gesture.

"Gimme another beer!!" scowled the drunk yet again.

The bartender was completely out of patience and this time he screamed!! "You've been here for four hours and you've drunk a fortune in beer! You have to pay for it now no matter how many legs you've lost!"

The barkeep glanced down at his tab sheet. "87 Marks!! Do you even have that much money?!"

"Germany owes me!!!" roared One-Leg. "Gimme another beer!!" Suddenly he grabbed one of his wooden crutches and hammered it explosively down onto the bar!

Every glass on the bar was lifted into the air and came down with a loud clanging!!

Wolfgang jumped with fright! Papa grabbed Wolfi's chair and pulled it close.

"Godddammit!" shrieked the bartender. He savagely jerked the man's crutch out of his hands and threw it towards the door! Then in a rage he grabbed the other crutch and One-Leg's raggedy black briefcase, walked over to the door and threw them out into the street! Next he bolted back and grabbed One-Leg viciously by his black leather lapels and began heaving him towards the door, his one foot dragging along the floor!

One-Leg then raised his fist and punched the bartender brutally in the mouth, drawing blood! The barkeep released One-Leg's lapels which caused the drunk to fall to the floor with a loud boom. Then he smashed his knees down onto both of One-Leg's arms to pin them to the floor, and hammered his face with violent bone-shattering blows!! Each punch made a thumping-snapping sound like someone smashing melons on concrete. Blood was now pouring out of One-Leg's nose, his mouth, and from his forehead.

When One-Leg's body went completely limp, the bartender seized him and threw him ferociously onto the sidewalk! There was a heavy thud and then a cracking sound as One-Leg's body and face met the concrete pavement.

"Asshole!!! Fucking asshole!!!" screamed the bartender, slamming the door shut and stomping back to the bar.

"They were trying to kill me too!!"" blared Papa, arching his back and waving his fists. He gulped down the rest of his beer, grabbed another handful of peanuts, stumbled over to the bar and slapped down 40 Marks. "No change," he said dryly.

Wolfi was aware of the stale smells of decades of cigarette and cigar smoke, spilled beer, peanuts, and dust, as Papa jerked painfully on his arm. His heart and stomach were filled with sheer gut-wrenching panic and he was shivering!

Outside the door One-Leg's black-draped body lay lifelessly towards the left.

"Is he dead?!" Wolfgang asked, his heart knocking fiercely against his ribs. "Is he?!!"

"No," said Papa gruffly. "Let's get you outta here!" He yanked on Wolfi's shoulder and teetered a bit before he shuffled off towards the bus stop.

"Rudi! Rudolf!" It was a gravelly high-pitched man's voice somewhere up ahead of them.

Papa looked around to see who was calling him.

"Hey, Rudi!!" There it was again, quite muffled.

Then off in the crowd, waist-high, they saw a man's face moving from side to side trying to peek between and around a couple lady's butts. When the ladies stopped at a window display, Wolfi saw that the face belonged to a man who was missing both legs, who was just a torso sitting on a four-wheeled square wooden dolly that was rolling this way! Thrusting his gloved fists against the concrete and locking his arms, the man stopped the dolly just as he was wheeling past them, then quickly swung himself around to face Papa and Wolfi.

Wolfgang jumped back in shock at this frightening creature!

"Rudi! You didn't see me hiding among the asses!" the torso-man hooted and laughed hoarsely, pulling up on the collar of his green army jacket.

"I should have known that's where I'd find your face, Felix!" answered Papa with a little snort. "You were always an ass kisser!!

"How are ya, youngster?! War still pissing you off, like me?" Felix asked Papa.

Wolfgang's heart was racing and his body was stiff. The stench of urine, poop, and whiskey that wafted up from inside the torso's army jacket made Wolfgang nauseous.

"No use complainin' any more, Felix, new world," Papa answered half-heartedly. "But, I've gotta get the boy home. We're already late. His mom will cut my dick off!"

"That's the only leg I have left," groaned Felix. "I get it, Sergeant."

Halfway down the block Papa pulled Wolfi into a kiosk which had thick black curtains in the front. Behind the curtains Papa put four silver Marks into a coin slot and a movie began to play.

Wolfi looked up at the film and could see a naked woman stroking and lifting her big supple breasts as she straddled a naked man who was lying on his back. Wolfi thought of the bartender straddling the one-legged man, but it was clear that these people were not fighting.

Papa seemed to be fumbling for something inside his pants pocket. He moaned softly and then quickly cleared his throat.

"Papa! We need to go home! Please! I'm tired! Mama's gonna be mad!" Wolfi pleaded, tugging on Papa's sleeve. "Papa!"

"Quiet!!" hissed Papa, and smacked Wolfi's hand.

Wolfi leaned lethargically against the wall and rubbed his stinging hand. He usually found it spellbinding to watch the naked people play when Papa stopped at these booths, but he was very tired, upset from the bloody bar fight and the torso-man, and he really hated it when Mama was angry!

Now the lady groaned and began pumping her jiggling pale nude ass up and down enthusiastically. Papa grunted, still groping for something in his pocket.

* * *

"Is your father coming to pick you up? To take you home?" asked Heidi. She wrapped her hand around his and leaned into him.

"He said he would come back in a few weeks," replied Wolfi. "But, it's been a long time since he was here."

"I think it's just been a few weeks," Heidi said hesitantly.

"Yeah? I dunno," Wolfi answered, almost whispering.

"Look!!" exclaimed Heidi abruptly pointing to hundreds of bluebells on the side of the road.

"Bwah! This is the place! Bluebells!!" Wolfi ran over to them and Heidi was right behind him. He could hear them again; hundreds of tiny blue chimes that were accompanied by intense euphoric vibrations in his tummy and groin. It was heavenly to him!

"Bwah!" he sang the word once more, and smiled brightly. Wolfi knelt down and deeply inhaled their fragrance which smelled exquisitely clean, a bit like grass with a touch of sweet powdery perfume. He picked three stems that were covered with bells and handed them to Heidi. She smiled, held them to her nose and savored their aroma.

"Do you hear them ringing too?!" Wolfgang said, searching for validation.

"Yes," she replied softly and touched one of the bells with her fingertip.

"Alright, please keep walking, Heidi! Wolfi! Come!" Fräulein Edel clapped her hands twice authoritatively.

"Tanks again!!" screamed Benjamin suddenly and sprinted up to the intersection ahead! Frank and most of the others raced after him.

"Tanks!!" Benjamin bellowed one more time.

Just like before, the earth began to rumble and Wolfi felt intense vibrations coming up through his feet and into his chest! He panicked and began running back the other way! Herr Schmidt was close enough to bolt after him and grabbed Wolfi firmly by the arm.

"We always have to stay together!" said Schmidt in a loud impatient voice. Briskly he turned Wolfi around and pushed him towards the tanks!

The blaring of huge engines was getting louder and Wolfi was gripped by fear! He felt the air humming against his body.

"Ahmeeeeeese!" screamed one of the girls. *"Amis!"*

"Yes!! The *Ahmeeeeeese!! Not tanks!!"* shouted Robert and danced around in a circle. *"Amis!!"* he shrieked again.

"They're trucks, not tanks, Wolfgang," explained Herr Schmidt bluntly. "It's the Americans. The *Amis.* No shooting today."

The Americans?!!! Wolfi trembled. *The Americans are killers!!*

Piles of bloody dead people killed by American bombs pervaded his mind again! Herr Schmidt blocked him from running away one more time.

Now Wolfi could see that appearing out of another huge cloud of dust and black smoke, was a long line of about thirty dark green military trucks! Most of the giant trucks were 10-wheelers with two tires in the front and eight double tires in the back. But, at the end of the line some of the trucks had regular tires in the front wheels, but then actually had tank treads in place of their back wheels! About thirty green-clad soldiers sat along the sides of the open wood-paneled cargo deck of each heavy half-track, which shook the earth almost as powerfully as the huge tanks had done some weeks ago. Diesel exhaust and dense dust now filled everyone's lungs.

After the half-track trucks had passed, one more huge 10-wheeler came to a quick rattling stop in front of the kids with a piercing high-pitched squeal. Then the air brakes bellowed a shrill "Yeowwwwwwww!!!!"

"Herr Schmidt, yes?" the American soldier shouted down through his open window.

"That's me," responded Schmidt.

"We have them!" sang the driver with a proud smile on his lips.

He then shouted back at the two other soldiers in the jeep behind him in words that Wolfi did not understand. The jeep drove off to catch up with the other trucks.

"That's wonderful, Sergeant Garcia!" Schmidt called up to the man in the truck.

"Yes, call me Miguel," the soldier offered and waved his hand.

"Can I ride?!!" Benjamin, standing on his tiptoes, squealed excitedly up at Miguel.

"Okay, Benji" Miguel called out to him. "Only two... you and, uh, this new boy next to you."

"Wolfgang!" bellowed Benjamin, who then grabbed Wolfi's arm, dashed to the passenger side, and shoved him up through the open door. Wolfi scooted over next to the driver and bounced excitedly up and down on the very warm seat which was vibrating fiercely. Intense heat from the huge engine was blowing up at him from under the dark green dashboard and the cabin smelled like diesel exhaust.

"I am Miguel," said the American, smiling warmly. Wolfi hesitated but then shook his hand politely. Very quickly Wolfi became fascinated by the instruments and levers and gadgets all around!

"We go!" Miguel heaved on the large black steering wheel and the giant machine lunged slowly around the corner.

Wolfi felt like he was looking out from the second floor of a roaring bouncing building that was hurling down the road!! Somehow he felt very powerful up here!

"Fun?!" Miguel beamed as he noticed the huge grin on Wolfgang's face. Miguel rammed the clutch down twice and gunned the engine as he shifted gears.

"Soooo gooooood!!" Wolfi shouted in order to be heard over the engine roar.

When they reached the orphanage, Miguel backed the truck up the incline of the dirt driveway and then helped the boys down to the ground.

"Good day!!" Frau Sandmann walked up behind Miguel and greeted him enthusiastically. "Thank you so very much, uh... Sergeant... Garcia!" She looked down at the cloth name strip on his green shirt pocket while shaking his hand vigorously. Her jagged yellow teeth seemed to dance as she smiled broadly at him. "This is truly wonderful of you! You are so generous to us!"

"We happy to help, Frau Sandmann," Miguel said proudly with a bit of a shy smile, and glanced up at the canvas-covered cargo area.

"Wolfgang, sit, watch," said Miguel as he guided him gently to a good spot on the grassy hill. His attention made Wolfgang feel very special right now and for the moment he grinned from ear to ear!

Miguel opened the rear gate of the truck and four more American soldiers jumped down to the ground! Many of the other kids now also sat restlessly near Wolfi in order to get a good view.

"What are you dumping here?!" asked Frank arrogantly. He poked Benjamin and whispered, "These guys are assholes! Their bombs killed my mama, my aunt, and my two cousins in Frankfurt, and they shot my papa in Africa!" Spit flew from his lips as he fumed. "Shitty *Amis!*"

Wolfi thought about the thousands of American bombs that had flattened Mannheim and killed so many people. Shitty *Amis!* Cousin Manfred always growled furiously when he said it. Shitty *Amis!*

The American soldiers unloaded the truck and worked for quite a while assembling numerous red metal poles using lots of silver nuts and bolts. Slowly and steadily it all grew into an impressively big 6-seat swing set, a very tall shiny slide, and a large jungle gym!

While he was working Miguel often glanced over at Wolfgang, smiled brightly and waved. Wolfi waved back timidly, but now he couldn't bring himself to smile because in his imagination he heard huge bombs exploding in Mannheim, and Miguel was one of them!! The shitty *Amis*!

The moment the soldiers finally picked up their tools and tossed them into the truck, dozens of kids raced down and climbed all over the gleaming new contraptions, screaming, giggling, and shoving each other playfully!

Wolfgang was still sitting quietly on the grass observing all the commotion. Miguel sat down and put one arm around him, pulling him close for a brief moment.

"You watching, you very patient," he said to Wolfi. "You like this new things?"

Wolfi looked at him and tilted his head a bit as it occurred to him that Miguel talked funny and he had a heavy accent.

"Yes," replied Wolfgang, now staring down at one of the chamomile plants that were spread all over the hill. The sweet scent of chamomile lifted his spirits, and he also liked how good it felt to have Miguel's arm embrace him. This soldier didn't seem like a shitty *Ami*. For a moment Wolfi leaned his head lightly against Miguel's shoulder.

Wait!! Americans are killers! Wolfi pulled away!

"Do you fly bombers?" he asked tentatively after a few moments. He smelled the stench of rotting dead bodies.

"No, never want that! That awful! I drive truck. Just normal man," Miguel responded reassuringly and stroked him on the back.

Wolfgang looked up at Miguel's face. He had smooth tan skin, warm brown eyes, thick black hair, and a kind loving smile.

"Look! I show you! Normal man!" Miguel said as he pulled his wallet out from his back pocket. He opened it to a picture of a very pretty lady with dark hair and big brown eyes, who had a bright vivacious smile.

"This - this is Carla, my wife. She probably love you much!"

Wolfi put his finger lightly on the picture and realized she looked a lot like Mama. Carla felt tingly to him. He wondered what her hugs feel like. *Miguel must love getting tingly hugs from her,* he thought.

Miguel stood up and pulled a black camera out of his pocket, pointed it at Wolfi and snapped a couple pictures.

"She probably love you much," Miguel repeated, patting Wolfi on the head.

* * *

"Wolfi, wake up!" A man was whispering intently and shaking him. "Wolfi!"

Wolfgang struggled to open his eyes. It was Herr Schmidt. Wolfi's heart pumped faster. *What's wrong?!"* he thought.

Schmidt smiled momentarily, which was a rare sight.

"Someone wants to see you," he whispered, and another subtle smile appeared on Schmidt's pink lips.

"Go to the toilet, put on your pants and shoes, and meet me by the back stairs."

"It's nap time," said Wolfgang softly.

"It's alright, Wolfi! You won't get into trouble. Someone wants to see you!"

"Who?"

"You'll find out! Go to the toilet!" Schmidt disappeared out the door of the boys' dorm.

After he'd relieved himself Wolfi tip-toed down the hall. He found Schmidt at the top of the back stairs leaning against the wall, softly playing an enchanting melody on a clarinet. Schmidt's eyes were shut tightly and his creamy white cheeks were pink with passion. Wolfgang stopped and listened with amazement! He had no idea that such lovely sounds could come out of gruff and authoritative Herr Schmidt!

Tears actually came into Wolfi's eyes as he felt the glorious tones caressing his tummy and his heart. The familiar faint smells of urine, poop, vomit, stinky feet, and a touch of bubble gum and lilac soap, all made Schmidt's magical music seem so very out of place.

"Wolfgang! How long have you been standing there?!" Schmidt opened his eyes when he came to the end of his splendid melody.

"Come! She's waiting!" Schmidt grabbed Wolfi's upper arm and led him downstairs. He jerked open the back door and gave Wolfi a gentle push. "Go!"

Wolfi looked up the steep hill and searched the bushes and trees with his eyes. Halfway up sitting on a thin carpet of dead leaves, was Heidi! Her light blond hair blew slightly in the breeze as she waved to him and whispered "Come!"

Wolfgang enthusiastically made his way to her and sat down with his shoulder touching hers. She leaned into him as if to hug him hello. He looked briefly into her affectionate jade green eyes and they both grinned.

It seemed very strange to Wolfi that she was sitting alone up here, but he was always so happy to see her that it didn't matter right now!

The odors of damp decaying leaves, funky smelling mushrooms, cut grass, the fresh afternoon breeze, and Heidi's sweet daisy aroma filled his lungs. Tingling feelings of connection flowed through his body and he felt very light. They sat staring down the hill without a word.

After a while Heidi turned her head and kissed him fondly on the cheek. Her soft warm lips felt heavenly against his skin. A few wisps of her fleecy blond hair blew in the breeze and tickled his nose. She laid her head on his shoulder and he covered her head with his. They sat like this in joyful silence for quite some time.

"Look!" Heidi suddenly said excitedly.

Wolfi opened his eyes as she handed him a tiny wild strawberry which glistened in the rays of sunlight that radiated through the trees. The berry was incredibly small, the littlest one he had ever seen, yet it was perfectly shaped and bright red. He held it to his nose. It had an absolutely luscious strawberry aroma! Wolfi grinned and put the berry under Heidi's nose.

"Bwah!" she whispered as she sniffed.

Wolfi gazed into her soft green smiling eyes again. He felt her love.

Heidi inhaled the berry's fragrance once more and beamed. "Bwah!"

"Eat it," said Wolfgang.

"No, I found it for you," she replied softly but firmly, and pushed the berry towards his mouth.

"But, it's yours!" he protested.

"Eat it," she said, and again gently directed his hand to his lips.

Slowly he placed it into his mouth. It was the most delicious thing he had ever eaten!! It tasted stunningly good and it warmed his heart too!

"Bwah!" he gushed.

Heidi grinned with delight!

Wolfi brushed his hand lightly over the green leaves of the very short plants which covered the ground where they sat. There! Another one!! It was even smaller than the first one, and also a bright luscious red! Wolfi picked it carefully and put it into Heidi's hand.

"Bwah!" she whispered. "Magical!" She put it under her nose and breathed it in for a while, then slowly wrapped her lips around it.

"Ahhhhh!" she sighed, savoring its mouth-watering sweetness.

Heidi put her arm around Wolfi's shoulders, gently kissed his cheek again, and leaned her head into his. He put his hand on her thigh and moved closer.

"I love you," Wolfi whispered faintly.

Minutes passed. Tingles moved in waves through his body, and he was floating.

"Heidi!!" A woman bellowed loudly from below.

Both Wolfi and Heidi remained motionless.

"No!!!" murmured Heidi intensely without looking up.

"Heidi!!" The irritating woman's voice was closer now.

"No!!!" whispered Heidi again, and squeezed closer to Wolfi.

The two kids continued their embrace without responding. Then the woman saw them.

"Heidi!! What the hell are you doing?! They've been waiting for you!!" It was Frau Reichert, the witch, angry as always. "You have to go!! They've been here for thirty minutes, waiting!!" she sprayed spit as she shrieked. A sunbeam bounced off the big jagged wart on her nose.

Frau Reichert smacked Heidi on the back of the head and yanked her angrily down the hill! Heidi stumbled and fought to keep her balance, managing only a quick glance back at Wolfi. She waved once, but her smile had been replaced by a look of fear.

After the back door to the boys building closed behind them, Wolfi could hear the witch still yelling at Heidi, "What the hell were you thinking?!!"

A crow cawed once above him, and he noticed a couple tree pipits tweeting in the distance. A breeze rustled the leaves on the trees. His shoulders and head were cold where Heidi had been hugging him, and he felt painfully alone and empty now.

Where's she going?! Who was waiting?! Why is she in trouble?! he felt panicked. *Where's she going?!!*

Something felt very wrong to him! Wolfi brought his knees up to his chest and rested his head on them. His heart ached severely.

Mama!! I miss you!! His chin quivered. Tears began running down his cheeks yet again.

Mama!!

Suddenly a twig snapped loudly. Wolfgang's body jumped in surprise!

"Wolfgang!" It was Fräulein Edel. "Wolfgang, are you alright?" she asked in a concerned tone.

"Heidi..." He burst into sobbing and pointed down the hill, unable to say more.

"I know," said Fräulein Edel. She sat down and put her arm around him. "I know, Wolfi, it's hard."

Fräulein Edel held him close as Wolfi bawled his eyes out, staring at the decaying dead leaves all around him.

"Where's she going?! Why is she in trouble?" he was finally able to ask.

"She's not in trouble, Wolfi. She was just late. Her new parents came to pick her up."

"What?!! Pick her up?!" His voiced cracked from panic and he began to breathe hard.

"She got adopted, Wolfi," said Fräulein Edel very lovingly.

"Add doppted?!" He questioned, between gulps of air.

"Yes. We should be happy for her," replied Fräulein Edel.

"What's add doppted mean?" he asked, very bewildered.

"It means getting new parents. A new home," she said, matter-of-factly, as if that was a completely normal thing. She put her hand on his head and pulled his face into her soft warm breast.

Wolfi's whole being howled with grief!

"Add doppted?!"

* * *

The big plump woman said words to Wolfi that he did not understand and she gestured towards the luxurious couch.

The tall thin man also said something completely unintelligible and pointed to the sofa. They were both smiling at Wolfi, but they seemed agitated.

"Sit!" The man finally said a word that made sense to Wolfgang, but Wolfi felt scared to move.

Suddenly the big woman laughed loudly and lunged at Wolfgang! She grabbed him, picked him up, and hugged him so tightly that he felt sharp pains in his ribs! Wolfi struggled passionately to get out of her vice grip but she squeezed him even more tightly. Then she started kissing him all over his face, kiss after kiss! She moaned with each disgusting wet peck of her lips. An electric jolt of pain shot up through his head because she was pushing her face against him so hard that it twisted his neck! Her heavy rose perfume was repulsive to Wolfi, especially mixed in with the putrid stink coming from her armpits. He gagged.

Then, she began to cry!! She was sobbing loudly! And still she was holding him in a painful iron grip, smothering him with kisses!

Why is she crying?! What's wrong with her?! Wolfi felt scared and he began to sob too, while trying desperately to free himself from her imprisonment!

"Doris!" yelled the skinny man, and then a lot of other words came out of his mouth that made no sense to Wolfgang. The man finally grabbed the woman aggressively by her arms and released Wolfi.

Clumsily he guided Wolfgang by the shoulders to a seat on the couch. The man then walked over to a piece of furniture with a screen in it and flipped a switch.

"Tee Vee," he said proudly.

Wolfi once saw a television in one of the store display windows in Mannheim, but he had never seen one in a home before. He was enthralled! The fuzzy black and white picture showed two men in wetsuits and scuba tanks under the ocean. Air bubbles that looked like long clouds of thick smoke were streaming behind them, and both men were pumping their legs furiously trying to swim as fast as possible.

The man in the grey wetsuit suddenly stopped and brought himself to a standing position by waving his arms through the water. He then turned around to face the man in the black wetsuit. Grey wetsuit pulled a knife from a holster on his ankle and swiped it at the other man! Black wetsuit grabbed grey's arms and the two grappled with each other, making flip-flops in the water, both struggling to control the knife. Grey wetsuit suddenly cut through the hose on black wetsuit's scuba tank! Massive clouds of air bubbles now streamed up to the ocean's surface!

Wolfi was panicking for black wetsuit, hoping somehow to help the man breathe! Wolfi's heart was racing and his chest heaved up and down rapidly! He was perspiring and his legs were shaking.

Large woman pounced over to him from her side of the couch and again hugged him fiercely, smothering him with more repulsive wet kisses! Her heavy frame crushed Wolfi's arm and again she bent his neck to the side painfully!

"Ahhhhhhhhh!!!" he screamed, furiously trying to shove her off of him!

"Doris!!" yelled the tall man! He lunged at her and yanked her brutally off of Wolfi! Then he sat down and put his arm on Wolfi's shoulders to try to comfort him.

Wolfi pulled away. He trembled and whimpered once, but then quickly suppressed his crying! Abruptly he stood up and got into a rigid pose to make himself big! He did not feel safe here!

The stinky woman was sobbing loudly yet again!

Why is this large creature crying?! I hate you!! Wolfi's face twisted into a fierce scowl.

The creature and the thin man yelled angrily at each other for quite some time, and then stinky woman shoved the man viciously into the door, causing a loud boom!

Wolfi thought of the one-legged man being beaten to a bloody pulp in the bar and he felt afraid! He moved quickly toward the corner of the room.

Shitty Amis!! he thought as he watched them vigilantly. *Shitty Amis!!* His heart burned with pain.

Mama!! Why?!

Mama!!

"Okay!!!" barked the creature to the man after he had bellowed at her a while. Wolfi had heard Miguel say that American word.

"Okay!" the man said emphatically to her.

Rancid thing walked over to Wolfgang in the corner and leaned down offensively close to Wolfi's face. Her breath smelled like a foul dish rag.

"*Bett.* Bed," she said callously. It was the first word she had said all day that Wolfi actually understood.

She led the way down a hall and tall man walked next to Wolfi with his hand on Wolfi's shoulder. Once they were in a small bedroom, the stinky one stripped Wolfi down to his underwear while the skinny one watched from the doorway. She lifted him onto the bed, tucked the covers around his shoulders, and slumped her heavy body onto him! And again she drenched his face with tons of wet kisses! The putrid stench of her armpits was horrendous! Wolfi gagged, shoved her on the breast as hard as he could, and scrambled away, banging his knee hard against the wall!

"Doris!!" shouted the man once more. Now he jerked her harshly off of Wolfi, pushed her brutally out the door, and said a few more angry things to her in American!

"*Gute nacht*," the man then said awkwardly to Wolfi in German. Good night.

"*Gute nacht*, Wolfgang," the creature mumbled from the hallway.

Wolfi's heart was pounding! He felt desperately sad, glaringly empty, agonizingly alone. *I don't belong here! I hate these people!!!*

But, where do I belong?!

A muffled high-pitched squeal escaped from his mouth.

"*Gute Nacht, Mama*," he whispered faintly as tears welled up in his eyes.

Soon he drifted into the world where he could fly. There he felt safe.

* * *

"Move over!" It was a soft woman's voice. She had lifted the featherbed cover and climbed in next to Wolfgang. He stirred and opened his eyes.

"Good morning," she had whispered and kissed his cheek three times.

Even in his groggy state, Wolfi had by then realized it was Aunt Monika, Mama's sister, but he hadn't understood why.

"Your Mama and Papa left you here last night because you fell asleep long before they were ready to walk home. Remember?" she asked quietly. "Uncle Werner is at work and your cousins are at school. It's just you and me, love." She smiled, looked sweetly into his sleepy eyes and kissed him tenderly once more on the cheek.

Wolfgang recalled now. He had been really happy that he didn't have to walk home so late! He snuggled close to Aunt Monika and put his arm around her waist.

She slipped her hand briefly inside his underwear and lovingly squeezed his naked butt. Wolfi giggled and lifted his bottom up to pull away! Now his bare leg rested on her nude thigh, just like he loved to do with Mama. Ecstatic vibrations were emanating from her skin into his body and his heart.

"I love you, Auntie," he said in a quiet voice.

Aunt Monika lifted his head up and put his cheek onto her voluptuous breast. He felt the hardness of her tall nipple underneath her nightgown and lightly rubbed his face against it a few times.

"I will always love you, Wolfi," she said very softly, almost singing the words. "Always! No matter what happens."

He felt her tingling love in his abdomen and down to his toes.

"Wolfi, wise and powerful, will always find his way."

"Wolfi, wise and powerful, will always find his way." Now she was actually singing, almost as beautifully as Mama does. Monika had heard Mama sing it to him since he was a baby.

They lay affectionately and quietly for a while, Wolfi's cheek still resting on her nightgown by her nipple, his naked leg up on hers.

Soon Aunt Monika arched her back, stretched her arms and legs, and then yawned, letting out a big sigh. Slowly she pulled on the string at the front of her nightgown and open it wide to expose her creamy nude breast. Gently, she slipped the erect nipple over into his mouth and he sucked happily. Strong tingles of love filled his groin and overtook his heart!

Then all of a sudden he pulled his head away from her and backed off!

What would Mama say?!" he thought and his stomach turned over.

Monika looked at him closely and saw the fear in his eyes.

"It's alright, baby! You won't get into trouble!" she insisted, whispering intensely. An uncomfortable smile crossed her lips. "No one will ever know! You won't get into trouble!"

"I love you, Wolfi!" She pulled gently on his head and guided his lips back down onto her ample satin breast.

She arched her back with pleasure a number of times as he savored her. After a while she moaned and put her hands on his shoulders, pushing him tenderly down toward her open legs.

"You won't get into trouble!" she insisted.

Wolfi scooted down and laid his cheek on the delicate black hair. He shifted his cheek around quite a few times before he found a place to settle. He was fascinated by how very soft the skin on the inside of her thigh was and he stroked it fondly. The aroma of her powdery rose perfume blending with her musty smell was mesmerizing. The pounding in his heart felt sublime.

From time to time Aunt Monika raised her hips and moaned.

In a little while Wolfi's head and body went completely limp and he was sleeping.

Chapter Five

It was long and hard. The man was pointing it, then swinging it back and forth, while holding it firmly near its base with both hands. Like a speeding bullet, a small white ball tore past the man and slammed loudly into the thick padded glove of another man who was crouched behind him! A tiny cloud of dust rose from the glove.

"Steeeee-rike!!" The muffled shout came from a third man who was standing behind the other two. His face was hidden inside a heavy metal-caged mask, and he held a bulky black pad over his chest which he poked up under his chin.

"Hey, batta, batta, batta, batta, batta!!" Miguel yelled at the man who was holding the long hard wood thing.

The wood man was dark brown. His white teeth and the whites of his eyes glistened brightly in contrast to his chocolate-colored skin. He smiled over at Miguel and Wolfgang and pointed his wood once at each of them.

Chocolate!! thought Wolfi and smiled back. He'd never seen a chocolate man in real life, but he had heard about them when Mama read to him from that children's book.

Spread out around this big grassy field were two more chocolate men, a few caramel-colored men just like Miguel, and a bunch of vanilla ones. Each man wore a folded leather glove on one hand, green U.S. Army pants, and a yellow shirt with a black number on it.

The chocolate man with the wood was wearing green Army pants too, but had on a bright red shirt with the number 7 on it. There were about ten more red shirt men sitting on a long bench to the side.

Miguel put his tongs down on the side of the grill, waved some of the thick smoke away, then turned to Wolfgang and grinned.

"You have good time, Wolfgang?" Miguel beamed.

"Yes, thank you," Wolfgang said with a shy smile. He adjusted his lederhosen self-consciously and scratched his nose. His eyes surveyed the funny-looking sizzling frankfurters that Miguel kept turning and moving around over the hot charcoal. They did smell pretty good and he realized he was hungry. Another man lifted a steaming hot cage of long potato sticks out of a big vat of bubbling grease. Those smelled really delicious!

"French fries!" exclaimed Miguel as he noticed Wolfgang eyeing them.

"Pommes frites!" yelled Julia with a big grin on her face, while struggling to sound as French as she possibly could.

All four of the other orphanage girls standing with her also summoned their very best French accents and shouted in unison, *"Pommes frites!!"* Then they laughed hysterically, poking each other's tummies and hopping around in circles.

Miguel grabbed a paper plate, put a big pile of salted french fries on it and handed it to Wolfi. Wolfi slowly put one of the hot potato sticks into his mouth.

"Mmmmmmm!" he grunted with pleasure and grinned from ear to ear. This was one of the best things he'd ever tasted! Julia and Miguel both giggled at him.

"Pommes frites!" shouted Julia in French again, both hands grabbing the plate Miguel gave her.

"French fries!" announced Miguel once more.

"Fensh feyes!" Wolfi tried his best to sound like Miguel.

Miguel grinned, grabbed a glass bottle of thick red sauce and poured some onto Wolfi's plate next to the potatoes.

"Stick in here," he suggested to Wolfgang. *"Ketchup."*

"Kesh upp," mimicked Wolfgang. He dipped a hot fensh feye into the thick red goo, and stuck it into his mouth.

"Yuuuchhhhhhhhhh!!" his face contorted into something resembling Rumpelstiltskin! The amazing fensh feye was completely ruined by that horrible-tasting red stuff!!

"No problem, not worry," reassured Miguel, gently patting Wofang's shoulder. "Eat french fry!"

Wolfi quickly ate all the fries off his plate, relishing the amazing crispy deliciousness of each one! Miguel squeezed a strip of yellow mustard onto one of the strange frankfurters that he had laid inside a long grilled bun. He set it on Wolif's plate and Wolfi devoured it immediately.

Miguel put sizzling frankfurters and a grilled bun on the plates of all the other very eager kids, and then doused the hot coals.

When Wolfi had finished sucking up his second big plate of fensh feyes, Miguel sat down, put his arm around him and pulled him close.

"Listen, Wolfgang," he said softly. "I want tell you something. I speak not good German, so this hard."

Miguel pulled out his wallet and opened it again to the picture of his wife.

She looks like Mama! Wolfi looked up at Miguel and smiled.

"Carla, my wife," Miguel reminded him. "She not live here with me. She stay America. I tell her about you, I sent picture. She say she like you much. I like you much also, Wolfgang."

"Carla, me, we talk very long time," Miguel continued. "We want son. Carla, me, we want you be son for us, come live America! You be adopted."

By now Wolfi was familiar with that word. Julia had explained it to him after he'd spent the night with the stinky plump woman and the tall skinny man.

Wolfgang looked silently at Carla's pretty face and into her eyes in the picture for quite some time. She felt very good to him. He imagined what Carla hugs feel like.

"You want be adopted, live America?" Miguel asked gently.

Mama! Wolfi actually felt one of Mama's hugs just then and his heart ached from missing her. He was extremely confused.

Every day since the train ride he still had an agonizing burning desire to just go home!! It always seemed so very simple to him. *Let me go home!!*

Home! But...Mama's not home. Mama's gone. Papa never came back. Papa's mean. But, I just want to go home! What if Aunt Monika comes to get me, Uncle Werner, or Manfred, and I'm not there?!

Miguel saw a tear run down Wolfi's cheek and pulled him close. Wolfgang's chin quivered as he looked up into Miguel's warm brown eyes and gentle olive face.

"Okay." Miguel tried to comfort him.

Wolfi felt too overwhelmed to speak. His heart stung and was racing with anxiety. He liked how Miguel made him feel, and he imagined that getting Carla hugs and kisses every day would be really wonderful.

"Wolfi, are you happy?" asked Miguel with concern in his voice. "You want live America?"

Aunt Monika! Uncle Werner! Home! He still couldn't answer Miguel.

For quite some time Wolfgang leaned into Miguel and relaxed into his loving embrace. Then he gazed up and searched for reassurance in Miguel's kind eyes.

With a motion that was barely perceptible, Wolfi nodded his head.

* * *

"Mama!!!"
"Mama!!!!"

Her screams were piercingly loud! She was covered in dark blue blood, which was gushing from the left side of her face, and from her crushed left arm and shoulder. A large patch of light blue skin hung down below her left cheek, revealing glistening meat, muscle and crushed bone! Her blueish-white eyeball was dangling on the end of a bundle of stringy optical nerves! Whenever she moved her head, her eyeball danced from side to side, bouncing off the flesh where her cheek used to be.

She turned her head far to the left to scrutinize the scene with her other eye. One of the giant spools of cable had burst through the back of the truck's cab. A sharp broken edge of the spool's wood rim was a mere two inches from her bloody face, and she was pinned up against the dashboard! Suddenly a fierce cracking sound filled the truck cabin like an explosion and the monstrous spool lunged another inch directly at her!

"Eeeeeeeeeeeh!!!!!" She screamed ferociously!

"Daddy!" Now she remembered he was driving. Maria gathered all her strength and leaned forward to try to see around the spool.

The driver's side door was hanging wide open, swinging slightly back and forth. The side window and the front windshield were shattered, and the floor was covered with a thick layer of broken glass. Hot white steam danced its way from under the dashboard through the spokes of the steering wheel. The cabin reeked of nauseating diesel fuel, filthy axle grease, antifreeze steam, muddy snow, and blood.

"I...want you more today than ever before..." The music started to fade and the DJ put his best smile into his fast-talking voice. "So much more, than ever before! Chicago radio time is 1:32 on a very cold afternoon..."

The radio was blasting at full volume and the truck's powerful diesel motor was still bellowing like a wounded beast!

Her father's savage grunts and howls were so loud they cut sharply through all the blaring noise. His right arm hung completely limp against his side. A section of white bone was protruding from his left leg and dark blue blood was pouring out around it. He struggled intensely in an attempt to move that leg with his good arm, and shrieked occasionally from excruciating pain.

"Must... get... help..." her father managed to say between tormented growls. Now aware that his words were barely audible over all the shrill noise, he stopped for a moment to shut the engine off.

He lifted his broken leg up and over successfully for a moment but then lost his grip! The limp limb plunged down towards the ground, pulling the rest of his broken body with him! He shrieked brutally from inconceivable pain!!

Maria screamed! Then her head suddenly slumped down against her bloody blue chest and her world went silent.

Wolfgang was floating just under the ceiling of the truck's cabin, and he looked down at her body. His heart was beating wildly and his chest heaved as he gulped anxious breaths of air.

"Can you hear me?" he asked her. His voice echoed back to him from a distance, "you hear me?"

The wind howled. It was freezing. Horror and agonizing loneliness seemed to be burning through his skin and exploding inside him. His heart thumped furiously against his ribs and its pulse hammered on his ear drums.

"Mama!" She seemed to speak but Maria was still motionless.

Then suddenly she was floating next to him by the ceiling of the cab! Her face looked beautiful just like before. She looked over at him and smiled. Wolfgang felt sparkling love coming directly out of her heart!

Maria looked down at the bloody body on the seat and back at Wolfgang. Her lips did not move, but Wolfgang heard her say, "What happened?!"

Wolfi gazed into her luscious dark blue eyes and felt mesmerized, immobilized. He was unable to speak.

When he finally looked down again at the body, it was laying on a table. Seven busy doctors and nurses in blue pajamas and white face masks surrounded it. Four very bright spotlights hung next to him and Maria, who were hovering up by the ceiling.

Maria turned her head and her dark passionate eyes connected with his eyes. She made him feel power, euphoria, and filled his being with grins and warmth! Wolfi became aware again of that magical perfume which somehow radiated the intense love he felt coming from Maria! Roses, lilacs, and baby's breath in a passionate sweet musty blend. Wolfi inhaled deeply, all the way down to his toes, again and again. H*eavenly,* he thought.

Maria grabbed Wolfi's forearm as she looked down at the bloody body on the table.

"Who's that?!" she inquired.

One of the doctors was holding two heavy blueish-white paddles against the body. He glanced around briefly at the other masked people and yelled, "Clear!"

* * *

"Watch out!!" screamed Julia. She lunged forward, grabbed his shirt with both hands, and jerked him back to the side of the street.

"Beeeeeeeeeeeuuuuupppp!!!" A black Mercedes-Benz 300 sedan blasted its car horn aggressively and swerved toward the opposite lane!

"Watch out!!!" shrieked Julia again, and pulled him very close. "Please don't walk in the street! I love you!" she begged passionately.

Julia noticed that he was shaking. She wrapped her arms around him even more tightly for at least a full minute, in an effort to calm him. But this hug was just as much for her as it was for him.

"I've loved you since your first day when I tucked you into bed in the store room! You were so precious and vulnerable and cute!" she continued. "And nobody here loves me the way you do, Wofi! I can't lose you!!"

She kissed him tenderly once on each cheek, and patted him on the back. "Today was really hard for both of us, we're tired, it's a long way back to Bliss Cottage. And, I don't want to miss supper. Let's walk."

The Marburg city street went uphill for many blocks. Their shoes made scuffling sounds on the gravelly pavement.

"Did you have to take tests, like me?" she asked him.

"Yes," he replied. "Colors, shapes, um... puzzles, counting... oh, and questions about stories... other stuff."

"Yeah, mine was questions about stories, math problems, puzzles," said Julia. "They asked me about my mama. Asked me how I feel about her." Julia's head drooped towards the ground as she walked silently for a few moments.

"My god!! I feel lonely, assholes! Every day! Why do these stupid doctors need to ask?! My mama and papa are both dead!! How do they think I feel?!" She kicked a piece of gravel that slammed into the bumper of a parked car with a loud ping.

"I don't even remember my mama," she grumbled. "I only know she and my papa died in Frankfurt when American bombs hit our apartment building. I was one year old and I didn't die. Now I'm twelve and I've lived at Bliss Cottage ever since then. How do they think I feel?!! Assholes!"

"My cousin saw piles of stinky dead bodies outside bombed buildings lots of times when he and my Mama went into the city." Wolfi grimaced as he spoke in a half-whisper.

"I don't remember any bombing," she said. "They only bombed cities, not here by the orphanage."

The uphill climb seemed very steep now and they were both breathing hard. They struggled to conquer the slope for a while in silence, looking pensively towards the ground.

"Did they ask you what you feel about your mama?" Julia asked in between gulps of air.

"Yes. The doctor gave me a doll and said 'pretend it's your mama'. I got mad and threw it down and I yelled 'she's dead!'".

"I'm sorry, Wolfi. I love you." She reached out and gently took his hand in hers. His heart beat faster and his hand tingled from the magic of her touch. He looked up into her teal-blue eyes.

"I love you," he said, squeezing her hand affectionately.

A bright red Citroen 2CV drove slowly past them and then pulled over to the side of the road. Gravel crunching under its rubber tires made muffled popping sounds as it came to a stop. A man stuck his head out the driver's side window, peered back at the two kids, and waved.

"It's the farmer! The one with the huge draft horses! Come on!" Julia tugged on Wolfgang's hand and raced toward the car.

"*Guten Tag, Julia!*" shouted the farmer through the open window. "You two are a very long way from Bliss Cottage! Come, get in."

He opened the passenger door, which in this car was hinged on the side closer to the rear of the car, so that it swung open at the front of the car. Julia climbed in first.

"*Guten Tag, Herr Bauer!*" said Julia with a huge grin and shook his hand enthusiastically. "Thank you so much for stopping!"

"Bauer means farmer!" gushed Wolfi as he stepped through the doorway behind her. "Farmer the farmer!"

Herr Bauer saw Wolfi's mischievous smile as he shook his hand, and he played along. "You're lucky that I've known Julia many years, boy!" He waved his index finger in a threatening gesture toward Wolfgang, but couldn't help smiling as he shoved the clutch down to the floor and put the car into first gear.

They began to move and pick up speed.

"Bwah!" said Wolfgang, as he looked out the window with his eyes wide open from excitement.

"First time?" asked Farmer the farmer, leaning forward to see Wolfgang's face.

"Yes, first time?!" Julia asked, widening her eyes.

Wolfi nodded. "I rode in a huge Army truck! But not ever in a car."

"How strange is that, a giant truck before a little car?!" remarked Herr Bauer. "Germany doesn't have many cars now. But, it will. There are lots of empty autobahns to fill."

Wolfi gazed enthusiastically out the front window, the rear window, and both sides, fully absorbed in how fast the buildings, trees, and sign posts were moving past him! He was spellbound!

Now on the right was the long sloping ramp of a railroad track. As the red bricks on the wall were speeding hypnotically past him, Wolfgang suddenly remembered a dream!

Neu Isenburg Girl!! There was always a red-brick railroad ramp!

He felt her presence in his heart now. She was always sad. So lonely. But he always felt her love in the dreams, and he really liked hugging her.

A rectangular white sign next to the railroad track whipped by them and disappeared quickly.

Did that sign say Neu Isenburg!?

* * *

"You got a fantastic fountain pen and pencil set and you don't even know how to write! That's stupid! You're stupid!" Frank stuck his face right up to Wolfi's face and yelled, spitting as he did, like usual.

Wolfi wiped his face off and dried his hand on the grass where he was sitting. He gagged.

"It was his birthday, Frank!" insisted Fräulein Edel as she walked up to them.

"Yah, but he didn't start first grade with us in August!" retorted Frank. He danced defiantly in a circle.

"That's not something I can explain to you now," replied Fräulein Edel. "You leave Wolfgang alone, now!! I mean it!!"

Frank danced closer to Wolfgang, then shrieked and punched him viciously on the shoulder socket of his arm. Wolfi jerked back and winced from the sharp jolting pain! Tears welled up in his eyes. Frank raced off to the other side of the meadow at full speed.

"Frank!!!" screamed Fräulein Edel as she lunged at him and missed, then sprinted after him. "Frank!!" He was already way ahead of her and disappeared into the woods.

Wolfi grabbed on to his shoulder and laid back on the soft grass. Some of the other kids were pointing and laughing. He felt agonizingly alone, his arm hurt, his heart ached. He closed his eyes. Soon he found fascination and comfort from breathing quickly in and out like the rhythm of a group of drummers. *Whuuuuuu...shaaaaaa, whuuuuuu...shaaaaaa* In...out, in...out... He sped up the tempo and increased the intensity of each puff, while taking in the vastness of the sapphire blue sky and fleecy white clouds.

Suddenly something big flew right past him and then was quickly gone again! Someone giggled.

Then hovering over the grass right in front of him was a girl in a white flowing gown! Astonished, he sat up immediately, but then relaxed a bit as he saw her tanned pretty face and her wavy brown hair.

Neu Isenburg Girl! Wolfi recognized her from his dreams.

The girl giggled, turned, and flew off to the far edge of the meadow where two massive round white oil storage tanks were now standing! Stairs spiraled up along one round side to the top of each white giant and a white ladder shot straight up the other side of the tank for access to the domed black roof. On their right and overlooking the meadow, two tall white apartment buildings appeared from nothingness!

She flew past the buildings, over a grassy soccer field, to a 3-story white house with a red tile roof, which she circled a few times. A teal-colored streetcar jingled its bell a few times as it plundered along tracks on one side of the meadow and soon disappeared into the shadowy green forest. That seemed very strange; a streetcar in a meadow!

Then instantaneously she was hovering right in front of him again!

Neu Isenburg. Wolfi heard her say it but her mouth did not move.

She reached out and took his hand. Wolfi apprehensively tried to pull it back, but before he could react he was suddenly flying right next to her over the soccer field and towards the big white house! She led him to a window at the top edge of the sloped red roof. Somehow they sailed straight through the glass and into a very small narrow room! There was a skinny bed and a tiny white desk and dresser near the window.

Just as they got past the window pane, her green eyes abruptly turned dark red, and intense hatred and fury spewed out from them! She directed her loathing down at the floor and was shuddering as she pointed! Screeching, screaming, horrifying voices were gurgling up through the carpet like scalding boiling oil!

Streams of tears poured down her cheeks. Wolfi felt her precious love in his heart.

Suddenly they were both flying toward a huge puffy white cloud high above the meadow.

Neu Isenburg Girl giggled. Then she was gone.

Chapter Six

Julia clutched his hand a little tighter. "Are you excited?" she asked him. "You got invited to a birthday party! That's amazing!"

"Who is this girl?" questioned Wolfi.

"Her mom is a friend of your mama's!"

"Mama!" His heart skipped a beat.

"Mama?!"

"Come, walk faster!" Julia urged and pulled on his hand. "There's the waterwheel! You love the waterwheel!"

Wolfgang struggled to keep up with her and he was breathing hard.

"Will Mama be here?!" Wolfi asked anxiously.

Julia stopped in her tracks. She looked at him in silence, puzzled. She shook her head a little to tell him no, but she was clearly bewildered by his question.

"The door is open, come!" Julia pulled him firmly past the heavy hand-carved wooden door and into the restaurant.

Three stuffed deer heads with large sets of antlers and bulging sad brown eyes stared dejectedly down at them from high on the wall to the left. Wolfi hadn't noticed them when he was here with Papa. It was poorly lit inside this place. The smoke from cigarettes and cigars was so thick you could barely see the wall on the far side.   Savory smells of roast pork, potato dumplings, sweet and sour red cabbage, and the pungent odor of beer pervaded the smoke-filled air. There was a constant loud blanket of noise from many conversations, occasional piercing laughter, and the clanging of silverware, plates, and glasses.

"Do you have a reservation?" asked the lady behind the brown wooden podium as they were walking past her. She took a huffy sniff through her nose and looked arrogantly at the two children. Her overwhelming perfume smelled of dead roses, and when she lifted her arm like a Nazi salute to stop them, Wolfi noticed her underarm smelled a bit like horse poop. He wrinkled his nose.

"He... he's here for the birthday party... um, Bischoff," announced Julia timidly, pointing at Wolfgang.

"Speak up, girl! What?! Bischoff?!" sneered the hostess.

Julia nodded.

"Bischoff, let's see... Yes, in the room next to the toilets!" horse poop lady commanded with a wobbling nod of her double chin. She pointed to her right.

"Wolfgang!" A short brunette woman in white heels and a beautiful yellow dress came bounding over to him with a huge grin on her face. She engulfed Wolfi in her arms with loving affection and kissed him on the cheek!

"Wolfgang!" she repeated. "I'm so happy to see you again!" She put both her hands on the back of his head and smothered his face between her pillowy breasts so firmly that he couldn't breathe. She smelled of sweet creamy jasmine. Her loving attention felt strangely wonderful to Wolfi.

"How are you, Wolfgang?! Do you remember me?" the woman asked him hesitantly. "Isabel and I were at your apartment quite a few times visiting your Mama. Remember?"

He looked into her face for a moment, then looked at Julia for guidance. He actually did not remember ever seeing this woman before! He thought for sure that if he told her so, that he would not be invited to stay for the birthday party. He just stared at her very uncomfortably.

"I'll pick you up in two hours," Julia said, interrupting the awkward silence. She touched Wolfi softly on the shoulder as she turned to the brunette woman. "Thank you, Frau Bischoff." Julia curtsied.

"Wolfgang, you've grown tall and you look so handsome! Your Mama would be very proud of you!" Frau Bischoff knelt down, ruffled his hair and beamed at him.

Mama. Proud of me. He stumbled on the thought. Didn't seem proud, she had sent him away. His heart raced and was now so heavy with pain that it felt like it sank down to his stomach.

He glared silently at the floor.

"Come see Isabel! You'll remember her! She's six today," said Frau Bischoff excitedly as she stood up and grabbed his hand.

In the party room, a girl in a white dress with a red ribbon in her brown hair was the center of attention for twelve other kids at a long table.

"Isabel!" Frau Bischoff extended her arm and waved her hand near the girl's face to get her attention. "Isabel! You remember Wolfgang, right?! The son of my good friend, Angelika."

Isabel examined Wolfi briefly with her eyes, let out a nervous giggle and asked, "The one who died?"

The room became completely silent and everyone's eyes were on Wolfi! A bolt of searing pain pierced his heart.

She's dead.

"Isabel!! You're being extremely rude!!" Frau Bischoff turned blotchy red from embarrassment. "Isabel!! I'm ashamed of you!"

Isabel peered down at the white table cloth for a few seconds, then smacked the table and said to the short boy sitting across from her, "Give me your spoon, I'm going to bend it with my mind!"

Most of the kids squealed with delight, but the boy challenged her. "You can't do that! Nobody can!"

She held the spoon in a horizontal position close to her eyes, made a very intense grotesque face, and exhaled loudly through her nose.

"It bent a little!!" shouted one of the kids. Isabel stuck her nose arrogantly into the air and squealed.

Frau Bischoff took Wolfgang by the hand and sat him down in the empty chair by the far end of the table. Her fingers trembled as she poured him a glass from one of the bottles of orange soda. Then she handed him a piece of mocha cream layer cake, patted him on the head, and hustled off to talk to one of the waiters.

Wolfi gulped down most of the orange soda right away, and quickly devoured the delicious cake - mocha cream was one of his favorites. When his plate was empty he stared blankly up at the blue and white porcelain dishes which were mounted on the wall.

At the opposite end of the table the kids were poking each other and fidgeting as red-ribbon girl opened presents.

Wolfi's heart ached. Always when the loneliness overtook him he felt very drained, exhausted.

Soon he laid his head down on the table and closed his eyes, easily tuning out the annoying clamor.

* * *

"Wolfgang!!" It was a very hoarse whisper.

"Wolfgang!!" There it was again, reverberating like it was coming from a large cavern. A shiver invaded his groin and ran all the way up to the top of his head.

"Wolfgang!!!" The voice was louder now, fiercely intense, terrifying! It was a bone-chilling hiss from deep in the blackness at the bottom of the stairs!

Suddenly two invisible hands were squeezing him firmly on the waist! He looked down - his feet no longer touched the floor! Painful spasms wrenched through his stomach. The cellar door creaked and opened slowly as Wolfi's body floated towards it!

Now he could see the vague outline of a man at the bottom of the stairs who was dressed entirely in black! Powerful buzzing waves of electric energy were rushing up the staircase from him, slowly and forcefully pulling Wofli down the stairs towards this terrifying blackness!! Wolfgang felt all the air gushing out of his lungs and his heart was on fire!

He tried desperately to scream! Nothing! Absolutely nothing came out of his mouth. And his body was completely paralyzed!! A freezing draft blew up from the cellar as the howling of the wind reverberated in the distance.

Now Wolfi was helplessly hovering a few steps from the bottom, just a yard away from the man!! Every part of his body felt as if it would explode from sheer terror!! He was dripping with sweat and trembling violently.

Then the nightmarish black form reached both its arms out to Wolfi!! In a penetrating chilling whisper it again said, "Wolfgang!!

A thousand razor-sharp daggers pierced Wolfgang's stomach!!

Suddenly Wolfgang's feet hit the concrete of the cellar floor and he instantly started running as fast as he possibly could!

"Wolfgang!!"

"Wolfgang!!"

Someone touched him on the shoulder!

"Wolfgang!!"

His back arched and he jumped in total shock, now opening his eyes widely!

"Julia!" he relaxed just a bit as he saw her face and inhaled her wildflower scent.

"Wolfgang, you fell asleep!" She ran her fingers gently through his blond hair.

"We have to go back. Did you have any fun?" asked Julia.

"No."

* * *

"No," said Frank in a dejected skeptical tone.

"You really don't think he came?!" Benjamin asked him once more.

"No," Frank said again, looking down at the floor.

"But it's December 6th. It's St. Nicholas Day!" Benjamin protested. He made a face like he was going to cry.

"Yeah, but you have to be good! Schmidt always tells us that we're not behaving, so fat Nick didn't stop by here, I'm sure of it," Frank clarified with a sneer.

Wolfi could see puffy flakes of snow drifting by outside the window and noticed that the sky was beginning to change from black to dark blue as daylight was arriving. He stood in his crib looking down at the one foot of soft blueish white snow that had blanketed the ground already. Herr Schmidt was trudging through the deep snow from the girl's dorm, lifting his feet up high as he walked.

"Schmidt!!" announced Wolfi in a loud whisper.

Frank and Benjamin quickly peeked out the window to confirm. Lightning fast, they tip-toed to their beds and slipped under the covers! Wolfi laid down and covered himself too.

Once inside the front door, Schmidt stomped his black boots to get the snow off and then clunked up the stairs to the second floor. He opened the door to the young boys' room, cranked the light switch on and the room lit up brightly.

"Morning!!" he bellowed. "Let's see what we've got!"

Twenty pairs of feet pounced out of their beds and thundered against the floor as the boys ran to the hallway! Schmidt backed up so they could all come out the door.

"Did you polish your shoes shiny enough? Were you actually good boys?" Schmidt said mockingly. "Did you get candy?!"

Lined up neatly against one wall of the hallway was a motley collection of 20 worn-out old, but very shiny, leather shoes. Benjamin found his shoe first and thrust his hand inside.

"Heeeeeeyy!" he whined. His face turned white and his chin quivered as he saw that his fingers were black! He reached back inside and pulled out a fat piece of pitch-black coal. Speechless, he raised his shoe and the piece of coal into the air and glared at Herr Schmidt in disbelief and anger!

"What?!!" demanded Frank as he also pulled a large chunk of dirty coal from his shoe. In spite of his dire prediction, he could not believe it! He stomped both feet loudly and scowled at Schmidt.

Wolfgang didn't bother picking up his shoe because he could already see the black edge of a piece of coal inside. A cramp twisted his stomach into a painful knot. He felt deeply hurt. *I'm sure I was a good boy!! I'm sure I was!!*

Benjamin was whimpering now and so were most of the other boys. Wolfi also began to cry.

"Well, I guess St. Nicholas agrees with me! You have not been good boys!" declared Schmidt. "He even left four willow switches for us to spank you with."

"Asshole!" Frank looked Schmidt defiantly in the eyes. "Asshole!"

"Well, I don't think St. Nicholas is the asshole here, Frank. You boys were the assholes for not being good," countered Schmidt.

"Asshole!!" Frank's face was filled with rage as he continued to glare directly at Schmidt.

"You should all spend today thinking about how you can be good boys! Then maybe if we put your shoes out again tonight, just maybe you'll get some candy," suggested Schmidt in an icy cold tone.

Frank was still staring furiously at Schmidt's face! He knew somehow that this had nothing to do with St. Nicholas.

"Asshole!"

* * *

It was a glistening deep red, and it seemed to pulsate as he looked at it. It was the most beautiful heart that he'd ever seen. "Love, Julia," she had written on the inside of the card. He grinned from ear to ear as he looked again at the beautiful words - these were words he already knew how to read. "Love, Julia." It was as if she had her arms around him now and he could feel her familiar magical vibrations on his skin. Her sweet wildflower scent caressed his thoughts and seemed to fill his body with love.

"I love you, Julia," he said softly. He looked through the window over to the girls' building and smiled.

Behind the trees on the far left he saw clouds of black smoke drifting toward the sky. It stood out against the backdrop of pure white snow that covered the ground as far as one could see. Soon the fat black puffs of diesel exhaust were directly below him as a huge dark-green U.S. Army truck roared and backed up into the orphanage driveway! Piercingly shrill screeches trumpeted from its air brakes as it maneuvered its way into a spot to park! The air smelled like freshly baking bread mixed with gasoline exhaust; that familiar odor of diesel fumes that Wolfi knew from the city.

The door of the giant truck opened and a man in dark green Army fatigues stepped down into the snow with his black boots. At least fifteen kids surrounded him immediately, looking for chocolate or other goodies, desperate for attention from one of the few adults in their world.

"Benjamin, here, give to everyone! Happy Valentine!" said the man handing him a big bag of foil-covered chocolate eggs.

As the man turned Wolfgang saw that it was Miguel! Wolfi jumped out of his chair by the window, slammed his feet into his shoes, and raced down the stairs!

When he got to the truck Miguel was nowhere in sight.

"You already got two!" commanded Benjamin, as he smacked the hand of one of the younger girls. He was clearly enjoying the power that he'd just been given. By now thirty or more kids surrounded him, all jostling fervently for position and clamoring for chocolate eggs.

Wolfi walked anxiously all the way around the huge truck three times and could not find Miguel anywhere!

Suddenly from behind him there was a hand on his shoulder! Wolfgang jumped in shock!

"Wolfi!" said a warm familiar voice.

"Miguel!!" Wolfi turned and fell into the secure comfort of Miguel's embrace. They were both beaming!

"Come, we take ride!" said Miguel warmly and began leading him to the passenger door of the truck. "Frau Sandmann say alright you go!"

"Really?!! Just me?!" Wolfgang could hardly contain himself.

"Yes, just you. Climb in," said Miguel matter-of-factly as he helped Wolfgang up into the huge truck.

Miguel shut the door with a loud metallic thud. Wolfi could only see the hair on top of his head peeking up over the truck's front hood as Miguel walked around the front. Miguel pulled himself up into the driver's seat, turned the key and hit the starter button. The massive diesel engine roared ferociously underneath them and the seat tickled their butts as it vibrated madly. Miguel smiled at Wolfi, gunned the engine three times, honked the blaring horn twice, and then slammed the gearshift forward.

Once again Wolfi felt like he was riding in a massive building which was bouncing and gliding through a world where everything was far below him and looked way smaller!

Farmer the farmer's big u-shaped courtyard and the massive barns and house which framed it came into view. The great complex looked almost miniature, and the draft horses and cattle in and around it looked tiny! But the walled-up square that was brimming over with an enormous pile of animal poop in the center of the courtyard still reeked with a nauseating stench that was huge!! They drove by the giant waterwheel at the mill and even it seemed to be the size of a toy! Wolfi grinned brightly and felt very powerful!

"Bwah!!" gushed Wolfi.

"Bwah!!" Miguel grinned as he mimicked Wolfi's favorite word.

About fifteen minutes into the ride Miguel pulled the truck off the road and brought it to a jerking stop at the edge of a big snow-covered field. The air brakes let out another piercing shriek, and Miguel shut off the engine. Suddenly there was complete silence.

"What happened?!" asked Wolfi nervously. The very serious look on Miguel's face gave Wolfi a bad feeling.

Miguel stared at the trees on the frozen white horizon. After a long tense silence, he sighed heavily three times, shifted his feet, and turned to face Wolfgang.

Wolfi's heart began to pound. He searched Miguel's face inquisitively for clues.

"Remember I tell you Carla and I want adopt you... want you, be our son?" Miguel asked slowly and softly.

"Yes...," answered Wolfi with a very faint smile, hoping for good news.

Miguel looked down at the floor and took a very deep breath, letting it out slowly.

"Army send me to other land... Korea... before Germany time finished... they say need me Korea, now." Miguel lovingly took Wolfgang's hand into both of his.

Wolfi's chin quivered a bit and his pulse pounded against his ear drums. By the time winter had set in a couple months ago, Wolfi knew in his heart that no one would be coming to take him home. That made it easy to decide that he wanted hugs from Carla and Miguel every day!

Miguel continued. "Agency needs interview me, Carla too, before say alright for you be adopted."

Interview. Carla too. Wolfi felt hope.

Adopted. That word always made him remember the day that Heidi got picked up and now his heart stung from missing her.

"But, Wolfi, Army send me Korea before interview day. And, Army say I can not come back Germany for interview." Miguel's voice was heavy and hoarse. His eyes were full of tears. He wiped his cheeks and was silent for quite some time.

Wolfi watched him for a bit and then stared blankly at the dark green dashboard.

Miguel put his arm around Wolfi's shoulders and pulled him close.

"Do you understand?" he asked, almost whispering.

"No," replied Wolfi, again searching Miguel's face for clues.

Miguel grimaced like he was going to burst out crying, but he held it back. He kissed Wolfi's forehead and laid his cheek on top of Wolfi's head for a few moments before he was able to pull himself together enough to look into his eyes and speak.

"Wolfi, that means... you not be adopted." Miguel cupped Wolfi's face in both hands and kissed his forehead affectionately. "I'm sorry, Wolfi. I'm so sorry!" Now he did sob a few times, but quickly suppressed his crying in order to be strong for Wolfgang.

Not adopted. Wolfgang's heart sunk to his stomach and then back up to his throat. Tears streamed down both his cheeks. He buried his face in his palms and sobbed loudly, his whole body heaving.

"Wolfiiiiiiii..." Miguel held him close and sang his name with love, hoping somehow, some way, to comfort him.

Wolfi heard Mama's song in his mind now, felt her loving voice in his heart.

Wolfi, wise and powerful, will always find his way.

Wolfi, wise and powerful, will always find his way.

All of a sudden he bolted into a rigid standing position, the top of his head bashing into Miguel's cheek!

Maybe she was wrong!!! What if she was wrong?!!

He sucked the mucus back through his nose with a furious snort, fell back into the seat again, and bawled uncontrollably. His mind wandered to the German soldier buried in the field and wondered if it felt this agonizingly lonely to be dead.

The freezing wind howled like the haunting wail of an air raid siren.

* * *

In the distance there was a hollow thumping sound as if someone was pounding on a large melon. It was becoming louder. Wolfgang looked below him towards the noise and saw seven doctors and nurses in cloth masks and light blue pajamas crowded around the body of a girl on a white operating table. One of them raised his fist high into the air and bashed her chest as hard as he could! That was the melon sound.

Like every time that he saw Maria, this was all in blue and white; like a black and white movie, but in blue and white.

"Clear!" shouted one of the doctors dressed in powder blue. With his hip he pushed aside the pounding doctor and quickly placed a defibrillator paddle above the girl's naked left breast and another paddle below her other one. There was a high-pitched squealing sound like a tiny siren continuously going up in pitch, and then an explosive booming blast of electric current shot into the girl's body! Her body rocketed violently up off the table and came down with a powerful thump! The defibrillator's hum began to rise in pitch again as it recharged.

"Once more, doctor," said the melon pounder.

"Who is she?" It was a soft whispering woman's voice to his right.

Even before he looked to the right and connected with her dark blue passionate eyes, he felt sparkling love emanating from her. It was Maria!

"You!! She's... um... you!" His voice cracked. It frightened him to see her in two places at the same time! His own heart pounded wildly as he looked down at the girl's body, and then back at Maria floating next to him!

"No, I'm here," she said quietly. She was very certain of that.

Wolfgang looked back into her dark eyes and suddenly became overwhelmed by a feeling of euphoria, total lightness, and powerful deep love like he never imagined was possible! Now his heart felt feathery as it continued racing wildly!

"Come," she whispered tenderly and then affectionately merged her hand with his. The magic of her touch and the sensual warmth of her silky skin gave him an ecstatic rush!

You feel amazing to me! Wolfi was in a heavenly trance.

Floating, flying, she guided him upwards toward an extremely bright white light not far away.

Wolfi felt blissful like he had never known as they approached the light! Suddenly his awareness was pervaded again by that luscious blend of roses, lilacs, and baby's breath flowers. This aroma was somehow intoxicating, angelic, and it seemed to energize him and everything around him with pure magical power! Wolfi inhaled it deeply, again and again, all the way down to his toes.

All of a sudden the brilliant light was immediately in front of them! She looked at him and let out a high-pitched squeal of delight and headed straight for the center of it!

"We can't!!" Wolfgang barked loudly! The light's fierce intensity scared him! He jerked on her hand to try to stop her. "We can't... Maria!"

It was too late! They were inside!! Instantly they were surrounded and encompassed by a world of indescribably resplendent beautiful colors!! Things were no longer only in blue and white, but radiated hues and tones and colors that were majestic and glorious beyond imagination!!

The white clouds and gorgeous white buildings below him were a white that was more pure and beautiful than even seemed possible! The astonishing greens of the lush grass, trees and bushes, the sensational blues of the sublime sky and the stunning lakes, the many spectacular shades of red, yellow, orange, purple, pink, violet, lavender, were all phenomenal, beyond belief!!

Wolfi's body, his entire being were enveloped and penetrated by what seemed like sublime heavenly protection and angelic nurturing! The air, the sky, the clouds, the grass, the lakes, the trees, even all the pure white buildings below; everything radiated this inconceivably gorgeous love!! It was a buzzing euphoric warmth, an ecstatic electrifying power, a sublime physical texture which caressed him, embraced him, and filled him with stunning divine love!

There were no words for this!! Even the word love seemed entirely inadequate! *Love, love, love, love, love, love, love, love, love, love, love...*

"So incredibly amazing!!" Maria squeezed his hand and gazed into his eyes. "Incredible!!" she exclaimed again. Enchanting pure love beamed out from her too now, and filled Wolfi's heart with even more delight!

"I love you!" Wolfi gushed. He wrapped his arms around her and pulled her close. *This feels like heaven.*

BOOOOOOM!!!! A thunderous explosion was accompanied by a brilliant flash of blue light, and the heavenly world suddenly disappeared!!

"There she is... She's back!" said one of the light-blue doctors down below with relief in his voice.

"Maria!"

Chapter Seven

"Maria!" The doctor called out to her in a loud hoarse whisper.

The nurse glanced back at him and stopped to let him catch up. She smiled and nodded a few times as the doctor said a long string of words to her that Wolfi didn't understand. Then the doctor put his hand over the pocket full of multi-colored pens on his chest and hurried away.

Maria was wearing a white cap, white nurse's dress, white stockings, and white shoes, but when her eyes met Wolfi's eyes, her smile shined even more brightly than all the white she had on! She said something to him in a light bouncy voice as she walked off, and then pointed toward the end of the long hallway. Wolfi did not understand even one word, but she had a pretty face and he liked her smile.

"Tuna fish!" the lady sitting next to Wolfi said as she poked his side. Then with a serious look on her face she pointed her curved index finger at the bread she was holding.

"Toooonfish," said the man awkwardly, trying to pronounce the German word *Thunfisch.* He didn't smile either.

Earlier today when these strange people had picked him up, Frau Sandmann had said, "Col. Bruce and Mrs. Bruce are nice people who are going to let you live with them for a while".

Mrs. Bruce now handed him the "toooonfish" bread wrapped in a paper napkin. It tasted like nothing he had ever eaten and he really liked the salty sweetness of the creamy sauce! He devoured it quickly.

Maria, the nurse, was back and approached them saying words in American to the couple. Mrs. Bruce stood up, took Wolfi by the hand and began following the woman. The nurse's flabby butt cheeks bounced and danced underneath her white dress as she strutted in the lead. At the end of the long hallway, her animated buttocks walked through an open door and she gestured to some chairs inside the room.

Gently she closed the door behind her and spoke to Wolfgang with a grin on her face. He understood nothing, and now her bright smile did nothing for the anxiety he was feeling as he wondered why they were here.

The nurse spoke to Mrs. Bruce again, and then walked over to a white table and picked up a large syringe from a silver tray. It was huge, with silver wings at the top of a fat open-sided glass and metal shaft, from which extended a long thick silver needle with an extremely sharp tip! To Wolfgang that looked like a serious weapon and he wondered what it could be for. He shivered.

Suddenly the windows began to rattle profusely! Even Wolfgang's chair was vibrating! An earth-shaking screeching roar was coming from somewhere outside! Wolfi jumped up in shock!

"Fighter jets," said the nurse, yelling to be heard over the tremendous noise. She pointed casually upwards with her index finger.

As the roaring subsided, the nurse picked up a small glass bottle of clear liquid and turned it upside down. Next she jabbed the syringe's jumbo needle into the bottle's cap and pulled outward on the plunger until the liquid was in the syringe. After shooting a couple of squirts into the air, she lifted the sleeve on Wolfi's shirt with her other hand and wiped his upper arm with an alcohol-soaked gauze. The pungent odor of the rubbing alcohol burned the inside of his nose and his eyes.

Then she suddenly raised the king-sized needle and aimed it at Wolfi's arm!! Wolfi screamed and tried to bolt for the closed door!! Mrs. Bruce and the nurse seized him immediately and confined him aggressively in the chair!

Wolfi began shrieking hysterically while fighting frantically to free himself! Mrs. Bruce got up, pinned his arms behind him, and tried to restrain his body by thrusting her chest down on his head, while the nurse held him against the back of the chair with one hand. But, he was still struggling so much that it wasn't safe to give him the shot. Both women yelled angrily at him! Wolfi didn't understand a word.

The nurse stepped back, held the syringe up in the air, and pointed at it vehemently with her other hand.

"Polio! No! *Nein,* polio*!*" said the nurse in a loud desperate-sounding voice.

"*Nein,* polio! No polio!" echoed Mrs. Bruce, also yelling and pointing her crooked finger at the syringe.

Poleeeyo. It meant nothing to him. The terrifying metal needle meant everything right now, and he continued fighting feverishly to get away from it!

The nurse let out a heavy frustrated sigh and put the silver syringe down. She whispered something into Mrs. Bruce's ear, who then got up and walked out the door. Mrs. Bruce came back very soon with the Colonel right behind her. He paused in the doorway to survey the scene, cleared his throat with a very loud barking sound, and then strode authoritatively into the room.

Without a word he kneeled down behind Wolfgang's chair and in a flash had both his arms locked around Wolfi's chest and torso! One of his hands reached around and held Wolfi's arm tightly against his side. His other arm extended up Wolfi's chest and behind his neck where the Colonel's hand pushed forward on the back of Wolfi's head. Now Wolfgang was completely immobilized! To be certain, Mrs. Bruce put her hands on Wolfgang's knees, and leaned forward with most of her weight to disable his legs.

The nurse brought her face close to his and sternly waved one finger at Wolfgang to admonish him. His chin quivered. She was breathing hard and her breath smelled like marzipan, cooked spinach, and vinegar. It was repulsive! Wolfgang gagged.

Again she wiped his arm with alcohol. The pungent smell burned the inside of his nose. Then without warning she jabbed the enormous needle brutally into his arm!!

Wolfgang let out an ear-splitting scream!! The pain was unbelievably excruciating!! Dark red blood oozed out one side of the puncture hole. Slowly but aggressively she pressed her thumb down on the syringe's metal plunger and emptied it into his body!

The pain was incredible! Wolfi was inconsolable for quite some time.

* * *

"Stillhalten!!" Mrs. Bruce bellowed! She had looked up the German word. "Hold still!!"

The back of Wolfi's neck stung brutally every time the man scraped the sharp edge of the buzzing razor against his skin, and Wolfgang simply could not prevent himself from flinching.

"Stillhalten!" snapped the barber, raising his black comb and silver electric razor into the air in frustration. He glared menacingly at Wolfi, who defiantly scowled back!

Powwww!!

Wolfi jerked back in shock as Mrs. Bruce angrily smacked the back of his head! The pain burned.

"Stillhalten!!" she commanded fiercely and swatted him again!

His head and neck sizzled, his chin quivered, and tears began streaming down his cheeks. The barber pressed painfully hard as he shoved the sharp razor in a straight line from the back of Wolfi's neck, over the top of his head and to his forehead.

Row by row like grass being mowed, Wolfgang's blond locks fell from his head to the floor, leaving only ugly rows of extremely short stubble. When he was done the barber slapped cold stinging aftershave onto the raw skin of Wolfi's neck. It burned harshly and smelled really disgusting, like lavender mixed with beer and mint!

"You said he's been with you three weeks?" the barber asked Mrs. Bruce as he spun Wofli's chair around. "Hasn't he learned any English?!"

"Doesn't seem to want to," replied the Colonel's wife indignantly.

The barber shoved a hand-held mirror into Wolfgang's palm. Wolfi saw awful red splotches all over his head, and the stubble that used to be his hair reminded him of the concentration camps! He looked ugly, absolutely horrendous! His mouth twisted spastically, his chest heaved, and he began to sob. But, then immediately he suppressed it with an intense fierceness. He was not going to let this woman see him cry!

"American boy!" said Mrs. Bruce pointing at him and smiling awkwardly. Wolfi understood those two words and she knew it. Four more times she pointed her crooked finger at him, "American boy!"

After she paid the man, she clenched Wolfgang's hand assertively, jerking him out the door and down the stairs.

"You here three weeks. American boy, Scott!"" she hissed at him with a creepy forced smile as she yanked him through the double doors of the cafeteria.

She shoved him into a chair at one of the tables and motioned authoritatively for him to stay there while she trudged over to the food line.

In a few minutes she reappeared at the table gesturing at him with a green ice cream cone in each hand. She did not see the grimace on Wolfi's face as she handed him a cone and stuck her tongue out to lick hers.

What?! GREEN ice cream?! he thought. *I love ice cream!! Chocolate! Coffee! Vanilla! Chocolate with brown nuts! But not GREEN!!!*

"Pistachio!" exclaimed the American woman between noisy slurps.

Wolfi gagged. *It smells like grass! I don't want to eat grass ice cream! Never heard of piss tashyo!*

"Pistachio!!" she declared again. This time she noticed his frown. "Eat it!!" she commanded.

"Eat it, Nazi!" said a curly-haired boy as he skipped past their table. "Nazi!" He gave Wolfgang a dirty look, then giggled and chased after his mother. Wolfi had seen him around the apartment building.

Wolfgang's heart stung and felt very heavy. Mrs. Bruce patted him briskly twice on the shoulder, but without much compassion.

"You - not kraut, not Nazi!" she announced with an arrogant chuckle, "you - American boy!"

He knew all those words and all of them made him angry!!

I am not a Nazi, my Papa is not a Nazi, my Mama was not a Nazi, kraut is something we eat, and I'm not an American!! He stared at her defiantly but was too scared to speak. Besides, she was stupid and did not understand German.

"Must learn English, Scott!" She gave him two more quick unsympathetic pats on the shoulder.

"Must learn English, Scott."

* * *

"Say what this is!" demanded Mrs. Bruce sternly. She waved the book up and down pointing vigorously at the picture of a locomotive and rail cars.

"Ein Zug," said Wolfgang confidently. He enunciated the German words for "a train" very clearly and was proud of his answer. *"Ein Zug,"* he repeated, and then looked down at the floor.

"No, in English!" declared the Kindergarten teacher. She moved to take the book back from Mrs. Bruce, who quickly jerked it out of reach.

"No, not Zug! It's a train, Scott! A train!! Don't be dumb!" Mrs. Bruce's voice was loud, agitated, and high-pitched. She shook the book at him again.

Wolfgang's heart ached and raced, from anger and from hurt pride. But the weeks of constant aggression from these American people had brought such rage into his heart that he was now much more inclined to be blatantly defiant than to break out in tears. He stared hatefully at the grooves between the tiles on the floor.

"Okay, then, so what is this?!" Mrs. Bruce barked as she pointed to a long-haired figure in a dress. She smacked Wolfgang firmly on his shoulder. He jerked back to avoid another one of her head slaps.

"Eine Puppe," he said quietly after a few moments of tense silence. Again he pronounced the German words very clearly and was pleased with himself for knowing the right answer.

"Goddamn it, Scott! It's not a Poopa, it's a doll!! Goddamn it!!" Mrs. Bruce shrieked, but then restrained herself in front of the Kindergarten teacher. Sweat was hanging off the tiny black hairs above her upper lip. Her cheeks were bright red.

"You are so incredibly stubborn! We've been at this for thirty five minutes now! Your teacher and I are trying to help you! Goddamn it!!"

"Doll," the teacher said softly in an effort to encourage him and to calm Mrs. Bruce.

Doll. Wolfi had never heard that word. *Puppe* seemed entirely logical and correct to him. "Doll" had a very strange sound to him.

"Dull," His voice fluttered as he strained to say it right.

"No!" yelped Mrs. Bruce.

"Dull."

"Not dull!! Doll!!!" shouted the Colonel's wife.

Wolfi sneered and put his best effort into it again. "Dull."

"You're not even trying, Scott! Goddamn it!! I've had eeee-nufff!" Mrs. Bruce was furious! She grabbed Wolfgang harshly by the neck and shoved him towards the classroom door.

"Thank you, Mrs. Albert," she said callously to the teacher without looking at her.

Once they were in the hallway Mrs. Bruce smacked Wolfgang so hard on the butt that his leg lifted up off the floor! His bottom smarted and buzzed intensely. Two young boys giggled at him as they walked by. Wolfi felt agonizingly alone, rejected, abandoned, devastated, and enraged!!

"You American boy now. Gotta learn English, Scott!" she hissed, pushing him harshly out the school's front door and then strutting towards the car.

He glared at the back of her head with utter contempt!! *I hate you!!!*

* * *

Mrs. Bruce released him from her hug and sat up again, while tucking the bed covers around Wolfi's shoulders.

"Scott, I can't believe it's already been four months since you arrived here! Time has flown by! We love having you here. You're a sweet boy, a blessing to our home!"

She bent down and planted a sloppy kiss on his cheek.

Wolfi pulled his pajama sleeve over his wrist and moved his arm to the top of his head. On the way up he wiped the spit from her kiss off of his face. He was pretty sure that she hadn't noticed.

"Do you like it here?" she asked him, straightening the collar on his pajama shirt.

Wolfi's eyes darted back and forth a few times. *Does she ever shave the black hairs above her upper lip?* he wondered. She stroked his blond hair stubble. He liked the aroma of the baby oil on her hands, but that was mixed with the awful warm-sour-milk stench coming from her breath. She let out a heavy sigh. He gagged and turned his head away.

"You don't know if you like it here?!" she whined. Her voice cracked slightly. "Scott? Don't you like it here?!"

Don't call me Scott!!" is what he wanted to say, but he didn't have the courage. She got angry a lot and then she was really an asshole! Wolfi thought of Frank; asshole was his favorite word, and Frank was really an asshole!   *So is this woman - an asshole!!* He glared at her.

"Scott!! We've given you lots of toys, new clothes, loving attention, a very nice new home, and a loving family. All the things that you did not have before! You really don't know if you like it here?!" she said, in a demanding tone that was also filled with sadness. "Scott, I'm certain that you like it here better than at the orphanage, right?"

Wolfgang continued to gaze at her in silence. His face showed no emotion.

"Well, I suppose it's best we know this before you start first grade next month," Mrs. Bruce said. She let out another foul-smelling sigh and a bit of a whimper. "I can't believe you don't know if you like it here better than the orphanage! For heaven's sake!!"

Now she was breathing hard and scowling at him fiercely.

"Would you actually rather be in the orphanage than here with us?!" she demanded between anxious breaths. "Where would you rather be?!"

Wolfi was expressionless and silent for at least another full minute.

"Orphanage," he whispered. He stared at the wall behind her.

"What?!! What?!! I can not believe it!! What an arrogant ungrateful selfish little shit you are!! After all that we have done for you?!!" she fumed.

Wolfi didn't understand all her words, but it was quite clear that she was furious. He pulled the sheet up over his head.

"You selfish little shit!!" she bellowed and ripped the sheet away from his face, scratching his neck badly with her fingernail.

His neck burned. He thought of Julia and how much he missed her affectionate hugs, how his aching heart longed to just be able to tell her what his day was like today, to look into her eyes and to once more feel really deeply genuinely loved! He really hated for the Colonel's wife to see him cry, but this time he was unable to suppress the tears. His chin quivered and he sobbed.

"Well, cry all you want, young man. You are absolutely not going back to that orphanage! Not after all the money and time and heartache that we have invested in you!!" she barked. She smacked him soundly on the chest twice to accentuate her words, then quickly got up and strode over to the door.

"You're an American boy now!! Good night!!" she fumed. She slapped the light switch and slammed his bedroom door shut!

Wolfi pulled the covers back over his head and bawled. "I hate this place!! I hate these people!!" he whispered vehemently into the blanket. The wildflower scent of Julia's skin and hair came into his mind. *Julia!! I miss you!! Julia!!* Four months. It seemed like it had been forever since he hugged her goodbye.

He missed Fräulein Edel's warm hugs too. He even missed Herr Schmidt just a little bit when he thought about him playing the clarinet. He missed Miguel from the Army. He missed Heidi. He missed Mama's hugs!! A chill shot through his heart. Tears streamed down his cheeks.

He imagined now that Julia had her cheek next to his, her chest laying on his body, just like she did in the storage room that first day. This time she didn't have to get up and leave. That made him feel a bit more safe, made him feel loved, and soon he was able to relax down into sleep.

There he felt very peaceful, protected, empowered, and loved. And he really liked flying, floating...

* * *

He was floating in the staircase again, and once more something massively powerful was forcing him slowly down, directly into the darkness!! Ferocious waves of electrified buzzing energy came racing up the stairs! Then, he saw him!!

The man in black!!

Wolfi tried to scream! No sound came out of his mouth! Nothing!!

One more time he put all the strength he could summon into a scream! Again, not even a squeak!!

The freezing wind howled outside the cellar windows. Whiffs of coal, potatoes, onions, mold, and dust filled his nostrils.

Wolfi's pulse pounded against his ear drums. Every part of his body felt as if it would explode from terror! He was paralyzed. And, he was almost at the bottom!!

Suddenly the black form reached his arms out!!

"Wolfgang!! It was a fierce whisper!!

Wolfi felt like he was being attacked!! Thousands of razor-sharp icicles seemed to pierce his stomach, his face, his entire being!

Somehow, some way, Wolfi landed just to the left of the creature!! Amazingly, his legs and arms were working now!! Horrified by the black creature, Wolfi stampeded through the storage area, out the back door and through a huge grassy field!

Wolfi looked behind him. The black form was only ten yards away!!

"Wolfgang!!" It was gasping for air, galloping after him.

Wolfi sprinted away like a bolt of lightning and he kept running!! And running, and running...

* * *

"I saw you running through the woods and I am pissed off!! Don't deny it!" Mrs. Bruce opened the apartment door even before he could ring the doorbell! She was waving a fat wooden spoon in his face. "I drove by in the car and I saw you racing out of the trees on Levin Street!! You are supposed to walk straight home and not take any shortcuts!!

He stumbled as she grabbed his upper arm brutally and jerked him through the door, threatening him again with the spoon.

Wolfi had been fantasizing about another delicious snack of cold chocolate milk and a banana on the path through the woods. He knew that the big spoon definitely cancelled that out.

"Miss Connors agrees with me that even though you're only in first grade, it's safe for you to walk home alone - it's just a few blocks. *But,* you are absolutely *not* allowed to take a shortcut through those goddamn woods!!" She was perspiring heavily, and panting. Wolfi gagged at the sour-milk stench coming from her mouth.

"Who knows what kind of creeps could be lurking in those woods! You deliberately disobeyed me and I am pissed off!" she thundered. "Royally... pissed... off...!!"

"It's only a block through the woods!!" Wolfi protested.

She grabbed him ferociously by his ear lobe and dragged him down the hall towards his bedroom.

"*Come* here!!' Her disgusting spit landed on his cheek and he tried to pull away. Lightning bolts of pain shot through his ear, down his neck, and into his back as she wrenched on his ear!

Even before they got inside his bedroom door, she tore his pants and underwear off in a rage! The fingernails on her other hand stabbed his upper arm like needles as she viciously held him in place! Wolfi struggled unsuccessfully to free himself, and his cheesy-white ass was now completely exposed.

"You are *not* to walk through those woods!! Ever again!! Do you hear me?!" she raged.

She plopped down onto a chair, slammed him face down across her lap, and raised the spoon high into the air.

"This is going to hurt me more than it hurts you." she declared.

She whacked and hammered his bare ass in a fierce rage over and over and over!!

Wolfgang screamed at the top of his lungs, numerous times!! He looked back across his shoulder and saw large red welts forming on his bottom. He tightened his butt muscles as solidly as he could in an effort to block some of the excruciating pain!

"Son of a bitch!!" screamed Mrs. Bruce. "You broke the goddamn spoon with your rock-hard ass! Son of a bitch!!" She threw him down to the floor, and charged over to her own bedroom!

Wolfgang scrambled to the far corner of the room and hid next to the tall dresser! She saw him disappear behind it as she stomped back into his room. This time she had a fat hair brush in her hand.

"Get your ass over here *now!!*" she raged, and grabbed him violently by the front of his shirt. Her fingernail dug into his chest, and his knee slammed against the corner of the dresser.

"Ow!!" he bellowed.

"I'll show you *ow,* you little shit!!" she blasted. Drops of her spit smashed into his face like speeding bullets. Then in a flash she had him face down bent over her lap again! She pounded viciously on his nude posterior with the heavy hair brush.

"Ahhhhhhhhh!!!" Wolfi screamed at the top of his lungs!

His screaming made her even more irate and she whacked his ass harder than before! The sharp edge on the back of the plastic brush sliced into his skin. Blood oozed out quickly, and then in another spot too. Mrs. Bruce noticed the blood and stopped.

Wolfi tried to yank his pants up while running toward the tall dresser. The top of his naked rump was still showing and he grabbed it in an effort to decrease the throbbing pain.

"You stay in your room until I say you can come out!!" the Colonel's wife fumed. She stomped over to the door and slammed it shut.

Wolfi fell face down on his bed and wailed, holding his bloody burning butt cheeks in his hands.

* * *

Papa had been fumbling in his pants pockets again, both front and back this time. Then he had lost his balance, planting his cheek and shoulder against their apartment door with a hard thud. Mama had heard the commotion and jerked the apartment door open from the inside.

"Where the hell have you been?!" Mama had demanded. "You're shitfaced drunk again... so loaded you can't find your keys in your pockets."

"I was... lookin' fer... thisss..." Papa pulled a crumpled white bag of chocolate-covered toffee out of his jacket pocket and shoved it in her direction. A few pieces fell to the floor as he lost his balance again.

Grabbing Wolfi's shoulder was the only thing that prevented Papa from a face-plant into the floor.

"Never mind the damn candy!! Where the hell have you been?!" Mama demanded. "I told you that when I'm having my really bad days, and I need you to take Wolfi to work with you, that you are absolutely *not* to stop at the bar after work!! But, over and over, you stop to get drunk, you expose him to bar fights, you expose him to those disgusting porno automat films, you put him in danger by barely being able to walk, and Wolfi has to help you find your way home!!"

"Angelika... It was... jhhusss a cupple 'a... beers." Papa put everything into trying to convince her. "Take... the cannndy, c'mon...," he slurred and burped loudly in her face. He pushed the tattered bag of candy up to her nose.

"Rudi, get that candy out of my face!" Mama ordered, pushing his fist aside. "Look, since Manfred moved out I don't have him any more to send looking for you and Wolfi. And, I am simply way too sick to be walking around in the dark myself!! *That's why Wolfi goes to work with you in the first place!!*" She was literally screaming as she said each word. Wolfi had never seen her so angry.

"Jhhusss have some... cannndy". A line of spit slid out of the corner of Papa's mouth and down his chin. He waved the bottom of the candy bag back and forth menacingly at both her eyes, almost hitting the tip of her nose each time.

"Get that candy out of my face!! You are so fucking drunk!" she bellowed.

"Angelika... I'm sayin'... I'm shorry... Jhhusss have some fuccckin'...," he burped again, and shoved the candy at her nose one more time.

"Get it away!!" Mama shrieked and pushed his hand down again.

"Angelika... Jhhusss take it...," he raised it to her chin.

"No!!"

"It's jhhusss... some goddamn cannndy..." This time he hit her nose with the bag.

"Rudolf!! I don't want any goddamn candy!!!" Mama screamed. With a furious powerful stroke she slapped the candy away from her face! The paper bag ripped and dark chocolate toffee wafers flew all over the living room floor.

Bam!!! Papa's raging fist suddenly smashed into Mama's nose!

Booomff!! His next hit exploded into her abdomen by her solar plexus!

Mama let out a breathy muffled scream! She bent over in agonizing pain. Several drops of blood from her nose dripped onto the floor. Quickly, she straightened up and tried to run toward the bedroom door! He grabbed her upper arm violently, painfully stretching and pinching her skin, and she screamed again!

Whack!! His ferocious fist slammed into the back of her skull! Mama ducked hoping to avoid the next punch, and tried to free herself from his crushing grasp.

Wham!! His fist landed directly on her left kidney.

"Eeeeeeehhhhhhhh!!!" Mama screamed from excruciating pain!! She tried furiously to get free, but his hand clamped down on her arm like a vice grip.

Boomff!! Another savage blow right under her solar plexus.

Furiously he rammed her through their bedroom door and hurled her onto their bed! Then he jumped on top of her, straddled her torso with his legs, and pinned her arms down with his knees. The bed frame squealed and thudded loudly against the wall.

Thoomp!! Thoomp!! Thoomp!! Papa pounded Mama savagely on her breasts!! Blow after raging painful blow he slammed into her chest!

"Eeeeeeehhhhhhhh!!!" Mama screamed at the top of her lungs!!!

"Eeeeehhhhhhhhh!!!" shrieked Wolfgang as loud as he possibly could. He ran over to the far side of the bed and grabbed Papa's leg trying to pull him off Mama. Papa's left fist flew in a wide arc around his back and smashed squarely into Wolfgang's neck, throwing him viciously against the wall. Wolfi fell to the floor with a resounding *Booooom!!*

Thoomp!! Thoomp!! Thoomp!! Again Papa's ferocious fists bludgeoned Mama's bosoms, and then he smashed into her face like a sledgehammer, again and again and again!! Mama struggled vehemently to get free, but his full weight slamming into her shoulders through his knees made it impossible for her.

"Eeeeeeehhhhhhhh!!!" she howled in utter agony.

"Eeeehhhhhhhhh!!!" screamed Wolfgang. But, he had no influence here, no power, no way to help his precious Mama.

Chapter Eight

"Wow!! That's where I used to live!" gushed Wolfgang, a little bit in shock. "Please, can we stop?!"

Mrs. Bruce touched the Colonel lightly on his shoulder, and said hesitantly, "I suppose there's no harm in looking..."

Col. Bruce pulled the 1956 Chevy Belair station wagon over to the shoulder of the autobahn and stopped.

"Wow!! That's my building! My apartment is the furthest one to the left on the first floor!" Wolfgang blurted out, fingering the car's door handle. "I want to go up there! I used to walk down here to the autobahn with my cousin, I can walk up there!!"

"No, absolutely not, you can not go up there!!" barked Mrs. Bruce. "There's nobody up there! Your mother is dead and your father moved away!"

"But, what about my cousin? Maybe he's up there? And, maybe my Papa did stay! I want to go look!" Wolfgang insisted. His heart ached again now. Any kind of connection to Mama was unspeakably precious to him, through cousin Manfred, or even one through Papa. *It's home!! This is where I'm from!!*

"Scott!! No!!" boomed Mrs. Bruce. "We pulled over here only as a favor to you so that you could look, but only look! Nobody you know is up there! You can not walk up there! Are you nuts?!"

'But... I just want to... go see!" Wolfi's chin quivered and he burst into tears. "I only wanna... if... anyone's home!!" he protested, barely able to get the words out through his contorted shivering lips.

"No! No! And, no!!!" Mrs. Bruce slapped him soundly on his thigh and scowled threateningly. "Just an hour ago we were in the Mannheim Court finalizing your adoption. Now you belong with us. Now you're an American boy, not a kraut. No one that you know lives up there!! Nobody!!"

"But... neighbors... friends... Elke..." Wolfi stammered.

"Your mother is dead, Scott!! Dead!!" Mrs. Bruce's tone was cold and harsh. "Your father left you at the orphanage. It is time for you to move on! Move on!!"

The Colonel barked, "With us you get a brand new life that is full of opportunities you never would have had as a German kid! You should be damned grateful, Scott. Damned grateful!!"

"Let's go. Drive, Otto," Mrs. Bruce ordered as she smacked the Colonel's bicep. "Let's just drive. This little shit is not the least bit grateful!"

She turned to face Wolfi in the back seat, grimaced angrily, and bashed her fist into the top of the vinyl seat with a booming thump.

"You are truly an ungrateful selfish little shit, Scott!"

* * *

"Scott!" Frau Sandmann grabbed him and pulled his head in between her ample cleavage. Wolfi was having a hard time breathing. "I can not believe you gone for one year! I very happy to see you! Wolfgang, you grow much! Wolfgang!"

Frau Sandmann was speaking English to him, as the Colonel and his wife had requested before this visit, but she could not bring herself to keep calling him Scott.

Wolfi recognized her scent of faint jasmine blended with dust and mold, and she was actually wearing that same greenish grey dress she wore on his first day. He didn't remember ever once being glad to see Frau Sandmann, but today it actually felt good!

The familiar aromas of boiled potatoes, green beans, and pork came wafting down the hall. Suddenly an attractive blond woman in a white flower-print dress charged through the double doors from the dining room. It was Fräulein Edel!

"Wolfi!! Happy... see you!!" she gushed as she careened towards him. She had a huge grin on her face and was breathing hard. She was also speaking her best English, as requested, but with a heavy German accent. She quickly reached the entry way where they were all standing, got on one knee and tenderly wrapped her arms around him.

"Wolfi... I... miss you!" Fräulein Edel barely got the words out before she began sobbing. She refused to call him Scott. This was her sweet Wolfi, not some stranger named Scott. "I miss you much, Wolfi!!"

Wolfi inhaled her familiar fragrance of fresh carnations as she cried and held on to him. Like always, her scent and her love seemed to caress him and comfort his heart.

"I missed... you!" Wolfi said very softly to her in English. Tears came flowing down his cheeks too now, and he fell eagerly into her loving embrace. He had desperately missed feeling genuine affection and love! He wanted Fräulein Edel back in his life!

"I... missed... you!!" he said again, between sobs. He trembled in her arms and his knees buckled. Both of them were sniffling and weeping loudly.

"Okay!!" said Mrs. Bruce rudely. She was clearly uncomfortable with this display and wanted very much for it to end now. She looked at Frau Sandmann hoping for some relief, but gave up the moment she noticed tears streaming down Sandmann's face too.

The Colonel cleared his throat loudly, making that barking sound that always comes out when he's trying to take command of a situation. But this time no one paid him the slightest bit of attention.

Just then Julia came racing thunderously down the stairs from the girls' dorm!!

"Wolfi!! Ich hab' dich vermisst wie die Sau!!" cried Julia! She was grinning from ear to ear as she grabbed him, kissed his cheeks numerous times, and lifted him up off the floor!

"Buah! Ich könnt' mir kaum glauben wenn ich gehört hab' ich darf dich wieder sehen!" she continued very excitedly. *"Es ist über ein Jahr gewesen! Ich hätt' mir gedacht ich seh' dich nie wieder. Aber, wie geil, da stehst du jetzt wohl! Wie geht's dir, lieber Wolfi?!"*

Wolfi felt huge panic!! He didn't understand a word she was saying!!! *Why can't I understand you?!! Julia!!*

You always said I understand you better than anybody! Julia!!!

When Julia put him back down on the floor, a massive chill coursed through his body and he shivered as he looked desperately into her eyes.

Julia stepped back and saw his confusion. Adoringly, she took both his hands into her soft warm hands and looked into his face. And again, as always, the instant that Wolfi's gaze met her sparkling teal-blue eyes he felt that nurturing deep love that had poured out of her soul ever since she tucked him into bed his first day. Julia was magical!

He grinned at her through the tearful wetness on his cheeks. He was tremendously happy to see her!! It felt indescribably amazing to be held by his best friend again, to feel her love!! And at the same time he was incredibly devastated!! He could no longer speak to her or understand her!! He was in utter shock! It had never occurred to him that he could forget German!! *What?!!*

"Ach...du...Wolfi..." Julia closed her eyes dreamily for a moment, then stepped forward and swooped him up into her arms again. The wildflower aroma of her skin and hair and her passionate love made him feel delightful tingles, like he was floating.

"Ich hab' dich so sehr vermisst, Wolfi! Wie geht's dir, denn? Wolfi!!" she gushed, her voice cracking from the intensity of her emotions. Her chin trembled.

Wie geht's? How are you? He still knew what that meant.

"Goo...," he started to give the automatic answer, but he could not finish the word in English or in German. Things were actually not good.

Vermisst. Missed. He remembered that word too.

"*Vermisst...*" he said hesitantly, and then kissed Julia on the cheek to show her that he had missed her. His chin quivered.

I have so much to tell you about, Julia! I want to talk and share and hug like we always do!! But Wolfi no longer had any idea at all how to say that in German! He stared at her blankly.

Julia looked inquisitively at Fräulein Edel, again at Wolfi, then back at Fräulein Edel, who simply shook her head no. Now Julia realized that Wolfi could not understand German any more! Tears began rolling down her cheeks.

There have never been any barriers between us, Wolfi!! she shouted out silently, just through the look in her eyes.

Wolfi touched his own chest and then hers, as if to say he knew what she meant.

She grabbed him again and held him close to her chest, her wet cheek resting on top of his prickly buzz-cut hair. Wolfi put his arms around her and enfolded her with his whole being. Both of them felt overwhelming love, and deep shattering sadness simultaneously. They hung on to each other and cried their hearts out for quite some time, sobbing noisily.

"That's enough, now!" commanded Mrs. Bruce when she could no longer put up with her own discomfort. She tried to pull Wolfi's arms off of Julia.

Julia reached out for him and Wolfi immediately wrapped both arms around her waist again, completely ignoring Mrs. Bruce!

Floating. Euphoria. Wolfi and Julia were briefly in heaven.

"I said that's enough, now, damn it!" barked the Colonel's wife once more. She jerked Wolfi off the German girl by grabbing his upper arm aggressively, painfully stretching and pinching his skin!

"We have things to talk over with Frau Sandmann upstairs! Come. Let's go," commanded Mrs. Bruce heartlessly and began dragging him up the staircase.

Wolfi stumbled and smacked his hand sharply against the edge of a step to catch himself. He turned and looked desperately at Julia.

"Julia!!" he cried.

Julia stood lifelessly at the bottom of the stairs, her mouth open in complete disbelief. "Wolfi!!"

Wolfi's throat closed up as tightly as a vice grip and sharp pains shot through his solar plexus. His heart wailed with agony, pounding furiously in his chest.

Suddenly raging anger overtook him! He stopped, yanked his arm defiantly away from Mrs. Bruce, and started running back to Julia!

The American woman stabbed her fingernails into his chest as she fumbled to snatch his arm again!

"Owwww!!!" yelped Wolfi.

"Come, you stubborn kraut!" fumed the woman, scowling at him and jerking painfully on his arm. "Come!"

* * *

"Come!! Wolfi!" Elke had bubbled in a very loud whisper just as her smiling face appeared speeding around the corner. "Wolfi! Come!"

"Elke!! You almost fell down the staircase! Slow down!!" her mom, Aunt Sasha, had demanded loudly, obviously annoyed. "Ten years old!! You are way too old to be racing everywhere you go, and you disturb the whole building sounding like a herd of elephants!"

"Oh vay, Elke, you seem as excited as a new bride when her husband just got home!" giggled Mama. She rolled her eyes at her best friend who lived upstairs, and who Wolfi called Aunt Sasha. Then Mama smiled at Sasha's daughter, Elke, and said, "It's actually really nice how loving you are with Wolfgang. Thank you for playing with him and always being so good to him, sweetie."

Elke smiled briefly at Wolfgang's mama, but moved quickly over by the cellar door where Wolfi was playing with his red toy car.

"It's bath day!" Elke whispered into his ear, her soft warm lips skimming the sensitive middle of Wolfi's ear. He tingled all over and stood up immediately! His cheeks were blushing and he was grinning.

"Let's go!" Elke grabbed his hand excitedly and stepped in the direction of the cellar door.

"Wait!" said Wolfi as he walked towards Mama to hand her his car.

Aunt Sasha leaned close to Mama and whispered, "Ingrid from the top floor told me she caught her husband having sex in the basement storage area... uh, with the new woman, what's her name?"

Mama put her fist on her hip and anxiously gestured downward with the palm of her other hand to signal Sasha to shut up!

"Have fun!" said Mama awkwardly as the kids headed downstairs.

"Leave it off!" Elke blurted. She swiped Wolfi's hand away from the light switch, then gently took his hand in hers and the two of them raced down the stairs.

"They are just so cute! Always so excited to see each other!" Wolfi heard Mama giggling.

"Cute," retorted Aunt Sasha sarcastically.

Wolfi and Elke practically flew down the stairs into the black cellar below! Elke always liked it to be dark. She stopped abruptly where she thought the last step was, probing the darkness with the tip of her shoe. Then she turned left with her arms straight out, carefully searching for the doorway to the storage areas.

The blackness seemed to have an eerie texture to it, as if it was touching them, almost embracing them. Suddenly Wolfgang realized he was not holding Elke's hand any more! He panicked. It was pitch black and she was gone!

"*Wolfgang...,*" hissed a voice, echoing somewhere in the darkness. *That didn't sound like Elke!! Who is that?!* A freezing chill ran up his spine to the top of his head.

"*Wolfgang!!...*" The sizzling whisper reverberated off the cinderblock walls in all directions.

"Elke?! Is that you?!" Wolfi's heart was thumping wildly against his ear drums, his body buzzing.

"*Wolfgang!!*" Another directionless hiss!

A few beams of light from a distant window danced on the floor behind him. He turned and suddenly saw Elke standing not far away! He let out a huge sigh!

"Elke!!!"

"Come, Wolfgang!" she whispered intensely, reaching out her hand. Elke led him to where a few sun rays were coming in from the cellar windows. Wolfi could see her now in the dim light as she turned around to brace her hands behind her back, then jumped up backwards to sit on the big potato bin. The musty odor of the earthy russets inside the wooden bin wafted up through the open slats as her butt flopped down onto it.

She put both hands on top of Wolfi's shoulders to pull him a little closer, and then scooted her bottom towards him, which caused her skirt to ride up. Wolfi gently put both his hands on her silky nude thighs. Her legs emitted wondrous blissful energy that somehow caressed his hands with love and made them tingle! The sweet aroma of chamomile soap drifted up from her legs. She smelled just like her mom. That fragrance blended in with the scents of potatoes, dust, mold, and coal which filled the air. His face felt warm from electrified excitement, and his heart was vigorously pumping euphoria into every part of his body!

"Mmmmm...," Elke moaned at the touch of his hands.

This game made them both feel blissful magic in their galloping hearts, and delightful sensations in their bodies! Ever since Elke had showed him how, he liked playing this game so much more than playing with cars!

Elke scooted closer to him so that her knees hugged his waist on either side. The amazingly soft skin on her warm thighs danced sensuously against his palms and fingertips as her legs moved. His solar plexus, the back of his neck, and his groin, all seemed to be purring like a cat in heat.

Elke opened her thighs a bit more, gently put a hand on top of Wolfi's and guided it sensuously up her inner thigh...

* * *

"Do you want me to touch it?" Wolfgang asked her again.

"Maybe... I dunno...," said Sandy softly and spread her legs a little more.

Suddenly someone bashed the switch on the wall very loudly and bright light flooded onto the two kids like on a movie set!

"What the HELL are you doing?!!" screamed Mrs. Bruce. *"What in the fuck is going on here?! What IS this?!!"*

Wolfgang jumped in total shock! He had not heard her coming.

"What the HELL are you doing, Scott?!!" Her face turned beet red as she roared at him, glaring fiercely. She grabbed Sandy by the lapels of her jacket and yanked her up into a standing position. Sandy lost her balance and almost fell down the stairs.

"Sandy! Pull your skirt down and get up those stairs to your apartment right now!" Mrs. Bruce yapped at her like a frightened Chihuahua.

"And, YOU!!" she shrieked at Wolfgang. She raised her hand and smacked him viciously on the ear!

Jolting sharp pain exploded down into his ear canal and shot through his head and shoulders. A very high-pitched squeal began ringing loudly in his ear.

"Owwww...," he protested and pulled away from her.

"I'll show you 'owww'!" she bellowed. "Get your ass up!! Now!!"

She locked ferociously onto his earlobe with her thumb and forefinger and dragged him into their apartment! Agonizing lightning bolts shot through his ear and his neck!

She threw him into his bedroom and then quickly grabbed the big hair brush from her room.

"You're absolutely disgusting, Scott!! Revolting!! You're *sick!!* I'm embarrassed to have you as my son!!" she yelled.

Then she sat down, slammed him over her knees, ripped his pants and underwear down, and began whacking his naked butt fiercely!

Wolfi squelched his tears right away, and angrily clenched his butt muscles as tightly as he could, in an effort to fight the pain! Each swat stung severely and it felt like the edges of the brush were again tearing through his skin! He was sure there was blood.

Chapter Nine

"I want you to damn well hold it!! You do NOT have to pee again already! Last week you held it for almost twenty-four hours!" Mrs. Bruce yelped at Scott, thumping him in the gut with her fist and blocking him from getting into the bathroom.

"But that was right after that doctor stuck a metal probe up inside my penis, and then it hurt insanely to pee!!" Scott protested vehemently.

"Don't be such a baby! We all have to go through some pain sometimes to be healthy," Mrs. Bruce countered coldly. "The doctor probed for obstructions and abnormalities to find out why the hell you still wet the bed at eleven years old!!"

"But, that was psychotic!! A metal probe up my penis!! It hurt like nothing I've ever imagined anything could hurt!!!" Scott barked at her, visibly angry.

Mrs. Bruce slapped him hard on the face, her wedding ring crashing painfully into his cheekbone! She was so fast he almost never saw it coming. His face stung fiercely and his ear was ringing!

"Don't you sass me, you little shit!" she growled and waved her finger at him. "You get your ass up to your room right now!! And don't you dare take a piss until I give you permission!! You have to learn to hold it so you stop pissing in your bed at night!!"

"Mom!" Scott pleaded with her. His bladder felt like it was going to burst. There was no way he could hold it! *I have to pee!!!"* he thought. Anxiously he shifted his weight from leg to leg and grabbed his penis through his pants hoping to shut off the flow.

"Get your hands off your penis!! You make me sick!!" Her face was dark red, her lips were contorted in a savage scowl, and her eyes bulged out as she spit the words into his face. "You're disgusting! It's time for this shit to stop, goddamn it!! You are eleven years old and you still wet the fucking bed!!"

Scott pleaded for mercy with his eyes. He continued shifting his weight back and forth, turning in a circle once like he was dancing.

"Knock it off!! Get your ass upstairs!" she bellowed, waving a crooked finger in his face.

Scott made his way up the steps slowly and deliberately in order to avoid peeing his pants. He laid on his bed for a minute, shaking his knees back and forth, still holding on to his penis through his pants. That wasn't working! Quickly he stood up again and danced the pee pee boogie. Very soon that also became totally ineffective.

After ten excruciating minutes of bouncing on and off the bed, he knew he was going to piss his pants!! Holding it was no longer an option!! Spastically, he slinked into the bathroom, briskly flung the seat up, whipped his zipper down and grabbed himself! Niagara Falls! He peed copiously for quite some time.

"Goddammit!!" Mrs. Bruce stomped up the stairs in a rage! "Ouch!!" She crashed her forehead into the bathroom door as she raced around the corner out of control!

"You son of a bitch!! I told you that you are not allowed to pee!! You bedwetting little kraut!! Did you not believe I would make you do it?!" she fumed.

Scott immediately squeezed his penis and shut the flow of urine off.

Fucking bitch!!! he thought to himself and grimaced at her.

She held an empty glass up under his nose and shook it threateningly! "This is what I told you I would do! But you just never listen! You stubborn kraut!"

The vicious woman dipped the glass into the urine in the toilet bowl and filled it up. Then she shoved it into Scott's hand and hissed, "Drink it!!"

Scott looked at her in disbelief! He started to put the glass down on the counter. She blocked his arm with her whole body!

"No, you don't! You will drink it!! Now!!" she yelled.

"No!!! It's pee!!!" he pleaded in a whining voice.

"I warned you!! Goddammit!! I told you that if you took a piss that you're gonna drink it, and I meant it!! Drink up!! Goddammit!! I'm tired of this shit!!" She smacked him brutally on his ear.

His ear stung intensely and was ringing. Scott's hand shook as he lifted the glass very slowly to his lips. He gagged.

"Hurry the fuck up!!" she commanded, and slapped him again, causing urine to spill out of the glass onto his wrist when he coiled back.

He took a very tiny sip. His abdomen jerked violently several times and primal sounds escaped from his throat. It was everything he could do to not vomit!

* * *

He was singing softly to himself, reading the lyrics off the sheet music and playing the chords on the piano. Something about this song made him feel fantastic! Somehow it was magical! He'd been singing it over and over for at least three weeks.

Scott had just turned fourteen and had no confidence in his new deeper voice, so he sang very softly. Besides, that was a lot safer. Mrs. Bruce always ridiculed him ruthlessly whenever he showed his real feelings or let himself be vulnerable, so there was no way in hell he was ever going to let her hear him sing. Ever!

"Maria... I fell for a girl named Maria..." For some very strange reason his heart was full of love when he sang this song!

Why do I have all these feelings with this one?! he wondered.

"Maria... I fell for a girl named Maria..." He continued singing and his voice actually cracked with emotion! *Maybe I'm going to fall for a girl named Maria? I don't know, what the hell is this?!*

He started at the beginning once more, singing quietly, but then suddenly it was too much! He got very choked up and singing was no longer an option! Tears ran down his face.

Wow, I haven't cried for a very long time! What the fuck?! Big boys don't cry!! You're fourteen years old!! Knock it off!!

But, he was overwhelmed with agonizing loneliness at this moment! His heart was aching from deep, profound sadness!

He thought of Mama. But only very briefly. He squelched it immediately. Scott didn't think of her much any more. Those memories made him angry these days. He was hurt and pissed that she left him, that she had never said goodbye, that she had never explained.

Who the hell am I feeling in this song?! Why the fuck does it make me so sad?!

"Maria... I fell for a girl named Maria...," he started at the beginning yet again and actually crooned to her! Inexplicably his heart was bursting with love for whoever this girl is!!

Suddenly his German cousin, Manfred, came into his mind and his heart sunk!

The movie!! The girl in the movie!! Was her name Maria?! Fuck, I don't know any more!! Was it?!

"What the hell movie did YOU see?!" sixteen-year old Manfred had roared at him as he kicked the soccer ball down the street.

"It was a blue-and-white movie. A really nice girl with dark hair was riding in a big truck with her dad. It was snowing, they skidded on some ice and had a huge crash. She got hurt really bad and later we saw the doctors operating on her!" Wolfgang had said enthusiastically.

""We never saw such a movie!!" Manfred had bellowed at him. "Wolfi, you're nuts! Stupid!! Shut up!!"

"It was a huge truck with spools of steel cable on it!" Wolfi had added, hoping to jog his cousin's memory.

"You're crazy, you're stupid!!" Manfred had shouted again. "I mean it! Shut up! You're stupid!!"

Wolfi had been absolutely positive that he was remembering it right. The girl was sweet and beautiful, and she had really touched his heart. He had been very upset that she almost died! And, in the movie it showed her going to that indescribably beautiful world beyond the light, which Wolfi remembered vividly!! He knew he was right, otherwise why would he remember so many exact details?!

To this day, Scott remembered those details and a lot more, but he had never mentioned the movie or the accident girl to anyone since Manfred. Nobody.

Was her name actually Maria?! Fuck, I don't know.

Whackkkkkk!!! Mrs. Bruce had snuck up on him and smacked him from behind, directly on the ear! Scott's ear screamed with pain!

"You did NOT take the garbage out yet!" she barked at him ferociously like a drill sergeant. "I asked you to do that two hours ago! One simple thing! One simple fucking thing!! Good Christ, you are stupid!!"

"I'm good, but not Christ. And not stupid," muttered Scott under his breath as he walked toward the kitchen.

"Don't you talk back to me!!" She slapped him soundly again, this time on the back of his head!

* * *

"You actually seem pretty smart to me, not stupid at all!" said Alexa. Her voice was soft and kind. Scott was sitting next to her on the hood of the car.

"They seem to be threatened by the fact that I'm different from them. They call me stupid kraut, stubborn kraut. They're violent too," responded Scott quietly.

She reached over and stroked his upper arm lightly. Her touch gave him mystical feelings which flew straight to his heart! A warm wind rustled the fronds of the many tall palm trees. A few wisps of her strawberry-blond hair gently caressed his face, sending tingles through his chest and gut. He really liked how she smelled, too, like fresh peaches and cream.

"I have to keep a log of every mile I drive with the family car, and they figure out exactly how many miles to my date's house, then to the indoor movies, then someplace for a soda pop, back to her house, and then home. If the log shows I drove more miles than that, then there's hell to pay, I lose my driving privileges, lose my freedom, and I get smacked around. And it's indoor movies only! Not allowed to go to drive-in movies because they're sure I'll have sex there. They say sex is disgusting! Don't touch any parts. Keep your tongue in your mouth! No sucking face, no sucking anything at all, ever!" Scott obviously needed to vent! His torso and head shook as he finished.

"But!!! Scott! You totally rubbed their noses in their own shit, didn't you?!" bragged James loudly, proud of his best friend's independence and rebelliousness. He and Emily had both been listening to Scott's tirade.

"Yeah...," Scott said and then hesitated.

"What?! Tell me!" protested Alexa.

"I figured out how to unscrew the car's speedometer cable so that miles don't rack up." Scott sighed. "I unscrew it after the number of approved miles that they calculated, and then I drive wherever I want! Add gas if I need to, screw it back on just a few blocks from home."

"Wow. So, how do you know how fast you're going when the speedometer's disconnected?!" Alexa sounded concerned.

"You just go as fast as everyone else is going!" announced James with a cocky smile.

"That seems crazy! You guys! That does not sound safe at all!" objected Alexa. "Seriously!"

"It's how we got here, all the way to LA from Redding," said Scott softly. He stared at the millions of lights below.

"No!! Really?!" Alexa was a bit shocked.

"Yep," answered Scott. "They said LA was too far, but amazingly, they said since it's my last year of high school I could take the car to the ocean near Redding for Spring Break."

James continued the story, looking at Alexa. "Emily had really missed you after she moved from LA to Redding last year, and she convinced Scott and me to instead come to LA for Spring Break with her! So, we disconnected the speedometer after the number of miles that the ocean trip would have taken. And here we are!"

"Amazing," whispered Alexa. She shook her head but was smiling.

"You do what you have to do to survive," declared Scott with another deep sigh, but thinking maybe that had sounded way too pompous. He admired all the palm trees lining the street, but scowled a little from embarrassment.

"What's this road called again?" asked James.

"Mulholland Drive," Emily exclaimed. "Isn't it fucking awesome?!"

"Totally," beamed James, leaning into Emily's face. Scott watched James lightly rub his chest against Emily's erect nipples which were stretching the material of her thin white blouse. James planted a lingering wet kiss on her mouth and Scott noticed their tongues dancing between their lips.

Son of a bitch!! I want some of that from a girl again too! Scott thought to himself.

He really hoped Alexa hadn't noticed that watching the other two had made him hard! For a lot of years now, Scott had been ashamed of his animal desires. *The only thing you males ever think about is sex!* That message was echoed over and over in his world ever since he met Mrs. Bruce.

Shit! He adjusted his legs in an effort to hide the bulge! His eyes followed a tiny pair of headlights on one of the endless boulevards far below. The warm night air smelled like car exhaust and bleach combined with the scents of jasmine, luscious jacaranda tree blossoms, eucalyptus tree leaves, and roses. And, then there was the delicious aroma of fresh peaches and cream coming from Alexa, combined with the captivating warmth he felt from her body and heart, which made him want to just grab her and press his embarrassing bulge against her!

Sensuous slurps and moans came from James and Emily's direction. Scott was doing his best not to look or even imagine what was going on there.

"It's 1968," said Alexa, breaking the awkward silence, also staring straight ahead. "Just fifteen or twenty years ago, except for a few towns, most of what you see here in the San Fernando Valley was orange orchards - almost all of it! Millions of trees growing delicious oranges all year round!" She waved her hand in a large arch from left to right, and continued, "In less than a generation it became boulevards, cars, and buildings as far as you can see. The only orange trees now are in people's yards".

"Wow. Really?! All of this? Mostly orange groves?!" questioned Scott with surprise. He looked into her passionate light green eyes. Alexa nodded her head slightly as she met his gaze, and then smiled warmly at him.

"I liked hanging with you the last couple days." Alexa leaned into him, whispering softly. "You're a very nice guy. I like that you're really sweet but also totally rebellious!" She looked away and giggled, a bit embarrassed by how direct she was being.

"Thank you," Scott murmured. He crossed his arms and looked up at the stars, smiling to himself. He still felt self-conscious about the lump in his pants.

"Last night I actually had a dream about you!" Alexa scooted closer, wrapped both her hands around Scott's bicep, and grinned excitedly looking into his eyes.

"No! Really?!" Scott was intrigued and beamed back at her.

She squeezed his arm lovingly and spoke in a serious tone. "You were a little boy, and I saw you on a bed in a big room where laundry was hanging. An older girl hugged you and kissed your cheek and tucked you in. But you were crying, and you kept crying after she left until you finally fell asleep. Later a brown-haired boy woke you up and scared you big time! The whole dream I felt amazingly sad for you, and this morning when I woke up I was crying! Can you believe that?! How crazy is that?!"

"Whoa... shit... whoa... wait!!" Scott's face turned white and his heart sunk. He pulled away from her a bit. "Sheeee-it!!"

"What?!" asked Alexa, confused by his response. She pulled him close again and leaned her head against his shoulder.

"Shit..."

"Tell me! What?!" Alexa was gentle but always fiercely passionate.

"That's fucked up!" Scott was breathing hard. "That actually happened to me!"

"No! Come on!!" Now Alexa pulled away. "Really?!"

"Remember yesterday I mentioned that I got sent to an orphanage when I was six?"

"Yes..."

"What you just described is exactly what happened on my first day at the orphanage!" Scott's voice choked and his shoulders tensed up. It had been many years since he had allowed himself to feel the pain of that first day. Alexa noticed a tear run down one of his cheeks.

"Holy shit!! That's... Wow! Holy shit!!! That's totally nuts!!!" Alexa's mouth was wide open in disbelief.

"Yeah..." Scott was stunned. No other words came to him.

"What?!!" Alexa was clearly shocked. "That doesn't make any sense!!"

"Yeah..." Scott murmured again. He was dazed. This made no sense to him either!

"I've never felt such intense sadness like in that dream - it makes my soul hurt for you, Scott. Wow!! Poor baby!!" Alexa kissed his cheek and stroked the back of his head.

Her empathy made him choke up even more, like a kid when mom finally pays attention to his scraped knee. His chest heaved a couple of times as he fought back tears.

"Thank you...," he managed to say softly. A full-body chill raced through him.

"You remind me of my friend in the orphanage, actually. Heidi was her name," Scott said pensively. "We were very much alike. It seemed like we read each other's thoughts, so we didn't talk too much, just held hands a lot. She heard the bluebell flowers chiming just like I did!"

"Oh, yeah?" said Alexa. She was beginning to have feelings for Scott and really did not want to hear about another girl.

"Even though we were only 6, I loved her deeply. Because we were so much alike, she became everything to me." Scott couldn't help himself, even though he'd noticed that Alexa was only half listening now. "On her last day the counselors woke me up from a nap to go sit with her behind the boy's building. She picked a tiny wild strawberry that was growing next to her and gave it to me. That day was the first time I heard the word adopted. I still miss her. Still adore strawberries."

"I'm not Heidi!" Alexa insisted. "I don't want to be her, I don't want to have to live up to your expectations that I remind you of her!"

"I know," replied Scott quietly, trying his best not to show that he felt rejected.

"Awwww..." Alexa noticed his head hanging down and turned her torso to hug him.

Scott put his arm around her shoulders and pulled her close. He felt her breast against his chest and the intense beating of her heart. It actually felt to him like they were floating together above the car.

Scott looked at the silky skin on her face, into her luscious green eyes, and at her slightly open supple lips. Alexa gazed passionately into Scott's eyes and then down at his smile. Scott took in the sensuous beauty of her soft mouth as he slowly moved his head closer.

The moment that their lips touched, the tip of her wet tongue slid forward to caress his.

No, you're not Heidi!

Scott was in heaven!

* * *

"I totally can not get enough of your kisses!" panted Scott, looking into her beautiful face. "You make me feel things like I never knew were possible! And, haven't I always known you?!"

Alexa giggled shyly, but then opened her mouth again and moved in for more!

Sorrento Beach was hot and packed with people. Scott and Alexa were in a passionate embrace on a blanket, alone in their own world. Her little orange bikini didn't cover much, and Scott's bathing suit was fairly short, so it felt almost like they were naked! Her soft skin radiated love and sex to him like he'd never ever experienced before, and he was totally aroused!

They were both breathing hard and kissing uninhibitedly. Scott was rock-hard, and suddenly he was poking out of a leg-opening and wedged between her silky nude thighs. Alexa sucked sensuously on his tongue and thrust her pelvis into him. They rocked back and forth slowly for quite a while, continuing to kiss with abandon. Scott was overwhelmed by his emotions and by lust!

"I love you!" he blurted out. They'd never said it before. He pulled back and looked into her face.

Alexa stared at her fingers as she combed through the hair on his chest. Scott smiled and looked over her shoulder at the breaking waves, trying to act like it was okay if she didn't say I love you too. He got lost for a while in her delicious peaches-and-cream scent and marveled how fantastically it complimented the fresh-fish smell of the ocean. He affectionately pushed a lock of hair away from her eyes.

"I love *you*!!" Alexa gushed finally! "You are *such* a sweet guy! How could I not?!"

Scott let out a huge sigh of relief, pulled her mostly-nude body close, and started kissing her sensuously once more.

"Wait!" Alexa whispered intensely. She put her palms against his chest. "We need to slow down!"

"Why?!" This feels fantastic! Doesn't it?!" Scott asked. His stomach sank to his feet and the top of his head buzzed from anxiety.

"Yes, it does. But, I totally need to slow down!" countered Alexa, pushing him away.

Now Scott's body went limp, like a deflated air mattress.

"Why would we slow down... when this is the best thing we've ever known?!" he stammered.

"I know I said that a few weeks ago, and I do love you," Alexa offered in rebuttal, "but, all of a sudden life is super serious and I need to put things into perspective for myself! Maybe into perspective for you too!"

"What perspective?!" he whined.

"Yes, we both graduated from high school in the last two days, and that's something we should totally celebrate," she said fervently. "But, how can we party when just three days ago Robert F. Kennedy was assassinated in the Ambassador Hotel right here in LA - a few miles from here!" She paused to see if he was listening.

"That perspective!! And, if this isn't serious enough, only two months ago Martin Luther King, Jr. was murdered, and four and a half years ago John F. Kennedy was killed!! My world is falling apart!!" she protested. "All that they wanted was to make the world a better place! I don't know what to believe in any more!!"

Alexa scowled as she sat up, folded her arms over her chest, and crossed her legs. Two little girls screamed with delight as they raced away from the surf.

"But, right now, we've got each other and it feels beautif..." Scott was cut off by her disapproving glance.

"Jeez, aren't we supposed to be optimistic when we graduate, excited about fulfilling our dreams, wanting to create a life where we can make a positive difference?" Alexa grumbled. "But, how the hell can we do that when there's nothing left to believe in?!"

"I believe in music, in influencing people's hearts, opening them to peace and to love through powerful music." He wasn't sounding very convincing because feelings of rejection had drained him. "I wanna get really good and become successful and then change a lot of..."

Alexa interrupted him and scoffed, "*Jeee-sussss!* That's not gonna do it, come on! As serious as things are now, we need to take action, fight for change, not sing pretty songs!!"

She had never disagreed with him before. Scott's heart burned.

"I don't believe we can change the system." Scott was doing his best to sound wise and informed. "The system is corrupt, it favors war over peace, and it's all about sustaining the military-industrial complex that Eisenhower warned us about seven years ago. As far as I can tell, one man or woman is never going to be allowed to make changes because too many powerful people would lose way too much money!"

Alexa was quiet as she processed his words.

"But through the power of music and the arts we can influence people's hearts to a place of harmony and love, to a place of cooperation and sharing knowledge,"

Scott went on. "Out of that we could create a system that's based on the power of love instead of the love of power."

"That's totally ineffective bullshit!" Alexa declared. "And stupid! If the system is broken then we have to fight to make things better, not stand around playing little ditties and hoping things improve!"

"Mmm...kay...," Scott muttered. His solar plexus tightened painfully as he forced the hurt back down.

Alexa stared silently at the horizon. Scott got caught up in the intense power of the waves hammering against the pilings of the Santa Monica Pier.

""Do you remember when we were reading from 'The Prophet' this morning?" Alexa pulled the book out of her purse and flipped through it. "The passage on marriage... here it is."

She read out loud from Kahlil Gibran's poetry:

"And stand together yet not too near together:

For the pillars of the temple stand apart,

And the oak tree and the cypress grow not in each other's shadow."

"What?! Why can't we be close?! Why do we have to stand apart?!" Scott complained. "I don't get it."

"If we get too close, go too fast, we lose ourselves in the relationship, we lose our individuality," she tried to explain. "If we become one person, or even just stand right next to each other, then we can't hold up the roof of this temple."

"Mmmm...," murmured Scott. He was already feeling rejected, hurt, and drained because disagreements always put him there. And now his heart throbbed with agony while she kept talking about being apart! *What the fuck?!*

A heavy silence weighed on them for quite a few minutes. They both stared at the ocean.

"Have you seen James recently?" Alexa tried to lighten things up with idle conversation.

"Why the hell are you asking about him?!" Scott was insulted. He frowned.

"Just asking," she replied, surprised and uncomfortable about his defensiveness.

Jesus H. Christ!, thought Scott. *Why the fuck is she asking about James?! Here we are standing far apart holding up fucking temple roofs and avoiding each other's shadows, and she wants to know about fuckin' James?!*

Alexa saw the pain on his face. "You're really pretty needy, aren't you?"

Scott stared at the horizon. He felt empty, very alone.

* * *

Scott stared expressionlessly straight ahead as he marched rigidly erect, snapping his legs off the ground smartly, perfectly synchronized with the rest of the 40-piece Air Force band. His glossy white snare drum danced vigorously up and down with his left leg. He was one of six in the drum line, all waving their sticks in bold graceful strokes while beating out a very precise and energetic cadence. At the front of the band the drum major blew one long and then four short tweets on his whistle, and suddenly 34 horns blasted out the powerful introduction to Sousa's "The Stars And Stripes Forever".

The Air Force band that Scott was in had flown from St. Louis to LA to march in the afternoon parade at this theme park. Thousands of enthusiastic people lined the length of the parade route at least five to ten deep, waving their hands, brandishing flags, and even clapping in time to the music. The band was now almost back to the assembly area where they had started, behind the palm-tree lined wall.

He hadn't seen her yet. *Did she decide to not come?!"* he wondered as his eyes searched right and left while his head remained facing straight ahead like a good soldier. And, of course, not missing a beat.

There she is!! Right on! She's here!! Scott's face broke into a huge grin as they made momentary eye contact - but it was all he could offer right now.

Alexa noticed from his grin that he'd seen her. She waved discreetly, but smiled excitedly.

Once the musicians were back behind the wall again, Scott changed out of his dark blue uniform and into civilian clothes on the bus. When he came bouncing down the steps of the bus's front door, he beamed as he saw Alexa waiting for him in the shade. Grinning back, she came dashing toward him the moment he appeared!

"I'm happy to see you!" she spurted. They embraced and kissed passionately. "A wet one!" Alexa joked.

"Jesus I missed you!! Six months! We've never gone that long without seeing each other!" gushed Scott. Again, they locked lips and tongues. Scott was elated to have her petite sensuous body against his one more time!

"You sure do look different in your striped bell bottoms and a peace symbol necklace!" she observed, smirking. "When did you start dressing like a hippie? While you were in basic training you seemed to like being in the Air Force - you kept writing about excellence. When did you become a hippie?!"

"I totally did not like basic training!! And, I hate what the military represents! Jeez, you know that!" Scott protested. "When I decide to do something, I like to be excellent at it! And I was proud of myself for becoming excellent in spite of all the incredibly hard challenges in basic. I was *not* there for fun! Jeez!"

"I saw you being really excellent at playing the drums and marching excellently like a soldier in the parade just now," said Alexa.

"Thanks," he said. He didn't notice she was smirking again.

She squeezed his hand affectionately. "Isn't all this Air Force band excellence promoting war?! Right here in front of thousands of people?!" The tone of her voice was sweet like it usually was, but she was definitely adamant about her opinions.

"Alexa, auditioning for the band was my way of avoiding war since there's a draft on! My way of not having to kill people!!" Now Scott was the adamant one. "You're all about peace - isn't me pounding on a drum a lot more peaceful than killing Viet Cong?!" Scott let go of her hand and moved away from her as they continued walking.

They stood separately in the long line of their favorite ride for twenty minutes of uncomfortable silence, avoiding each other's eyes. Alexa finally wrapped her silky hand around his, intertwined her fingers with his, and gazed adoringly at his face. Scott felt a rush in his groin as she pulled his torso into her soft breasts. She leaned her head close and looked at his lips, then opened her mouth and planted another erotic wet kiss on his face.

The underground water ride had very dim lighting, so it was perfect for making out and groping in the dark, which they did the entire way. Scott felt a ton of love coming from her again and he was happy! *Just like the old days,* he thought sarcastically, *a whole year ago.*

After the ride they enjoyed soft ice cream and soda pop at a table under a bushy eucalyptus tree.

"I want to come back to LA in a few weeks and spend a week with you," Scott announced.

"I know," answered Alexa, without looking at him. She stuck her tongue out and gave her ice cream cone a long slow lick.

"It's really beautiful to see you again!" Scott grinned at her. There was romantic fire in his eyes, but also lust in his groin as he watched her tongue. She stared at the leaves on a nearby eucalyptus branch while she licked. The air smelled like caramel corn, grilling hamburgers, eucalyptus, that bleach-like odor of LA smog, and her delicious peaches-and-cream scent. To him, right now, these were the aromas of love. He felt fantastic!

"So, can I come visit in a few weeks?" Scott asked again, biting into the last of his vanilla cone with a crunch.

"I don't know...," Alexa mumbled.

Scott stopped chewing and wiped his mouth with a paper napkin. He frowned. The french horn section was blasting out an intense movie theme accompanied by huge cymbal crashes over the loudspeakers behind her. A chill ran up his spine.

"You don't know?!" His eyes probed her face for information.

She stared at the white table top, then blankly at his face, and again back at the table. Scott's heart was racing from uncertainty.

Finally she spoke, very softly. "There's somebody else".

Scott glared at her for a few moments.

"What?" he asked, hoping fiercely that he had heard her wrong.

"There's somebody else..." she repeated. "My ex... Bob... He's in Vietnam... We've been writing to each other since he got there."

"What?" Scott's face turned pale. "*Jesus! What the fuck?! Your ex? Writing since when?!*"

"About nine months," she went on. "He's in the infantry, fighting in Vietnam, and I started writing to him because he needed moral support. He needed somebody."

"Nine months! That's about when we graduated from high school!!" Scott felt hugely betrayed! *So that's why she kept insisting that the oak tree and the cypress can't grow in each other's shadow! Fuck!*

"Wow! I don't get it!" The truth was that Scott didn't want to get it. "Every time I left LA you cried your eyes out at the airport, and blubbered about how very much you'll miss me!" He felt numb, weak.

"I know," she said in a matter-of-fact tone.

"He needed somebody, huh?" Scott asked after a painful silence. His voice was shaky. "I need somebody too, you know. I need you. But to me, you just say that I'm really needy!"

Alexa's eyes remained silently fixed on the white metal table.

"You and I are in love, Alexa! You've *said* that we are! That's why I need you!" His voice cracked a bit and tears filled his eyes.

"I know... I did fall in love with you, Scott! I really did!" Alexa reached over and took his hand affectionately into both of hers. "Two months ago I went to Hawaii for a week when Bob was there on R&R from Vietnam," she explained tenuously. "I think we fell in love again."

What the fuck?!! I had no clue that an ex named Bob even existed?! Scott was in shock, incapacitated. His chest pounded in agony.

"You'll be in St. Louis for another few years, and I don't really want a long distance relationship. After Vietnam, Bob's moving back home to LA - in about four months... and then..."

Scott didn't hear another word, even though she kept babbling on and on about Fuckface Bob.

Scott's heart felt like he'd just been beaten senseless.

The wind howled in the frigid void.

Excruciating loneliness pervaded everything.

Chapter Ten

The trip was coming up in seven days and already he was totally nervous! Scott had the stack of letters in his hand and was reading them for about the fifty-ninth time. His heart still raced with excitement, but it also ached from painful memories.

"Dear Mr. Scott Bruce, The Consulate of The Federal Republic of Germany in St. Louis wishes to inform you that we have received a response to your inquiry of 2 March 1973, which was forwarded to the Office of the Assistant Mayor in Mannheim, Germany. We have enclosed the original response as well as a translation from the German to the English... "

Scott flipped over to the actual letter from him. The man's writing was barely legible and it looked like his hand had been shaking. Scott couldn't read the German anyway, so he turned to the awkward English translation from someone in the consulate.

"Dear Scott,

I was made exceedingly happy by the receiving of your letter, and for the knowledge that you are well and alive! Yes, the memories that you have writing to me are showing me that you are my son Wolfgang. Yes, we lived in Hirschberg in apartment on first floor at end of long building overlooking Mannheim. Yes, sometimes you were coming with me to work and spending entire day on construction sites. Yes, I visit you in orphanage on motorcycle. Yes, we ate in restaurant at the mill and watched the waterwheel..."

Scott's hand was shaking as he continued reading. *"Today I live in Mannheim with your Mama's sister, Aunt Monika, and husband, Uncle Werner. I have very hard life since seventeen years when you got taken away from me. This make much pain in my heart and make worse my health. Monika and Werner have been like brother and sister to me...*

Scott took in a long deep breath and let it out in an angry huff. *Really, he's the one who had a hard life when I got sent to an orphanage?! Really?!* Scott thought about all the times he had watched this man beat the shit out of Mama, and the only thing he could feel for Papa is hate. *And, why would Monika and Werner help him - didn't they know about the beatings?!*

Scott felt the incredible loneliness of all these years and he sobbed, but stuffed it back down immediately. Long ago he'd gotten in the habit of suppressing those feelings so that no one could see any weakness in him - especially after Alexa had accused him of being needy a few years ago. He wiped the tears from his cheeks, and snorted through his nose so he could breathe.

At the bottom of the page Papa had written: *"With your cousin Manfred I have not contact since your mother died. He very angry then and he disappear. However, I find him now through the Einwohnermeldeamt (Citizen's Registry Office) and I have send him letter about you..."*

Scott switched over to his friend's translation of the most recent letter he got from cousin Manfred.

"Dear Wolfgang..."

Rrrrrrrrrring!!!!! Scott jumped as the kitchen phone startled him. He was feeling way too emotional and vulnerable to talk to anybody so he did not get up. *They can call back.*

He read more from Manfred's letter. *"Dear Wolfgang, Sabina and Margareta and I anticipate anxiously your visit..."*

The phone seemed to be ringing off the hook and he got distracted for a while, mindlessly watching it vibrate.

Wow, I think that was seven rings! Something made him feel he needed to answer it. He hustled across the kitchen to the phone on the wall and grabbed the receiver.

"Hello," he said curtly, a bit out of breath.

"Hallo. Hier ist Ehrhardt, Manfred. Ist da Wolfgang?

It was a bad connection with a ton of hissing noise. Scott was pretty sure he had heard the name Wolfgang. The man spoke again through the hiss.

"Hallo. Hier ist der Manfred. Ist da Wolfgang?

This time Scott heard the name Manfred too! His throat closed up in a painful anxiety-filled cramp. His heart was racing now and so were his thoughts.

Is someone fucking with me?! Manfred knows I can't speak German!! He wouldn't call me!! It's got to be one of my wise-ass friends! Goddammit! This isn't funny! This hurts, you asshole!!!

"Wolfgang?" said the faint voice again, seeming to plead for a response.

"Um... Yah... *ich...* Wolfgang," Scott finally stammered, trying his best to say "Yes, I'm Wolfgang" in German. He felt humiliated by his inadequacy, and he was still pretty sure this was a prank.

Who's fucking with me?! Who is this?!! Scott's heart ached. *Son of a bitch, this is NOT funny! I'm totally vulnerable right now and this fucking hurts!!*

The faint voice continued, "*Wolfgang? Ja, echt? Du bist es?! Ich kann's mir kaum glauben! Ich hab' mir die ganz' Zeit gedacht du bist verschwunden!*"

Scott was dazed. *This guy's speaking perfect German! Whoa, shit!! This must actually be Manfred!! Oh, wow, what the fuck did he just say?!*

"*Wolfgang? Bist du noch da?*" the man asked.

Are you still there? He understood that, but Scott was panicking, breathing hard, unable to speak! He'd forgotten German a long time ago and remembered very little from that course in high school.

"*Wolfgang. Hörst du mich? Hast du mich verstanden?*" Manfred asked.

These words Scott understood too: Do you hear me? Did you understand me?

"Ummm... *nicht verstanden...,*" stuttered Scott finally. Not understood.

The background hissing noise was still dominant and Scott realized now that this actually was a trans-Atlantic call! Manfred remained quiet for a few moments, then finally spoke slowly.

"*Ah... Wolfgang... hör mal zu... wir sehen uns wieder Dienstag, ja? Wolfgang... wir sehen uns... wieder Dienstag.*"

We'll see each other again Tuesday. That had also registered with Scott.

"*sehen... wieder Dienstag...,*" Scott stammered. See... again Tuesday. Goosebumps covered his arms. He was shivering and in tears.

"*Wieder Dienstag...*"

* * *

"*Jeden Dienstag!!*" Scott beamed and pointed at the radio in the Mercedes 280-S. It was blasting that same song he'd heard so many times on the airplane last night! It had a nice groove with a totally memorable hook, even though it was a schmaltzy pop song.

"*Immer jeden Dienstag, kommst Du in meinem Sinn...*"

"Always every Tuesday, you come into my mind..." Scott understood these words. He found himself humming along for a few moments. Then the chorus came around again.

"*Immer jeden Dienstag, kommst Du in meinem Sinn...*"

Scott waved at the radio once more and beamed over at Manfred in the driver's seat. "*Heute Dienstag!!*" he spilled out. Today Tuesday!

"*Jawohl.* Today is Tuesday!" Manfred answered in German. "*Mindy und Kurt,*" he said pointing at the radio.

The rest of the ride from the Frankfurt airport to Manfred's house was uncomfortably silent because of the language barrier.

Manfred's wife, Margareta, and their 12-year old daughter, Sabina, met Scott at the front door of their house with wide grins, nervous handshakes, and awkward repetitions of *"Guten Tag"* accompanied by a half curtsy.

Margareta served mouth-watering mocha layer cake and delicious aromatic coffee, which all of them focused on intently, since conversation didn't seem to be an option. None of them could speak English, and Scott's German was pretty much useless.

Fuck! he thought. *These people are family, yet I don't feel the least bit like I belong! I have pretty much no idea what they're saying, or even if they want me here!*

After cake and coffee, Manfred disappeared for five very long minutes. Scott and Margareta occupied themselves tracing the woven patterns in the white table cloth with their fingers. Occasionally they made unintentional eye contact and smiled stiffly at each other. Young Sabina sat beside him, staring impudently. Her face was expressionless and her eyes were fixated on him.

You're being amazingly rude!! Scott said to himself, feeling totally uncomfortable. *Stop it!!!* He threw a brief scowl in her direction, but she continued her audacious glare. Sabina seemed to have no clue that staring was rude, or if she did know she truly didn't give a shit!

Scott muttered under his breath in English, "She's probably thinking, 'Stupid fucker, can't even talk'".

He noticed for the first time that the radio was playing in the background, and it was that damn song again! *"Immer jeden Dienstag, kommst Du in meinem Sinn..."* Always every Tuesday, you come into my mind...

"Heute Deinstag!" he said to Margareta with an awkward smile. Today Tuesday.

"Ja... Mindy und Kurt" replied Margareta, nodding her head up and down a few times without smiling. She let out an uneasy sigh. *"Kommst Du in meinem Sinn."* You come into my mind. Scott wondered what she meant by that.

Thank God, Manfred came through the front door just then! A tall thin man was right behind him. Manfred looked back at the man, pointed at Scott, and said, "Wolfgang".

Then, he looked at Scott, pointed at the man, and said, "Wilhelm".

"I can some English," Wilhelm said as he shook Scott's hand. "Manfred, he ask me... translate. Okay for you?"

"Oh, good!!" Scott was very relieved, but he wondered how much help "I can some English" would actually be.

Manfred poured a large mug of cold beer for Wilhelm and the three of them sat down at the table. Manfred spoke a few sentences to Wilhelm in German and then gestured toward Scott.

Wilhelm slowly lit a cigarette and exhaled the first big puff in a billowing cloud of white smoke. He took a few gulps of his beer, glanced briefly at Scott, and stared pensively at the table cloth for a few moments.

"Manfred... He tell me, when he say you bye-bye... you boy at train station... he cry, much sad," Wilhelm said. It was definitely broken English, maybe even shattered. "Every day he think you, and he very sad... he think he never see you again... many years sad... many times cry."

Scott shivered a moment and he blushed. It occurred to him that he had been so completely absorbed in the excitement of riding a train that he never said goodbye to Manfred! He inhaled deeply and let it out with a whoosh between his flattened lips.

"I missed you," Scott said to Manfred. His voice cracked.

Wilhelm translated.

Manfred spoke with his eyes on Scott, occasionally glancing sideways at Wilhelm.

Wilhelm translated more. "Manfred say... your mother... she die... uh... *Krebs, wie heisst das?!*... uh... yes, uh... cancer."

"I know," replied Scott very quietly. That was one of the few things Mrs. Bruce had been willing to share about his past.

Manfred stared at the floor intensely, choosing his words very carefully.

Wilhelm tipped his face back and gulped down more beer. He wiped his lips with the back of his hand, glimpsed at Scott, took a deep breath, and then went on.

"Mother, she *schwanger*... uhhhhhhh... pregnant... baby number two... Your father, he beat her many times, many days... she not want more baby from him..." Wilhelm glanced inquisitively at Manfred who then repeated the last of what he had told him.

"Ah..." Wilhelm belched loudly into his closed fist. "So... she make abor... abortion... self... metal clothes hanger... much blood... never heal... become *Krebs*, uh, cancer..."

Holy shit! That I didn't know, thought Scott. He imagined Mama with her legs spread far apart in the air, panting and sweating, her hands shaking, sticking a wire hanger through her vagina up into her uterus.

Mama. Holy shit! You must have been incredibly scared and alone! A chill ran through his crotch, and his heart ached for her.

Wilhelm sounded genuinely moved now as he continued translating. "Your mother... she know for one year she will die... she sign papers so you go *Kinderheim*... uh... orphanage."

Wilhelm put his cigarette out in the ashtray. "Papers say your father... not allow to take you... mother never marry him... Papers say only American can adopt you... Germany very bad after war... she think you live much better America."

Wilhelm paused to watch Manfred pour him another beer, and then he proceeded. "Manfred say he hate your father... Manfred say your father kill her... from many times beat her... from make her pregnant."

Scott felt nauseous. He shivered.

"I remember watching my father beat my mother often," Scott said in a shaky voice, looking directly at his cousin. "I remember screaming at him, trying to stop him, and being shoved against the wall. I hated him too!!"

"Ja," Manfred muttered after he heard the translation. Manfred stared at the floor a few moments, then spoke again through Wilhelm.

"Manfred, he ask, have you more remembering?" Wilhelm queried.

"You mean, do I have more memories?" asked Scott.

"Ah, yes, memories," replied Wilhelm.

"I remember that a very large stinky lady took me on the train, and she was dressed all in white," Scott said softly.

Manfred nodded and smiled as Wilhelm translated Scott's words.

"I remember Mama going crazy because some boys from your soccer team came to our house to say you broke your leg. Mama acted like you had died!" Scott kept his eyes on cousin Manfred to observe his reactions.

Manfred clearly looked amazed that Scott had remembered his broken leg.

"You told me many times that, from our cellar windows, you watched the American and English bombs exploding in Mannheim. That you and Mama saw piles of dead bodies whenever you went into the city," said Scott.

Scott thought for a moment and then continued. "I remember that you moved out of our apartment to go live with the man who worked at the newspaper, you were his apprentice."

Wilhelm was enthusiastic now. "Manfred say you remember much! He surprise, you remember very much!"

Scott looked at cousin Manfred and said in English, "My memories were the only thing I had to hang on to".

* * *

"Immer jeden Dienstag, kommst Du in meinem Sinn..." Scott could hear the radio playing on the other side of the townhouse door.

"That was Mindy and Kurt with *Immer Jeden Dienstag,"* said the DJ stiffly in German.

Always every Tuesday, you come into my mind. *And, it's Tuesday again, fuckers! Pretty weird!!* Scott noticed his hand was shaking as he pressed the doorbell. He wiped the sweat off his forehead and upper lip and took a deep breath.

A short brunette lady pulled open the heavy front door and screamed!

"Wolfi!!" the short lady shrieked. *"Ich kenn' Dich sofort!"* She grabbed Scott aggressively, locked her arms around his waist and pushed her ample breasts against his stomach. Then she looked up at him with love in her eyes and a huge grin, and gushed, *"Wolfi!!"*

I recognize you immediately, she had said. More and more of Scott's high school German was coming back to him after the past week of immersion in the language. But, he didn't recognize her.

"Monika, let 'ze boys greet each uzzer," said a short man in English with a thick accent as he walked towards them.

"Wolfgang," the little man said, pointing at Scott's chest and grinning from ear to ear. Then he pointed to his own chest and said, "Werner!"

"Ah, Uncle Werner!" Scott beamed, and gave his uncle a big hug, then shook his hand. Scott was shocked that his uncle was speaking some English! That was totally unexpected!

"Welcome! *Wilkommen!* Monika und I, we are happy you come, Wolfgang," said his uncle enthusiastically and put his arm on Scott's shoulder.

Whoa, shit!!" Scott suddenly had another memory and his heart raced. *Aunt Monika used to crawl into bed with me and play naked! Holy shit! And, she's my Uncle Werner's wife!* Scott wondered if his uncle ever suspected anything, if he ever knew. Scott's face turned red. He felt like he'd just been busted for being a bad boy.

Standing behind Uncle Werner in the dimly-lit dining room was the silhouette of another short man. The figure took a long drag off a cigarette and his face lit up from the red glow. Scott shivered again, *that must be him!*

Scott didn't recognize him even when his face came into the living room light. The man put his hand out for Scott to shake.

"Paps," said the man in a faint gravelly voice. He pointed at his own chest, and then let out a harsh cough.

Paps?!" thought Scott. *I never called you Paps, I called you Papa.* Scott looked Papa in the eyes for only the briefest moment, and then felt nauseous and had to look away.

You fucking asshole! Scott's mind was reeling. He could still hear the vicious *Thoomp!! Thoomp!! Thoomp!!* sounds of Papa's fists slamming into Mama's breasts and face. *I hate you!!! You killed my Mama!!!*

Papa noticed that Scott couldn't make eye contact. He gave Scott a very awkward self-conscious smile and sucked on his cigarette.

Scott wasn't able to hide his scowl when he did look in Papa's direction. *My aunt and uncle act as if they have no clue that you used to beat the shit out of my Mama! What the fuck?!*

"Come!" said Aunt Monika waving her arm. She led them all downstairs to the party room, where she had laid out a spread of pink-colored lox on buttered kaiser-roll halves, several delicious-looking cheeses and more bread, celery-root salad, and lots of beer.

"Wie alt bist du?" Papa smacked his lips disgustingly as he chewed a huge mouthful of lox. He pushed his thick glasses higher with the knuckle of his index finger and lifted his chin inquisitively towards Scott.

Wie alt bist du? How old am I?! thought Scott. *You're my fucking father and you don't even know how old I am?! What a cunt!!* Scott glared at Papa in disbelief before he could answer.

"Twenty-three," Scott finally replied quietly in German. He stared into his beer mug as he took a big swig.

"Seventeen years! I missed you!!" Aunt Monika said in German. She slammed her beer mug down, walked over to where Scott was sitting and wrapped her arms around him passionately once more. She pulled his head into her considerable breasts, and Scott felt quite embarrassed again. He couldn't see Uncle Werner past her powdery-rose-smelling breasts, but Scott hoped very much that Werner wasn't pissed off about Monika's affection for Scott.

When she released him, Scott turned bright red and couldn't make eye contact with anyone, especially not Uncle Werner. Scott stared at the floor and grunted as he struggled to chew a big bite of kaiser roll with lox, which was one of his favorite things from childhood!

"Eat that son of a bitch!" gushed Uncle Werner in English with a huge grin! He had noticed Scott's awkwardness, emotional vulnerability, and his sweaty face, and had hoped to make him laugh.

Scott giggled, covering his mouth to prevent spitting lox all over, and gave Werner a thumbs up.

"Wolfgang! Look!" Uncle Werner swallowed a big bite of lox roll, and then took a large gulp of beer. "The fish swim!"

He took a second bite of lox, pointed to his stomach and dramatically chugged some more beer. "The fish swim!!" he said again, and then exploded into a huge laugh!

Scott laughed loudly too. He didn't actually find the joke funny, but Werner's performance was so damned cute that it really cracked him up! And, he felt hugely relieved that his uncle did not seem suspicious of what Scott had done with Monika as a kid!

"Wolfgang!!" said Werner. He looked Scott warmly in the eyes.

"Wolfgang!!" his uncle said again and raised his beer mug like he was making a toast.

"Ja, Werner?!" answered Scott playfully.

"Wolfgang!! I nevah forget you!!" beamed his uncle with a thick accent. "I nevah forget you, Wolfgang!!"

Suddenly Scott's heart was beautifully full, knowing that Uncle Werner had always thought about him, had never forgotten him. Scott felt genuinely loved, like he actually belonged here! Like he actually had a family!

I love this guy!!" Scott thought to himself as he grinned hugely back at Werner and tears welled up in his eyes.

"*Danke!* - thank you!" he was finally able to say.

Werner noticed how emotional Scott was, and he leaned over to tenderly put his arm around Scott's shoulder.

"Uncle Werner," Scott asked after he took another big swallow from his beer and wiped his eyes. "Why can you speak so much English? That surprises me!"

"*Ah, ja!*" answered Werner. He continued in English with a heavy German accent. "All us, we must be soldier for Hitler in war, no choice. American army capture me in Africa, take me to USA. I very fucking lucky, I spend rest of war in prisoner of war camp, Idaho, and Montana! Rest of fucking war!! For three years, American army feed me good, treat me good, learn me bad English - all bad words first!" Werner let out another huge laugh, lifted his beer mug in salute, and then sucked down three gulps.

"Your Papa, not lucky like me," Werner continued. "He Hitler soldier in Russia, Russian army capture him, make him work dirty coal mine every day four years. Danger, very dirty, very hard. He get black lung sickness."

Scott glanced towards Papa but again could not make eye contact, and he did not feel one bit of sympathy for this asshole wife-beater. Papa didn't understand a word of what Werner was saying anyway.

"Stand up!" Monika ordered Scott in German with a smile on her face. "I mean it! Stand up!"

Scott got up slowly, adjusting his shirt on the way.

"Buah!!" Monika bellowed and let out a boisterous laugh. *"Buah!!* Just look at you!! How did you get so tall?! How tall are you?!"

Scott felt awkward as they all looked at him. "I'm 6 feet tall, um, 183 centimeters. Why?" he said in German.

"Why?!!" roared Monika, still laughing and slapping her thigh loudly. "Have you looked around the room? Your Papa is 5 feet 5 inches if he stands on his tiptoes, your beloved Uncle Werner is only 5 feet 6 inches, your Mama was barely 5 feet tall, I'm your Mama's sister and I'm also barely 5 feet, and our brother (your uncle) who got killed in Italy was short! Your Papa has four brothers who are even shorter than he is! How did you get so damned tall?!"

"I think I needed to be big, there was no one to protect me." Scott had never known that his parents and family were all so tiny, and it had not occurred to him today until just now!

My family actually is the Seven fucking Dwarfs! Who knew?!

"I needed to be big," he said again.

The others nodded in silence.

* * *

Booooommm!!!

"Hit the bass drum again," said a faint voice through the big monitor speaker to his right.

Booooommm!!! Scott laid into the bass drum pedal once more and the huge speaker towers on either side of the stage exploded with massive sound which pounded against his body!

Fuck!! What an amazing feeling of power!!" he thought, grinning from ear to ear!

"I'm so glad you're here!" said Walter from the other side of his electric grand piano. He was sorting through some written music, but he'd noticed Scott's grin. "First gig! How does it feel?!"

"Fanfuckingtastic, Walter!" beamed Scott. "Thank you for turning me on to this!'

"Man, you're the one who passed the audition!" Walter yelled back across the stage smiling. "Thank you for being here!"

Scott was 31 now and six months ago he had moved back to Germany to find his roots. He was proud of himself for having become relatively proficient with the language, and had already begun to see himself as German again, at least sometimes.

But, at his first job in Germany he worked 16-hour days, 6-days a week, for a household goods moving company with a tyrant for a boss. He'd been completely exhausted and truly miserable for six unbelievably long months. *I fucking hate Germany! This shit is not what I dreamed of!!* he had thought to himself all day long at work.

Scott had brought a drum set to Germany with him, and recently he'd played a couple gigs with some guys he met who had a jazz band. Walter happened to be at one of those gigs and asked Scott to audition for his show band which accompanied recording artists at big-venue concerts!

No shit?!! Scott had thought. *Big-venue concerts?! That would be incredible, a dream come true!*

"I like how you play!! Can you read music?" Walter had asked that day. "Can you sight-read music?"

The Air Force band had required everyone to sight-read music. Even though Scott got out of the military ten years ago, he hadn't lost that skill.

"No problem," he had said to Walter very casually, but inside, he had been so overcome with excitement that he got tears in his eyes!

It looked like there could be a thousand people packed into this field, and they were getting antsy to hear some damn music! Scott was reading over the hand-written music notes.

Okay, 100 beats per minute, heavy 2-beat, he thought, and sang the beginning pattern to himself again.

"Okay! They're ready!" whispered Walter loudly at Scott. "You count it off!"

Scott's heart raced and his drumsticks were a bit slippery in his wet hands. *Okay... 100 bpm... 100 bpm... 100 bpm...* Finally he heard the exact tempo ticking in his head.

"Now!!" hissed Walter and glared at Scott with his eyes flared open!

"1...2...3...4!" yelled Scott, clicking his sticks together above his head. The speaker towers pummeled the crowd with massive vibrations as the band blasted out the introduction to the opening song.

"Ladies and gentlemen!! Mindy and Kurt!!!" yelled the announcer into his mic.

A huge roar went up from the crowd as a handsome brown-haired man and a beautiful woman with long blond hair rushed past Scott to the front of the stage. They smiled brightly and waved at the audience, then turned toward each other in their tight blue-sequined jumpsuits, and began to sing the first verse of the song.

Scott lifted his sticks high into the air as he played, smacking the drums and cymbals crisply, passionately, and loudly!! His grin couldn't have been any wider, and he really was playing his ass off!

Then they broke into the chorus.

"Immer jeden Dienstag, kommst Du in meinem Sinn..."

"Always every Tuesday, you come into my mind..."

Tears streamed down Scott's face and he was grinning radiantly.

Holy fuck!!! he thought. *I get to play music again, and my first concert in Germany is with fucking Mindy and Kurt, and that song I kept hearing years ago when I visited the first time!! Holy fuck!! Today's not Tuesday, but who gives a shit?!*

He glanced up from his music stand briefly to look at Mindy and Kurt's sparkling backs under the multi-colored flood lights and the huge crowd beyond them.

Oh my god!!! A humongous chill ran through his body.

I've been here before! he thought. *This is another dream coming true! I had no idea it was Mindy and Kurt when I dreamed it, but this is exactly the way it looked and how it felt!! Holy shit!!!*

He wiped the tears out of his eyes very quickly in between strokes so he could still see the notes. He was playing with all his heart and rockin' it!!

Fuck!! Look at me!!

Mindy caught a glimpse of Scott's huge smile as she was singing and dancing up front. She gyrated slowly towards him with her blond hair blowing glamorously in the wind. Scott glanced up from the music a few times to look into her eyes as she sang directly at him. She was also grinning broadly, as if she was saying "thanks for playing your ass off, dude!"

Scott, still beaming, briefly nodded his head at her to say "Thank you too!!"

Another huge full-body chill shot through him. He felt high, amazingly high, and happier than he ever thought was possible!!

Fuck!! Look at me!!

* * *

The streetcar pulled away from the South Frankfurt Train Station and was clunking along slowly, occasionally clanging its bell. Scott's butt vibrated harshly on the hard plastic seat. It was an old boulevard with old tracks and the ancient streetcar's glass windows rattled severely with every little bump. Autos, vans, buses, and trucks of all sizes weaved quickly in and out around them. An old woman sitting near him saturated the entire streetcar with her overbearing rose perfume. The air coming through the open windows smelled like diesel exhaust and freshly baked bread.

In the distance on the other side of the river Scott could see the tall Frankfurt TV tower which was right by his apartment. The tower, with its huge concrete shaft and big disc at the top which looked like an alien space ship, had become a very familiar site in the past year. He felt at home in Frankfurt and liked his neighborhood. Besides, it was only about an hour and a half from Mannheim and Hirschberg, where he had been born.

A blue Volkswagen Jetta passed them with an "I [heart] Frankfurt" bumper sticker, of course with a bright red heart. *Me too!!* He stuck his thumb up in the air to show his approval.

The lady in a silver Mercedes right next to him saw his upraised thumb and quickly adjusted her pink sweater to cover her cleavage.

Well, yeah, thanks for sharing, he thought, and he smiled when she made self-conscious eye contact.

Scott looked again at the tower across the river. Suddenly, a powerful memory flashed through his mind! His heart pounded! An intense heaviness took over his body.

Whoa!! This is another repetitive dream coming true!! Wow, I forgot about this one, where I live near a tall tower with a spaceship disc on top! Damn!! I had no idea it was Frankfurt when I had the dreams.

He tried his best to remember what happens in those dreams. Nothing came back to him, so he focused on what he feels during them.

I feel good, he thought, it *feels like I'm playing music for a living, which I am, and I like that a lot. But, I'm always lonely in those dreams. Yeah, well, shit, I am lonely today, most every day, aren't I? Life is life.*

The thought of his loneliness made him remember the excruciating feelings of rejection and abandonment from childhood and tears welled up in his eyes.

He was getting really angry too! *Dreams coming true feels like I'm a victim, like I don't have control over my life, like things are pre-destined and I don't have choices!! Makes me feel powerless, like somebody's fucking with me!!! I'm pretty sure that's the intense heaviness I get when I remember one. Fuuuuck!!!*

He decided to think instead about the streetcar museum where he was headed, wondering if that will be any good. Oh, cool - there was a sign, "*Verkehrsmuseum Frankfurt - 3 km*". Frankfurt Streetcar Museum. Getting close.

Now he was focused on watching street signs and he noticed a yellow one with a black arrow that read "*Neu Isenburg - 1 km*". To the right was a long red-brick ramp with railroad tracks on it.

Fuck!! A huge rush of energy shot through him again!

Another dream!!! Neu Isenburg and railroad tracks and dark red bricks! And, I feel her right now - the Neu Isenburg Girl, always dressed in white. She's been in lots of dreams, and she was with me sometimes in the meadow at the orphanage! Wow!!! Neu Isenburg.

Then the same heaviness hit him and he thought about how he absolutely can not handle feeling powerless!! *Fuuuck!* He shivered and distracted himself with looking at the tall high-rises across the river.

After a short distance, the tracks angled through a wooded area which then gave way to an expansive grassy meadow. Off to the right were two big round oil-storage tanks with staircases that spiraled up along one side to the top of each white giant. Not far from them were two tall white apartment buildings, and over on the far right was a big green soccer field. Beyond that were a bunch of white houses with red-tile roofs. The smell of fresh-cut grass and warm summer air drifted in through the streetcar's windows.

He looked at a small window near the peak of the roof on one of the white houses and thought about how that room must have a very steeply-sloped ceiling and that it's tiny, probably only big enough for a kid. Then it hit him!

Holy shit!!! Is this where she lives?! Neu Isenburg Girl?!, he thought. *Is it?! I think so!! This sure looks like the place I saw when we played in the meadow at the orphanage and that I see in the dreams of her! And, I feel like I've been right here before!! Fuck!! This is craaaaaazy!! Does she live here now?! And, who the fuck is she, anyway?! Fuck!!*

Even in the uncertainty of not knowing who she could be, Scott remembered what her love felt like in the dreams, and it filled his being right now. It was euphoric, familiar, comforting. Yet, she was always totally sad and lonely, and he felt that from her each time too. He fantasized now that he was hugging her, trying to make her feel better.

That warmed his heart and other things, and he got aroused. He imagined looking into Neu Isenburg's loving green eyes and down at her luscious mouth. He brought his lips slowly closer until they met hers and then he sensed her erotic tenderness through their softness. When he opened his mouth a bit, she erotically caressed the tip of his tongue with hers...

* * *

"I forgot! I can't chew gum on the air! Where do I put it? Scott, you want it?" Carrie asked as she pranced over to his drum set.

"Yes, but only if you give it to me with your tongue!" he responded, smiling mischievously. He stood up and moved closer to her, his eyes on her full pink lips. *She won't do it,* he thought. He wasn't even sure that he wanted her to in front of all these people! Carrie tossed back her black curly hair and looked him over for a moment with one hand defiantly on her hip.

"Alright!" she quipped, making it sound like a one-syllable word: "ite". She gave him a seductive bad-girl smile, ogled his lips, and leaned in.

"Well, yeah!" gushed Scott.

He felt her soft mouth tenderly caress his and smelled her powdery makeup and heavy hairspray. It was long and hard and it tasted like cinnamon; he quickly moved the gum over to one side of his mouth, and began to sensuously stroke her receptive wet tongue with his. In his imagination he was also cupping her silky naked tits, gently squeezing them, fondling the shafts of her erect nipples...

"Sixty seconds! Places, everyone!" commanded the TV studio floor manager.

Scott lost his balance and almost fell forward into his bass drum when Carrie pulled away to hurry back to her spot! His heart was pounding excitedly in his chest and in his groin too. Carrie looked back at him and grinned sheepishly.

"I can't believe you've never fucked her, dude! She's hot, and she clearly likes you!!" said Stefan, adjusting the strap on his red Gibson bass.

"I dunno, man, it's just not there. We're great friends," he replied, shrugging his shoulders and trying to sound carefree.

Stefan was looking at Scott's package to see if he had a hard-on from kissing her. So was Greg the keyboard player. Scott's face turned cherry red, but there was no wood in his package. Ever since he started dating at sixteen, his penis got gloriously hard making out with a girl in clothes, or when he was fantasizing and touching himself, but with an actual naked girl, a nude aroused woman, or if he thought people might see or hear, like now, then he couldn't rise to the occasion.

Scott still felt guilty that he really liked playing naked with Aunt Sasha, and with Aunt Monika back then. Even to this day he fantasized about them sometimes when he beat off, and then he felt totally creepy and guilty afterwards.

Fucking asshole Mrs. Bruce had told him over and over that men are just pigs who want to fuck and only fuck and who think about nothing other than sex, and that they show no respect for women. *And, fuck, the bitch was right*, Scott did think about sex a lot, a whole lot, and he loved it!! So, he felt guilty for that, guilty for always wanting sex, guilty for jerking off, guilty about having sex when he actually did get to have it, and guilty afterwards about having had sex. Sex was never a beautiful or fulfilling event, ever, but, fuck, he loved sex!! Have a nice fucking day!!

Carrie was practicing her dance steps, and his eyes focused on the smooth curves of her heart-shaped ass as it seduced him through her skin-tight black leggings. He sighed. His groin tingled.

Really good friends, no benefits. What the fuck is wrong with me?!

"We're coming back," announced the floor manager. "Four, three, two..." Silently he held up his index finger for "one," and then pointed assertively at the band.

A huge cheer went up from five hundred people as Scott and the band began rocking loudly. Lots of fans were clapping their hands over their heads, or gaping wide-eyed at the band, some were singing along, and occasionally some dude screamed "whoooooo!!" as if he was about to cum.

Hot young babes were gyrating their perfumed bodies, sometimes offering sneak peeks of bare titties and nipples through their scanty outfits.

This is a good time! thought Scott, beaming over the drum set!

Above and behind him, the lamps and spots suddenly burst into super warm and blindingly intense blue light! A dude with a big shoulder-held camera was kneeling below the hi-hat and aiming a close-up shot up at Scott. That lasted all of three seconds and then the lights and focus changed back to Carrie and the other two singers.

When the song was over, even before the applause and whistles ended, the floor manager waved them aggressively off stage. Backstage a line of about forty fans looking for autographs pushed and shoved to get close to the band.

"You guys hit number 18 today!! Billboard Pop Chart!" gushed a gorgeous freckled girl after Scott had signed her maxi-single. "And, number one in Berlin

Discos!! Number one!!" She smiled so big from excitement that she drooled.

"Fuck yahh!!" yelled Stefan with a thick German accent that made Scott wonder if he was doing comedy. You could never really be sure with him, he was a bit strange. Stefan grinned as he looked up from signing his name to a record, "I heard we've sold over 200,000 singles! Fuck yahh!!"

"I think hot young freckles here is more excited than I am," mumbled Scott, scribbling his name on vinyl records and various other things that fans handed him. "Does hitting number 18 mean that I'm really good now? I'm not actually sure if I am good enough to be here."

"Awww fuck, man, of course you're good enough to be here!" insisted Stefan, clearly annoyed by Scott's buzz kill. "You wouldn't be our drummer if you weren't good! You're kicking ass, dude! Look!! You're on TV!!"

"Yeah... I dunno... you guys are all really good," Scott murmured.

"Relax, man! Enjoy the ride, fucker!" said Stefan.

Scott, the good drummer, was definitely a bummer. "Enjoy the ride, fucker!"

* * *

"One, two, three, four!" Scott clicked his drumsticks together aggressively high above his head. He and the backup band started rocking out on the introduction to the next artist's opener. The gigantic speaker towers boomed with an explosive sound that reverberated loudly through every part of the domed stadium and pummeled Scott's body and face!

The huge stage was blanketed with racks of multi-colored flood lights, strobe lights, black lights, and laser lights, all glaring and dancing over low-lying fog. From the darkness high on the far side of the stadium, eight long spotlight beams skimmed bright circles of white light all over the grandstands, the infield, and across the crowd, like searchlights looking for B-29 bombers in the night sky.

Holy shit!! thought Scott. *Look at all these fucking people!! 27,000!! Standing room only!! Holy shit!!*

His arms and legs tensed up noticeably as the significance of that thought hit him, as he felt the immense power radiating from the crowd!

Don't fuck up!! he yelled at himself in his mind.

Oops, that wasn't working! He knew the tenseness made his playing lack confidence at this moment and that had to be fixed right now!!

Relax!! You wouldn't be here if you weren't good enough! Relax!!

Okay. That worked its magic - he'd been practicing his mindset a lot recently. Now his playing was smooth, bold, and powerful once more. A cocky smile crossed his lips.

Enjoy the ride, fucker!!

"Ladies and Gentlemen!! *Meine Damen und Herren!!*" shouted the Master of Ceremonies over the band.

"Dortmund, Germany... Please welcome... Jacob Schumacher!!!!!" He stretched the last syllable out for at least three seconds.

The huge cheer from 27,000 screaming fans actually overpowered the mammoth speaker towers!

A tall brown-haired man with an intensely radiant smile came bounding onto the stage, one hand high in the air, singing at the top of his lungs. Eight powerful spotlight beams converged on him, creating a brilliant white aura around him. He looked like a Greek god!

"Who the hell is this guy?!" Scott had asked Udo the guitar player after rehearsal earlier that day. "He's pretty good!"

"What?! You don't know who Jacob Schumacher is?!" Udo had replied indignantly.

"Dude! I know I live in Germany, but that doesn't mean I have to subject myself to German music!" Scott had answered, indignant to the same level.

"He's a friend of Johnny Cash, and he's been cranking out German country-rock hits for about 13 years. He's a household name! Huge!" Udo had informed Scott. "The crowd will go crazy for him - you watch!"

Jacob Schumacher was really singing his heart out! Udo had said he always does, and this time was no exception. When Scott glanced up from his music, he saw women, girls, and a few men all over the infield screaming and swooning over him, some crying their eyes out as they felt the magic and the sexuality that was Jacob Schumacher in person!

When the chorus of the song came around, many thousands of fans began stomping their feet in rhythm so loudly that it actually shook the entire stadium!! Each thundering stomp sounded like an exploding bomb!

"Hey!!! Fuck!!! Are you feeling that?!!" yelled Udo without missing a note. "The ground is moving! The whole fucking stadium is moving!!"

"Fuck!!!" Scott felt his drum set moving, and glimpsed quickly up at the stadium roof. "Holy Fuck!! What if it doesn't hold?!!"

But, the passion from the audience and the performers, and the magnificent allure of the rocking music were soon over-riding the sense of danger, and besides, the show must go on! Scott grinned broadly as he realized what mammoth power that thousands of people have when they move together!

And, it's MY hard-driving rhythm on the drums that's inspiring this massive force of 27,000! How fucking cool and awesome and powerful is that, dude?!!

"Fuuuuuuck!!!" he screamed again, but this time beaming with joy and awe!! Scott was having the time of his life!

When the song ended, the massive crowd went absolutely nuts with applause, screams, and whistles, as they did for every song after that! This guy was truly adored, and they loved his music with a passion! Following the sixth song, Schumacher sat on the edge of the stage and told a quick story about Johnny Cash.

"Hey!!" It was a very heavy whisper from the other side of the big ride cymbal. Scott pushed down on one side of the cymbal to see beyond it, but no one was there.

"Hey!! Drummer!!" The hissing voice was agitated and louder! Now Scott saw him behind the china crash cymbal, crouching by Scott's monitor. It was Jacob Schumacher's assistant sound man!

Shit! Did I fuck up?! What did I do?! Scott's heart was racing!

"Drummer!!" the sound man whispered loudly and intensely, as he moved closer. He was not smiling. "We end up working with a lot of drummers who aren't any good."

Did I fuck up?! Scott was really full of anxiety now!

"But, you're playing your ass off! You're great!" An exhausted smile appeared on the sound man's face. "Thanks for putting so much heart into it, for helping Jacob have a great show!"

"Wow!! Thank you, man!!" Scott beamed. His heart was full and he felt very high!

The next one was a slow song, and quickly many thousands of high-held lighters glittered and shimmered magically in the blackness!! The mass of lights reminded Scott of the most colossal Christmas tree that anyone could imagine, and this titanic Tannenbaum glowed and radiated love and power from the crowd with an intensity that brought tears to Scott's eyes!! He felt the passionate love from this enormous audience for Jacob, for his music, for the musicians, for Scott!! Scott's entire being was floating and buzzing with bliss and connection to Source and with love!

This is righteously incredible, motherfuckers!! Scott thought, as tears streamed down his cheeks. *Whoa!! Shit!! Can't see the music!!* He swiftly wiped his eyes dry between drum strokes, and continued playing with a most righteous grin on his face!

Wait!! I've been here before!! Deja vu!! Deja fucking vu, again!! Another dream!! Scott swooned just a bit himself now, but then immediately put all his focus on following Schumacher's written music so he didn't fuck up!

Scott was truly playing from the depths of his soul! Goose bumps rose all over his skin. The hair on his arms and the back of his neck stood at attention.

Enjoy the ride, fucker!!

Chapter Eleven

"No one ever claps here!!" Scott slammed down a thick stack of file folders as he rushed back to his desk. He got there just in time to answer the phone on the seventh ring.

"I called you an hour ago! I need the cost, availability, and shipping time on that rebar!! Can't wait any more!" It was Sam on the line. Sam was one of the company's high-rise project managers, and he was pissed off!

"Sorry, man, been workin' on four things at the same time, and people are waiting at my desk for answers," said Scott into his headset. "I'll call him right now, and call you back." Scott hung up and dialed out immediately.

"Volutski Steel, how may I direct your call?" sang the sweet feminine voice on the phone.

"Hi, this is Scott from Bergerside. May I speak to David, please," requested Scott. The line rang only once when she transferred him.

"Thiiiiiiiiiiiiiiiiiiiiiiiiiis, is David!!!" gushed a man's voice on the other end. He sang it loud and dragged out the first word. It was like the dude was announcing himself at a huge concert! Even after four years of hearing it daily, Scott still giggled sarcastically to himself whenever the man answered. The funniest part was that David was dead serious!

The moment Scott got off that call, someone stuck a long list right under Scott's nose. Scott had to back away to focus. It was Harvey, the owner's son.

"I need everything on that list by Thursday!" demanded Harvey, aggressively pointing his greasy finger in the direction of Scott's chest. "Everything!" He did not smile.

"Yep. Will do," responded Scott matter-of-factly, pulling away from Harvey's belligerent finger. He thought about amending his words with "you arrogant little prick," but Harvey was already waddling across the big office so Scott was saved from self destruction.

"You wanted to add, 'you asshole', didn't you?!" Jennifer said, having just witnessed Harvey's fastidious finger fiasco. She smiled.

"Busted!" answered Scott. "I was thinking 'arrogant little prick', but 'asshole' has a nice *ring* to it!"

"That was a joke, right?! Asshole - ring, round, right?!" Jennifer giggled and slapped him on the thigh. "You're funny! You should be an entertainer. Oh, wait. You were, weren't you?"

"I were," answered Scott sarcastically. "Thousands of people used to clap and cheer and appreciate me! You fuckers never clap!!" He smiled, but there was obvious pain in his voice.

"Why the hell did you quit?!" asked Jennifer.

"Bands kept breaking up, not enough gigs, too hard to make a consistent living," replied Scott. "Met a bubbly hot girl here in Chicago when I visited from Germany four years ago, went gaga over her. Actually quit music for her, moved to Chicago, got married, started working here. But I ended up being totally miserable without music, so I was a horrible husband, we got divorced, and I got stuck in this shitty job."

"Well. I'm glad you're here. You make my days brighter!" Jennifer said grinning.

"Yeah?! But, ya don't ever clap, ya bastard!" teased Scott, smiling but raising his eyebrows menacingly.

"Well. Maybe I haven't clapped yet because you haven't shown me how good you really are!" She looked his body up and down a moment.

Whoa! She just implied that I might be a good fuck!

Scott's face turned bright red and his hands were sticky wet as he fingered the phone nervously. He glanced at her chest and no longer had any idea why his hand was on the telephone.

Aw, man, she's too hot, she'd lose interest! My life is boring now and so am I! Fuck, I'm not any good at sex anyway. But, damn, wouldn't I just love to bury my face in those bouncy soft titties, thank you ever so much!

Her tall hard nipples were protruding out from under her thin white bra, and Scott could see the brown areola vaguely visible through her white blouse. He kept taking peeks at her breasts, and ogling the back of his hand on the phone, but he was too embarrassed to make eye contact with her.

"So, I actually did come over for business," Jennifer said, thankfully breaking the uncomfortable silence. She pointed at two work orders she had just put on his desk. "I need this aluminum tubing and this order of reinforcement bar from David at Volutski. Can you please get me pricing on those, and get the shipping costs to Manchester, New Hampshire?"

"Oh, fuck!!! And I forgot Sam!!" Scott spurted out. "Alright. Wait here while I call David." Scott was relieved to get his mind off her tits.

"Volutski Steel, how may I direct your call?" The receptionist had such a soft feminine voice, and really sang those words sincerely. For four years now Scott had wondered if she was hot, but he'd never talked to her.

"Hi, this is Scott from Bergerside Construction. May I speak to David, please," asked Scott. She transferred him and David picked up right away.

"Thiiiiiiiiiiiiiiiiiiiiiiiiiiiiis, is David!!!"

Scott had to take a moment to suppress his giggles before he could speak.

* * *

"Okay! Drop what you're doing!! Now!! I need fourteen 60-foot i-beams yesterday!" Good-time Harvey had just come racing down the stairs from his father's office. He was breathing hard, sweating, and again pointing his finger aggressively at Scott's chest! "Find out if your man at Volutski can get us that many today! Don't wait! Now!! Call me when you have the numbers!" Harvey snorted loudly through his glistening flared nostrils, and then waddled quickly back upstairs to dad.

Jeez, I hate how he treats me! Fuckface!! Scott wrinkled his nose, shook his head, and mockingly snorted loudly himself. His fingers punched the key pads on the phone irately!

"Volutski Steel Company, how may I direct your call?" It was that beautiful sweet voice again. So soft, inviting, and totally sexy!

But this time Scott was super pissed off and venting steam!

"Hi, this is Scott from Bergerside Construction. May I please speak to *Thiiiiiiiiiiiiiiiiiiiiiiiiiiiiiiiiis, is David!!!*" Scott belted it angrily, holding the first word out really long like David always did. There was no smile in Scott's voice.

The phone was dead silent on the other end.

Oops!, thought Scott. *Is she still there? Did I fuck up?! Did I piss her off?!*

He heard one deep wheezing breath. Then complete silence again, as if she had him on 'mute', but he could still hear her chair squeaking.

"Oh my god! I just realized you're trying not to laugh!" blurted Scott into the phone.

That did it! The dam ruptured! She let out a long passionate high-pitched squeal, and then burst into uncontrolled raucous laughter!

She infected him easily, and within moments Scott was wheezing and laughing his ass off too!

"Just a moment, I'll..." She couldn't finish the sentence, and fell into another round of adrenalized gasping, squealing, and cackling!

Scott was laughing so hard he couldn't breathe!

"Just a mo..." She tried once more, but immediately lost it again!

Holy shit, she's adorable and fun!!" thought Scott. *She feels fantastic to me!*

"Okay... 'kay... 'kay," she was still cracking up, gasping for air between the '"kay's". Then she exploded into another wheezing *heeeeeeee!!!*

Finally, she was able to control herself long enough to form a whole sentence. "Just a moment, I'll transfer you to David." she said in her professional voice.

"Oh my god!! Not now! Not yet!" objected Scott, laughing loudly.

Again, she wheezed boisterously!

"I need to find out what happened to you!!" asked Scott, pretending to be very concerned. "Are you ok?!"

She squealed and giggled once more before she could explain.

"Holy...   He   drives   us   nuts   with   his *'Thiiiiiiiiiiiiiiiiiiiiiiiiiiiiiis, is David!!!'*... does it super loud, every day, all day, and disturbs everyone in the office!" the receptionist said. "He's one of the vice presidents, and he's grumpy, so no one has the guts to ask him to tone it down. And, for sure, no one ever dared to ask for 'Thiiiiiiiiiiiiiiiiiiiiiiiiiiiiis, is David!!!' the way you just did!! God, that was hilarious! I really needed that today!"

"Wow. I'm just realizing that the only words you and I have ever said to each other in the four years that you've worked at Volutski have been 'may I speak to...', 'one moment please...', and 'thank you'. I had no idea you were this fun!" said Scott.

"I had no idea you were this funny!" she replied.

"Hey. What's your name? I don't even know that after four years!" asked Scott.

"Maria," she said softly.

"Hi Maria, I'm Scott."

"I know... I've heard," she whispered sarcastically. Then they both cracked up again!

"Oh, yeah!" retorted Scott. "Jeez, I love your laugh - it's delightful! And you've always touched my heart just by how very sweet and inviting you sound when you answer the phone!" he blurted out.

But now he felt awkward. "Oops, sorry. That was probably too much! I have a tendency to gush. Sorry."

"No! I liked it!" she responded in that angel voice. "Really! No one's ever said anything like that to me - that I touch their heart! Wow, that was really nice. *Really* nice!"

"I really mean it," maintained Scott.

"I know. I feel that," she said warmly. "I've always really loved hearing your voice. Wondered what you were like, Scott from Bergerside in Chicago. I had no idea you were a babe!"

"Whew! It's getting hot in here! You better transfer me to *Thiiiiiiiiiiiiiiiiiiiiiiiiiiiiis, is David* so I can get some work done," said Scott with a huge grin in his voice. "Can I call you later?"

"Yes. Thank you. I'll transfer you now." She had switched immediately back to business mode, but with that heavenly sweet voice.

In the next couple hours Scott called the boss's sweaty son with the figures on the i-beams, returned eight other phone calls from messages, answered five new calls, and submitted four Inventory Availability Reports for Sam's high-rise projects.

But he was barely able to concentrate; he could not stop thinking about that receptionist!!

What was her name? Oh, yes, Maria. Jesus, she felt good! Wow... I feel her right now... Wow!... His chest and abdomen tingled and he was breathing fast.

Feeling her presence so vividly was overwhelming and he couldn't stand it any more! He dialed Volutski.

"Yes. May I please speak to Maria?" Scott said in a very stiff and formal voice when she answered the phone. She let out another one of those childlike precious squeals and laughed with her whole heart!

"I knew you were going to call me just then! I felt you right before I answered! That's pretty strange!" she said in amazement.

"Wow, very cool!" said Scott, opening his eyes wide in disbelief. "I feel like I know you, like I know you really well, somehow... already. You're super comfortable to me! How weird is that?!"

"I know!! I get it, actually, and I can't even believe I'm saying that!" she responded. "I'm feeling like I've always known you too, and yet, all we've done is laugh our asses off together once. It's freaking me out a little, maybe a lot... but it also feels super good..."

"Tell me about you! I want to know you!" Scott spurted out.

"There's really not much to tell," she replied. "I'm twenty-four. I was born and raised in the Chicago area, here in Cicero where Volutski is. Had one short job before this one. My dad's a truck driver, my mom's a teacher. All very boring stuff. But, you, you're not boring!! *Thiiiiiiiiiiiiiiiiiiiiiiiiiiiis, is David* told me once that you were in a band that had a hit record. Is that really true?"

"Yup. That was in Europe, Germany," he said, laughing. "A one-hit wonder. We got up to #18 on the

Billboard Pop Charts, sold about 250,000 singles, and then died a tragic death..." He happily told her that whole story and a couple more of his music war stories.

Maria kept putting him on hold to answer incoming calls, but they talked and giggled and connected hearts for well over an hour. Scott was having a fantastic time!

"Thank you!" she said after announcing she had to go. "That was good for me! You give good phone!"

"I'm in deep squat!" Scott blurted out, while laughing at her joke. "I absolutely have to talk to you some more... a lot more! You feel so totally familiar to me!! Who the fuck are you?! Can I call you again?!"

"I'm all over it," she said warmly.

* * *

"What are you wearing?" Scott began breathing faster and his groin tingled. He was imagining her in red four-inch heels, black garter belt and stockings, no panties, and her naked breasts pleading to be fondled and sucked.

"Are you at home?" she asked.

"Yes. Are you?"

"You just called my home number, goofball!" She laughed.

"Yes, I did, goofball yourself. What are you wearing?!" he insisted. He imagined the feel of her erect nipples on his palms as he slid them lightly across the silky skin of her titties.

"I'm wearing the same thing I've been wearing the last five weeks when I'm on the phone with you!" she answered. "Red heels, black garter, nude pussy, bare tits. Exactly how you like it, fucker!"

"Yeah, but you're not actually ever wearing that!" he countered. "What are you really wearing?"

"Right now?"

"No, Maria, this coming Tuesday!" he retorted sarcastically. "Yes, now!! What are you wearing?!"

"Well... actually... I just took a bath... um..." Her whispering voice became sultry.

"Yes?!" A euphoric buzz shot into Scott's cock, through his nipples, his heart, and his tummy. He was rock hard. Her erotic whispering always put him there.

"Go on!! You know how much I love freshly-washed pussy! Maria!!..." Scott was begging.

"Um..." She took a deep breath and let out a lustful sigh. Now sex oozed from the words that her mouth and tongue formed.

"I'm sitting in a chair... wearing four-inch red spiked heels, a very short black miniskirt... no panties... no bra... a white satin blouse that's unbuttoned down to my navel so my bare tits are almost hanging out..."

She was taking short quick breaths now.

"I'm kneeling on the floor in front of you," Scott said in a low half whisper. His voice shook with desire and his heart pounded heavily.

"I'm resting my cheek on your right knee... grabbing and massaging the underside of your ass... you spread your legs a bit and I'm stroking the inside of your thighs with both sides of my face, kissing and licking occasionally... your miniskirt gets pushed up to your hips as you eagerly move your ass forward in the chair... you open your legs wide, and thrust your throbbing wet groin toward my mouth..."

She let out a long passionate moan.

Scott went into vivid detail about what he was doing to her in the fantasy, and then said, "And, while I'm doing that, my hands are stroking your velvety naked titties and your nipples..."

"Uuuuhhhhh!!! Uuuuhhhh!!!" She groaned and actually squealed at the same time. "Uuuuhhhhhhhhhh!!"

"You just came, huh?!" exclaimed Scott. "Fuck, that was fast!!"

"Don't embarrass me!" She giggled uncomfortably, then sniffled three times.

"You're crying?!" he asked.

"Yes," she whispered. "No one has ever turned me on so much! That makes me come really quickly and really hard too!! Plus, these feelings!! I get overwhelmed by emotions and feelings for you! You bastard!"

"Nice!!" Scott felt like a stud. "Maria... I have overwhelming deep feelings for you too! Like I've never felt with anyone."

"Wow," she sighed and moaned at the same time.

"Don't you think we should do this in person some time?! Face to face... uh, part to part?!" asked Scott.

"Um... yeah?" she replied. The pitch of her soft voice slid up as she spoke, so her response sounded more like a question.

"Maria!! We've been having phone sex for five weeks now. I've never felt so deeply close to anybody, ever!! I want way more!! Lots more!! Don't you?" asked Scott.

"Um... yes... but... I'm really shy, actually... I would be scared... I'm probably not any good," she answered very hesitantly. "I feel safe enough to let go sexually only because this has been a fantasy."

"Wow. Uh... honestly... I get it..." Scott offered in a warm understanding tone. "I get scared when I try to have sex in person, actually, I totally lose confidence. And, I feel guilty afterwards."

"You're just trying to make me feel better," she protested.

"No, really!" He paused, uncertain about how much to admit to her. But her gentle soul did make him feel safe somehow.

"I'm all fucked up in the head from being sent to an orphanage, like I mentioned before," Scott admitted. "I loved playing doctor as a kid before the orphanage, but I've never had much real sex, even though I feel like I'm totally sexual. I'm horny all the time, but I feel guilty for even thinking about sex, and if I'm with a naked woman I get scared shitless, even though there's not much more exciting in life to me than a naked woman!!"

"Wow. That's sad, Scott. I'm sorry for you." She sounded very comforting.

"Thank you," he murmured.

"Um... something bad happened to me too," Maria said very reluctantly. "It's why you and I have not met in person..."

"Wow! Can you tell me?" Scott asked. "I promise I'll be understanding."

"I know. You're the most understanding man I've ever met... well, not met. You're sensitive and more kind to me than I deserve," said Maria. "But I don't know if you can handle this."

"Maria!! Please! I can handle it... tell me!" Scott was whining.

"I'm scared!" she protested in a throaty whisper.

"I promise, I'll keep my heart open!" said Scott in his best reassuring voice.

He remained totally quiet for a while so that she could have every possible chance to speak, but all he heard was her anxious breathing on the other end of the phone line. He wanted to know her secret!! He wanted to know all of her secrets, to know everything about her! His stomach growled, sounding like an underwater lion's roar.

"Scott." She took a huge breath of air and let out a long whistling sigh. Then speaking very slowly and quietly, she began to share.

"I was in... a really bad accident... about six years ago..." White noise hissed in the background of their phone connection.

"A car accident?" Scott asked after hesitating a couple moments.

"Truck accident," she answered, again very softly. "I got crushed."

You got crushed?! he thought. Scott's imagination ran wild.

The ghostly hissing sound in the phone line made his stomach jittery, like the eerie music in a horror movie.

Maria's voice cracked as she continued. "The left side of my face is covered with scars... my head is shaped funny... I'm blind in one eye... I can't smell anything... I have a deformed arm..." She snorted quickly to clear her nose. Then she was quiet for an uncomfortably long time.

"Wow." Scott broke the silence. He was stunned. She always sounded so totally beautiful and sexy on the phone. *She can't be saying she's ugly, doesn't seem possible! Is she ugly?!*

"Wow," he repeated. Nothing else came to him.

Maria went on. "I was eighteen, riding in my dad's semi truck on a delivery. It was winter, snowing, and the road was icy. My dad lost control on some ice, we slammed into the base of a highway overpass, and the load of steel we were carrying came crashing forward and crushed us."

"Wow." Scott felt totally inadequate with his responses, but had no idea what was appropriate to say.

"My dad's leg was broken in multiple places, one arm totally crushed, and the whole right side of his rib cage was caved in," she continued. "A huge spool of steel cable tore through the truck cabin. My left arm and shoulder got mangled, and the left side of my head was crushed. My eyeball was out of its socket, dangling against my bloody cheek."

Scott took in a deep gasping breath, and in a very raspy voice he said, "Wait!! Wow! That sounds like a dream I used to have all the time when I was a kid!!"

"What?!" she asked.

"Yes! Holy shit!!!" blurted Scott. "I thought it was a movie I had seen, but then I kept dreaming it over and over. I watch this very sweet brunette girl with her family, and I really liked her. On her birthday she goes for a ride with her dad in his semi. The road is icy, the Dad loses control and they skid into the base of a bridge. Their load of steel cable spools smashes into the truck cabin and crushes them! I remember seeing her eyeball hanging out. I used to have that dream over and over!!"

"What?! No!!" she protested. "That's fuckin' nuts! It was my birthday! My eighteenth."

"Really?!" Gut-wrenching feelings were coming up for Scott, about memories of Maria in the accident, and memories of being abandoned by his family. His heart was hammering fiercely and his face was hot. "Are you brunette?"

"Yes," she answered, her voice rising in pitch like it was a question.

"Wow..." Scott took a long deep breath.

"In my dream, at one point she's floating by the ceiling of the truck cabin, looking down on her own mutilated body," he continued. "Then, suddenly she's back inside her body and desperately screaming 'Mama!!!! Mama!!!' A few moments later she's up by the ceiling again looking down at herself."

"How the hell could you know that?!!" Maria snapped.

Scott felt dazed, overcome by the incredibly intense feelings in these memories. He laid his right palm on his head, and was breathing hard.

"How in the fuck could you know that?!!" she demanded again. "I've never ever told anybody about looking down on myself from the ceiling, and I never told a soul that I was screaming insanely for my mom!! What the fuck, Scott?!!"

"Wow." Scott rolled his eyes. His rapid anxious breathing was the only sound for quite a while. She was speechless.

"Except for my cousin when I was really little, I've never told anybody about these dreams!" Scott paused to see if it seemed like she was receptive. She still said nothing. But Scott was now feeling fervently that he had to finally tell at least somebody about the accident girl!! *Maybe she'll listen*, he thought. *And, shit, this is totally fucked up, but what if it actually really is her?!*

"The girl gets rescued by helicopter and taken to surgery. I see her die on the operating table, and watch the doctors trying to revive her with a defibrillator. Then she's floating next to me by the ceiling of the operating room, and she asks me, 'who's the girl?'. I tell her that it's her!" Scott paused again, leaving space for her to say something, anything. Her silence persevered. He gathered his courage and went on.

"Then we both float, fly actually, to a long white tunnel that has a super bright light at the end. We enter the brilliant light and suddenly we're in a gloriously beautiful world that has the purest of pure white buildings and magnificently radiant lakes and meadows and trees and flowers. All the colors are rich and dazzling beyond belief. It feels to me like it's heaven, and indescribably euphoric love is emanating from everything in that world. Even the air encompasses us and fills our beings with spectacularly blissful love, and with happiness, and peaceful power.

And then, suddenly there's an intense explosion like a bolt of lightning, and she's gone, back in her body, and I'm watching the doctors from the ceiling again."

"Fuck you!!" snapped Maria.

"What?!" Scott didn't understand.

"Fuck you!!" she repeated harshly.

"Why?! What did I say?!" pleaded Scott.

"Fuck you! That happened!! I got rescued by helicopter, I died in surgery and they used a defibrillator. How the fuck could you know that?!" Maria seemed upset.

"Holy shit!!" exclaimed Scott, his heart racing.

"And, I *never* told *anybody* that I was up by the ceiling of the operating room watching the doctors, or that I asked who the girl was!!" Maria blurted out. She was becoming indignant. "And, I sure as fuck never told *anybody, anywhere, any time,* that I went flying over pure white buildings in a place that looked and felt like heaven!! I knew that no one would believe that shit, not even my parents, so I never said a word. What the fuck, Scott?! What the fuck?!"

Scott felt weak, incapacitated. His heart was pounding furiously and his body was buzzing with fear. *Who's fucking with me here?! This is impossible!!*

"This is way too fucked up!! I'm totally freaking out, Scott!!" Now her tone was aggressive, as if she suspected him of running a scam. "How could you possibly know these things?! Who the fuck are you?!"

"I don't know." Scott truly had no clue. He was panting, and his sweat-soaked shirt was cold against his chest. He shivered.

"I can't do this!" she barked. "This is scary, and this is way more fucked up than I can handle!! I have to go!"

She was replaced by a harsh dial tone in his ear. Scott heard the wind howling through the frozen void.

* * *

Okay. Here we go. She didn't know where they were going to transfer her. But I remember a dream where she's in the basement.

The top of Scott's shaved head tingled, and he scratched it as he walked down the steps. The moment he opened the double doors he was accosted by the foul stench of human funk and rubbing alcohol! The uncomfortably warm air was incredibly stale, even putrid. He wrinkled his nose up and breathed through his mouth to avoid the nauseating stench.

Fuck, I hate hospitals!!! He remembered visiting Mama in the hospital after she had been taken there in an ambulance. He'd been scared to death, and the repulsive odor of rubbing alcohol mixed with human rancidness had made him gag.

His heart raced uncontrollably as he walked, and his running shoes squeaked loudly on the gleaming green linoleum. His stomach felt queazy and he was nervous as hell.

About halfway down the hall he thought he felt Maria! He stopped. There were no names in the plastic slots by the door, so he wasn't sure.

Fuck, I'd be totally embarrassed if I'm wrong! he thought to himself. Scott felt a super high-pitched sensation and intense feeling coming from this room. *It does feel like Maria.*

He stifled his fear. *Fuck it! I'm usually right. Let's do it.*

"Maria? Is that you?" he asked peering over to the bed on the far left.

"You came!!!" Her full pink lips and straight white teeth formed a big grin. White gauze bandages covered her left eye and cheek. "Scott, right?"

"Yes, it's me!" he said, running a hand over the top of his bald head to prove his identity. He walked over to the bed and took her soft warm hand in his.

For quite some time, they were speechless. They held hands affectionately and gazed into each other's eyes. It seemed like having their first meeting here would be completely awkward, but it actually felt mysteriously comfortable. He felt her soul, her sensuality, and her deep passionate love for him, in the radiating warmth of her delicate hand.

"You're so awesome to come!" Maria broke the beautiful stillness. "Were you nervous?"

"Yes. Until I actually saw you and held your hand. And then, no," Scott giggled. "Were you nervous to meet *me*?"

"No," she responded.

"You lie!!" whispered Scott, pretending to be angry as he leaned forward. "I know you were! You know you were! Ya bastard!"

Maria squealed with delight! *Heeeeeeeeeeeeeeeee!!*
Scott's heart melted every time she cracked up. She seemed to laugh with her whole soul, uninhibited like a precious child, somehow radiating the love of the entire Universe from her depths.

"I'm amazed that you're so chipper!" marveled Scott.

"Chipper, am I?!" she joked, in a very bad English accent. "I'm on morphine... Otherwise, it would hurt way too much to laugh!" She pointed to the white gauze that covered half her face. "Morphine also makes me very sleepy... so I'll be crashing soon!"

"You look good, Maria. You're beautiful!" he gushed in a whisper.

"You look good, Scott. You're beautiful!!" Maria whispered back dramatically, like an old-time Hollywood actress. Then she squealed once more, very proud of her own humor!

Scott's heart was happy and light! That fact seemed very amazing to him, considering he was in a hospital. She truly was beautiful to him. The uninjured side of her face was gorgeous, she radiated burning love from her good eye, and the smile on her luscious lips was to die for! "So, tell me again what they did this time?" Scott asked.

"It was the seventeenth time I've had surgery," she answered. "Built up the cheekbone... below this eye."

"Will you ever be able to see out of that one?" asked Scott.

"No. Not unless I get a donor... But, that means I could end up with my own dark blue eye here... and a green or brown donor eye on the other side," she said, obviously straining to be lucid. "Too fucking weird... Like I don't look weird enough already... assholes!"

"Hmmmm..." Scott stared at the wall, not knowing what to say.

"Have you had many visitors?"

"No... I don't have many friends... My parents, brother were here, but mostly... I've been sleeping," said Maria. Her speech was slow and her eyelid was getting droopy.

Scott lightly caressed the back of her hand for a while, and then cupped her palm and intertwined his fingers with hers. He gazed into her radiant blue eye and adored her with all his soul. Silently, holding hands, they made love with their hearts. The clock on the wall ticked each time the red second hand jumped.

"I'm just going to rest my eyes a bit," whispered Maria.

Scott stared tenderly at her beauty. Even with her eye closed, and on morphine, it felt like she was loving him with all her being.

Soon her fingers went limp.

* * *

"I fell asleep on you, didn't I?" she asked.

"I wish you had! Uh, fallen asleep on me... uh, naked... on top of me," answered Scott. He held the phone closer to his ear as if it was her breast.

"Cheesy joke, dude," she answered.

"Be nice!" demanded Scott.

"Um... that does sound pretty awesome, actually... naked, me on top..." offered Maria, letting out one of those heart-moving childlike giggles!

"But, of course, you'd have to see me in person to be naked with me," said Scott. He was trying not to whine.

"I just let you see me in person, dude! And, at my worst, after surgery, high on morphine! Whadaya want?!" she protested.

"You and me. Naked. Making love with ecstasy. Fucking our brains out," he said.

"Oh... Well... now that you put it that way!!" She squealed again. Then she moaned sensuously.

"So?? You just saw me in person for the first time ever. What did you think?" Scott asked her anxiously.

"You're ugly," Maria answered in a dead-serious tone, and then was silent.

Scott's stomach sank down to his toes. His heart hurt. The phone dropped to his shoulder.

"Hey!!" Her voice was faint.

"Hey!!" Another muffled cry. Scott slowly brought the phone back up.

"Hey!! I was kidding!! Oh, my God!! I was joking, and I totally reeled you in!" Maria insisted. "I'm sorry! Really! You're handsome, Scott! You're cute as hell!" But, she was proud of her joke and couldn't help laughing still.

"Now I don't believe you," replied Scott. His crotch was buzzing.

"I'm so very sorry, Scott! Wow! I totally did not mean to hurt you. Gosh, you're sensitive as hell!" Maria continued. "You need to learn to roll with the punches, dude!"

Scott's solar plexus cramped into a painful knot and his throat closed tightly. He heard the thumping of his heart against his left ear drum. Each beat seemed to have an echo somewhere in the distance.

"I guess you actually do know a lot about that - rolling with the punches." Scott broke the silence, his voice cracking. "Clearly, you've kicked ass at that, considering everything you've endured, and I have a lot to learn from you." The hurt in his heart did not allow him to sound very convincing.

"Yup, you do." Her voice was intense, but somehow still sweet. "Ya know... because I look so fucked up, people punch me with their stares, they punch me with their hurtful comments and questions, sometimes they punch me by quietly laughing to each other, they punch me by not hiring me, they punch me by not wanting to date me or even be seen with me... I have to roll, and duck and roll, and duck again to avoid getting clobbered emotionally. You need to do that too, dude! You're way too sensitive!"

I've survived and done ok, fuck you, he thought. Criticism always devastated him. He quickly put the focus on her.

"I'd be honored to be with you! I've seen you in person now, and you're gorgeous!" gushed Scott.

"Oh, come on!" protested Maria. "I was bandaged up, my face was swollen, and I was fucked up on morphine! I was not gorgeous!"

"I found you beautiful."

"I find you crazy, Scott."

"You may be right... I may be crazy... But, I might just be the maniac you're looking for!" joked Scott, almost singing the lines.

"Yes, you're fucking nuts," deadpanned Maria, and was silent again for a few moments.

"I do feel like I've known you before, as if we've been intimately close for a very long time," she admitted reluctantly. "And that is really nuts to me, because I don't actually fucking know you! The way our connection is so vivid, how I know what you're doing and feeling at any given moment - that does not seem even possible! Totally crazy, actually!"

"You were my friend at the orphanage," Scott said. He was hoping to explain why she felt like she knew him. "I remember laying in the meadow, or in bed as I was falling asleep, and I would fly with you to the clouds. We'd feel their moist fluffiness against our bodies, and chase each other through them. You always made me feel happy and comforted and not alone."

"Alright. Speaking of fucking nuts!" Maria sighed heavily. "Get real, Scott! I wasn't even born then!"

Scott felt totally rejected, deeply hurt. Those memories were as real to him as anything else in life was real, and talking about them brought up overwhelming emotions.

"I remembered something else from my dream, " said Scott softly after a few painful moments of silence. He was hoping he could reach her heart again.

"Do I really want to know this?!" asked Maria, prepared to shut him off.

"I need to tell you! I can't hold it in!" pleaded Scott. "Please!!"

"Fucker! You're gonna to tell me anyway, so what choice do I have?!" complained Maria. "Fucker!"

Scott took a long deep breath and sighed.

"Ok... In the dream, the girl's head is wrapped in bandages, only her eyes are showing. The doctor walks in saying this is the big day, the day her bandages come off. When he's done unwrapping her head, her mom gives her a hand-held mirror. I see her hand trembling as she slowly brings the mirror close to her face.

Suddenly she lets out a piercing scream and she rages at her mom, 'Why the hell did you let me live?!!! I'm deformed!!! I'm horrifying!!!!' Then she violently throws the mirror down and it shatters into hundreds of pieces on the floor."

There was only heavy breathing on the other end of the phone line.

"Are you ok?" asked Scott. "Did you hear all of that?"

He wondered if she was about to hang up.

"Fuck this! Fuck this!!" Maria finally barked. "This is way too fucked up!! I'm sorry. WAY too fucked up!! You just described in detail another thing that happened to me that nobody else knows about! Fucking hell!! That scene with my mom and the mirror happened exactly like that, and I absolutely never told anybody!! I would have been far too embarrassed. But no, you... you know precise details of like five things that happened to me that I've never mentioned to another living soul!! Fuck!!! How is that even possible?!!!"

"I have no idea." answered Scott, almost whispering. He truly had no idea how it was possible, and even that fact was painful.

"Well... I can't do this any more, Scott!!" bellowed Maria so loudly that her voice echoed through the phone. "I could never explain this, I could never talk about this, or about you, to anyone, could never explain you to my friends and family. Shit, I can't even explain you to myself! This is just way too fucked up!!"

"Mariaaaaaa!" Scott pleaded passionately. He hoped to touch the part of her that loves him. But his heart was exploding.

"No!!!" she commanded angrily. "I'm done!!! Gone!! I am truly sorry... I am. I don't want to hurt you, but, Scott, this is way too fucked up and I simply can not do this any more! I have to take care of myself. For all I know, you might be bat-shit crazy!!"

Dial tone.

He felt incapacitated, excruciatingly alone, abandoned, like the first day at the orphanage. Tears came from deep inside his soul and exploded in his eyes.

Mariaaaaaaaaaaaaa!!!

The freezing wind howled in his ears. "Maybe I actually am bat-shit crazy."

Chapter Twelve

"You're not crazy, bat-shit, or otherwise!" said Laura with an understanding grin on her beautiful light brown face. "Really! You're not crazy, you're psychic, which is crazy to a lot of people, but you're not literally crazy!"

"I'm actually psychic?" asked Scott.

"Yes, you are!" responded Laura. Her shiny black shoulder-length hair seemed to bounce in slow motion waves as she nodded her head with passion. She turned her still-youthful body to the right and pointed to the wall behind her. The front of her white and blue pin-striped blouse separated between the buttons as she turned. Scott felt an intense rush in his own chest and groin as he saw her velvety tear-drop-shaped breast and part of its dark erect nipple.

Her nude C-cup jiggled a bit when her arm stopped at the top of her gesture, and Scott had to suppress a moan. She turned her head to face him again and saw that he was staring, but she didn't adjust her blouse. Scott's heart thumped as he thought, *that was very erotic of her!* But his face turned red when he realized, *she busted me! Pun intended!*

"Look," she went on, still pointing behind her. Scott looked up from her nipple to see that she was smiling warmly and looking into his eyes. He smiled sheepishly back at her.

"I know," she said in a soft but deliberate tone, and paused for a moment. Scott's face turned even more red as he thought, *you know I like titties?* He felt a drop of sweat trickle down the front of his chest. His heart was racing as she continued.

"I know the diploma on the wall says, Laura Santos, Master of Science in Psychology, but I actually have credentials as a psychic too. My dad was a native Mexican shaman in the Toltec tradition. It's the same ten-thousand-year old shamanic lineage that you read about in those Castaneda books. My dad taught me awareness of the psychic realms, and he actually took me with him to other realities, just like don Juan Matus did for Carlos Castaneda! Believe me, I know what psychic is, and you are definitely psychic!"

"I feel like I know stuff sometimes, but I don't think I'm an actual psychic," whined Scott.

"You are!! But, you truly do not know how to give yourself credit for anything good! No credit at all!" she retorted in a soft but firm voice. "We'll fix that."

"Scott," she continued, "you have no idea how beautifully and deeply you effect people! When you walk into a room, you light up the room and most every heart in it, just by being the sweet loving courageous and very strong person that you are! Those qualities shine brightly like spotlights radiating out from your deepest self. People usually find you fascinating and inviting. That's exactly how you affected me the first day you walked into my office, and every week since!"

Scott fell into the heaven of her dark brown loving eyes as he noticed that his heart was beating faster. He was embarrassed by her admiration, yet the delightful tingles he felt in his abdomen and groin, his heart, and on the top of his head, let him know that this angelic wise woman was connecting with his soul. *She actually does see me as amazing!*

"Look," proceeded Laura with wisdom and love in her voice, "you've made yourself very vulnerable, opened your heart to me in a big way, and shared a lot of exceptionally deep stuff over the past eight weeks, so I know you pretty well now." She took a deep breath.

"The biggest proof that you're psychic is the visions, the repetitive dreams, and the actual other-worldly experiences that you had with Maria 15 years before she was even born - 33 years before her accident! You knew details about that horrifying accident which she had never told another soul! Every time you interacted with her as your 'imaginary' friend, you experienced her across time and in a different world than the physical world. And, the person who is now the real live Maria gave you undeniable confirmation of the fact that what you saw did happen to her. That makes you psychic, Scott!"

"Wow." Scott sighed heavily. A slight smile appeared momentarily on his lips. He wasn't sure he believed her, yet he was fascinated.

"My shaman father took me across time, to the past, to the future, to eerie other worlds, and it was so intense it usually scared the shit out of me," continued Laura, leaning in close to him with a comforting smile on her beautiful face. "You did the same kind of a thing. You saw Maria's life in the future, saw an event that would change her life completely, and you experienced it with her vividly in your present time too!"

Laura was quiet for a few moments to let that sink in. Scott stared blankly at the floor, but his heart was pounding. The aroma of that mystical perfume which was always in the vision filled his being with a heavenly glow. He smelled it now as vividly as the first time, the energizing sensuous musty blend of roses, lilacs, and baby's breath. Every time he thought of her accident, or of her, that fragrance was there.

"And, jeez, Scott, just consider the fact that you were floating with her when she was out of her body in the truck cabin and in surgery!" Laura's passion caused her voice to crack.

"Then, even more amazingly, you actually flew with her to the light at the end of the white tunnel, and the two of you floated and played in that indescribably beautiful world you told me about; glimmering white buildings, glowing green trees and meadows, gleaming blue lakes, all of which enveloped you and pervaded you with glorious love like you never knew existed!"

Her soft brown eyes widened and her nostrils flared a bit as she magnified the already intense look on her face.

"Scott!! Do you realize what that means?! You actually went with her when she died in surgery!! You actually had her near death experience with her! You bet your sweet ass you're psychic!!"

Scott almost laughed but he was too overwhelmed by the feelings exploding in his chest. He laid his right palm flat across the top of his bald head, still staring at the floor. Tears filled his eyes and his body buzzed with a massive chill as he saw that world beyond the light again in his mind, and remembered that powerful blissful love!

"You and Maria both experienced unbearable agony and fear in your own lives, which caused you to somehow connect across time. You both were in desperate need of a companion to soothe your excruciating loneliness in the nightmare you were enduring, or going to endure, in her case. That overwhelming need caused you to open your souls deeply to each other through the portals of time, way back when you were young, and then again when you recently met in the physical world."

"Think of it," Laura continued with an excited smile on her face, "she remained your friend in the psychic realm for many years. You used your psychic power to take care of yourself by magically manifesting a comforting understanding companion! Maria was the only person from home that you could actually take with you!"

"You won't be going home any more." The orphanage Headmistress's voice reverberated in Scott's mind and sent an ice-cold chill through his body. He smelled the disgusting stench of poop coming from Frank's butt as he pinned Scott down and pounded on his face that first night. Scott felt the stinging pain on his body again, and the agonizing loneliness and horror of being abandoned by his family. He looked into Laura's eyes, suddenly let out a blaring yelp, and began to sob loudly. A bit of drool fell from his contorted lips.

It took quite some time for him to compose himself. When he finally did, as Scott looked deep into Laura's tender brown eyes, in that moment, he loved her with all his being! Suddenly he was grinning! Never once since the orphanage had he actually felt understood! And it seemed incredible to him that Laura knew his deepest feelings and darkest secrets, and in spite of it all she still approved of him! *She even thinks I'm amazing!!*

"Fuck... this is the first time... that anything... makes... sense to me!!" He could barely get the words out between happy sobs.

Laura leaned forward to hand him the tissue box. His skin felt the warmness of her body as she got close. Scott snorted loudly to clear his nose, and his lungs filled up with her delicious sweet perfume which smelled like Freesia flowers. Her scent and the heat from her body intensified the love he felt for her. He was light, he was floating, and his heart was glowing.

"You also said a few times that you've had dozens of dreams come true," Laura said warmly, her dark brown eyes radiating love. "You said that deja vu is a regular occurrence in your life. Right?"

"Yeah. Deja vu, how do you do." Scott was dismissive. He hated the fact that dreams coming true made him feel like everything is predestined, and if things were predestined then he didn't have choices, didn't have any power.

"And this experience with Maria is beyond deja vu!!" Laura ignored his attitude. "That's totally being psychic, dude!! Beam me up, Scotty!"

Scott laughed with his whole heart as he wiped his tears away. Right then he felt a peace and calm like he had never known.

"Your being psychic and attracting her as your friend way back then is actually the very thing that prevented you from going bat-shit crazy!" said Laura chuckling.

"And then, when you met Maria in real life, it literally put you into a state of shock because it just did not seem possible. And that, sweet Scott, is the very thing which made you finally realize there was no way you were going to figure all this stuff out by yourself. So, you conquered your fear and opened your heart to seeing a shrink! That would be me!" Laura beamed at him silently for a few moments.

Scott felt the glow of her love as he processed her words.

Laura took a long deep breath and forced it out quickly. Scott admired the softness of her puckering full lips. The alarm clock ticked persistently behind her as Scott watched her chest expand and contract for a while.

"I know you don't really want to hear this, but she's not in your life to be your girlfriend, she's here to play a different role," Laura said lovingly.

Scott's stomach jumped up into his throat and his body sank under the floor. Anxiety filled his gut.

Shut the fuck up!!! He felt like screaming at her!! But he didn't have the courage to look into her eyes.

"And, she just recently played that role for you, that different role," Laura went on. "Besides being your childhood companion, you brought her into your life now to awaken yourself to your own power! To awaken yourself to your psychic abilities, and to the fact that you could no longer resist confronting what happened to you. That was the only way you were going to finally heal - by facing it, by confronting your deep emotions and darkest secrets! Having her as your girlfriend is truly insignificant compared to all of that!"

"But, why can't we have both?!", he whined. *Shut the fuck up,* is what he really wanted to say.

"We fell in love!!" He hadn't talked to Maria since she hung up on him a few months ago and his heart was still in agony. His chin trembled and tears rolled down his cheeks once more. He snorted to prevent snot from dripping onto his lips.

I need a hug!! He felt Laura as he got another whiff of that delicious Freesia-smelling perfume, but she didn't move. He glanced at her chest, into her eyes, and then stared at the wall she was leaning against. His palm traced a circular motion on the top of his head. He winced and pouted.

"Sweetie... I feel how much you're hurting," said Laura in a genuinely loving tone. She leaned slightly towards him and smiled awkwardly. "I'm sorry. Someday you will understand what a beautiful thing she did for you. Really! Incredibly beautiful! Think about it, she sees herself as an ugly freak and she lives with constant ridicule and painful rejection because of how she looks. In spite of her overwhelming fear, she found the courage to open her heart to you and to share some of her most vulnerable secrets. Even if it was only for a while, it was still the most beautiful gift that she could have ever given you. Ever!!"

Scott gazed at the floor between his legs, hoping Laura would not notice he was still crying and feeling sorry for himself.

"Scott! You never even went on a date with her, never had sex with her except in your fantasies!" She searched his face for comprehension.

"In fact, you told me you've never been able to be uninhibited and allow yourself the passion and pleasure of sex with a woman - ever!! That's in spite of the fact that you think about sex all the time!" Laura's voice was full of love. "I'm positive this is because of the guilt you feel from having had sexual encounters with your Aunt Sasha and your Aunt Monika."

Scott's face turned deep red from embarrassment and his forehead was glistening with sweat.

Laura continued with love, "In your subconscious mind you thought that being sent to the orphanage was punishment for the fact that you liked the erotic nakedness with your Aunt Sasha and Aunt Monika. Even though they were loving and tender with you, what they did with you was child abuse! Sexual abuse, Scott!! You were sexually abused!!"

Scott laid his palm across the top of his head again. He had known for a very long time that his feelings were twisted and maybe kinky, but those times with his Aunts were his favorite sexual memories. He had never again felt so much love during sexuality. Never. His heart ached from loneliness right now.

Laura took a deep breath and looked at him with intense softness in her eyes. "We will fix that - we will get you sexually healthy."

Scott continued staring at the floor, his face warping from pain. Teardrops were streaming down both cheeks. His chest and shoulders heaved. But Laura's words gave him hope as they reverberated through his whole being: *We will fix that - we will get you sexually healthy.*

That would indeed be fucking awesome!! Sexual pleasure without guilt, he thought, *being able to receive... fucking awesome!!!*

In his mind he felt the smooth skin of Aunt Monika's breast under his palm, the warm firmness of her tall brown nipple against his cheek. Her scent of powdered roses filled his nostrils and he felt that familiar glow of deep love that radiated from her skin.

* * *

The bartender's elbows were propped halfway across the bar and she was leaning close to him, her wavy long brown hair right near his face. Her white low-cut dress draped down towards the bar and Scott could actually see most of her plentiful right breast from the top. Scott felt the warmth of her body radiating against his face, and he got a whiff of her patchouli perfume. He grinned as his heart raced from the excitement of how closely she had leaned in and from the sexual tingles that he felt in his groin and his own nipples.

Briefly, she glanced down at her own cleavage when she noticed his eyes were there. She didn't change positions.

"So? You haven't answered my question. How are you feeling?" she asked directing a soft grin at him.

"Like, right at this moment, or generally?" Scott asked her, looking up into her luscious dark green eyes and that magical smile. He did his best to stay focused there, but couldn't resist glancing down at her breast again.

She grinned and blushed a little this time, as she saw that his eyes kept wandering to her chest. "You're such a horn dog! I mean generally." She continued leaning close, grinning, clearly enjoying his attention.

"Well, Sonja, generally, I'm feeling pretty combobulated, thank you ever so much", he answered with a very serious look on his face. "Earlier, as I was setting up my drum set I was feeling rather discombobulated, but now I'm pretty combobulated."

Sonja stared at him blankly for the briefest moment, then shrieked with laughter and pulled away to a standing position behind the bar, her bosoms bouncing as her chest heaved. Then, beaming with delight, she leaned down close to his face again. Scott's serious appearance changed into a mischievous smile.

"You *are* actually nuts!" She leaned closer and whispered into his ear, her warm lips lightly caressing the inside of it. Scott's body buzzed with sexuality down to his toes!

They both laughed with abandon! But, now as Scott gazed deeply into her dazzling green eyes and felt her laughter radiating in his heart, he felt a powerful connection! An intense euphoria! It seemed like her soul had somehow entered his and was sparking and tingling and on fire right there inside him!

Holy fuck, you feel good to me! He heard the words in his head.

"I can't believe what I just felt when you...", Scott leaned in trying to whisper into her ear, but she interrupted him.

"Why the hell do I feel this deep connection with you, feel like I've always known you?!" she asked him with her loud high-energy voice and an inviting smile. "Who the fuck *are* you?!"

"Wow! I was just thinking how looking into your eyes makes me feel like I'm floating! But I hardly know you! We've only talked on the phone once!", Scott gushed. "And, yeah, who the fuck are *you?*"

*S*weat formed on Scott's forehead and his heart pounded. He actually felt overwhelmed by the love that gushed out from her luscious half-Asian eyes! The light scent of her patchouli perfume seemed to envelope him with adoration. His heart hovered blissfully somewhere inside her soul.

"No, I mean it, who the fuck *are* you?!!" Sonja insisted, with only a hint of a smile this time. "Who the *fuck* are you?!!"

"Awwwright," Scott said half-heartedly. His voice was high-pitched and uncertain. "Who am I? Ok, well, I wasn't always Scott. I used to be a German kid named Wolfgang."

"Shut the fuck up! Really?! No! You're just messin' with me now, right?" she protested.

Suddenly the entire room thundered with a massive wall of sound from a screaming guitar!! It was the raunchy opening line of "Smoke On The Water". Everyone in the place jumped in surprise and held their ears! One of the servers dropped a tray of empty glasses which shattered explosively onto the floor.

"Sorry!" yelled Dave as he turned around to adjust the knobs on his guitar amp. "It goes to 11!" he shouted to no one in particular.

"No, really, you were a German kid named Wolfgang?!" asked Sonja, fanning her face with her hand to portray her shock from the guitar.

Scott noticed her patchouli scent again, but then became aware of the pungent smell of beer and stale cigarette smoke which hung in the air in this place and in all nightclubs. The odors made him think of the bars that Papa took him to so many times. Scott's taste buds remembered the Spanish peanuts and the beer he sipped back then. In his mind he heard the jukebox music of the schmaltzy German singers and the *oompah oompah* of their bands.

"I was born in Germany as Wolfgang Ehrhardt. My parents were both German. My mom died when I was 6, she wasn't married to my dad. About a week before she died I was sent on what I thought was going to be a cool train ride, but that ended at an orphanage where I lived for a year. Then I was adopted by Americans who changed my name to Scott Bruce, and they turned out to be abusive assholes!"

"Holy shit! That must have been super hard on you emotionally! So much rejection. Holy shit!!" said Sonja in a completely loving tone. "Now I get it. We're kindred spirits!"

"Yeah?" asked Scott.

She pointed to the plastic name tag on her lacy white dress. "Sonja Wu. You can maybe imagine, my life too has been full of rejection because I'm half Chinese in a white country. Plus, I had a totally traumatic rejection experience living in Germany for a year!"

"Really?!" retorted Scott, giggling a bit. "In Germany?!"

"Yes, fucker, there are Chinese people in Germany! Even Chinese restaurants, you dick!" Sonja smiled but was clearly annoyed.

"Sorry. I didn't mean it that way, fucker yourself!" Scott shot back and laughed. "I meant that I don't meet many people who have lived in Germany! And, yes, I've eaten in Chinese restaurants in Germany! Fucker!" He let out another short laugh.

Sonja Wu had a sad empty look on her face now as she quietly wiped the bar with a white towel.

"Do you want to talk about it?" asked Scott warmly and softly, hoping he hadn't hurt her feelings. Sonja ran the towel across the bar a few more times in silence, then her green eyes locked onto his.

"When I was 13, I was a foreign exchange student in Germany for a year," she said quietly. "I stayed with a family where the parents didn't like me, their two kids were totally mean to me, and I was never so scared and lonely in my life! I was not allowed to go back to the US until my year was up, my German language skills were really shitty, and I felt defenseless, helpless, imprisoned, abandoned, insanely lonely."

"Wow. That's awful! Where in Germany?" asked Scott.

"Part of Frankfurt," she said, "near Neu Isenburg."

"Neu Isenburg?!!" he blurted. He remembered the powerfully deep feelings he used to get whenever he felt Neu Isenburg Girl. His body buzzed. "No shit? Near Neu Isenburg?!"

"Yeah. Why?" asked Sonja hesitantly, taking a quick glance around the room.

Scott thought of the streetcar ride through that strange meadow in Frankfurt about ten years ago, when he was on his way to the Frankfurt Streetcar Museum.

"Did you live near two massive white oil storage tanks?" he asked her.

"Yes!!" Sonja pulled her chin back and up in surprise. "How the hell would you know that?!"

"They were round, sat at the edge of a huge meadow, and had white staircases that spiraled up along one side to the top. Near them were two white apartment buildings that were about as tall as the oil tanks. Over on the far right of the meadow was a big soccer field, and beyond that were a lot of white houses with red tile roofs.

"Wow!!! What the *fuck*?! How could you *know* that?!" said Sonja, clearly shaken.

Holy shit!!!! thought Scott, his heart pounding. *What if she IS Neu Isenburg Girl?!*

Now he couldn't restrain himself, and at the moment he didn't care if she was upset. He had to know!!

"On one side of the meadow," he continued, "at the edge of the forest, was a streetcar track which went to a streetcar museum."

"Yes!! What the *fuck*, Scott?!" protested Sonja again.

"You lived in one of the white houses by the soccer field, right?" Scott asked.

Sonja took a long deep breath. "Yes?" Her voice slid up in pitch.

"I see you in a tiny white room with a slanted ceiling, like it's in the attic," Scott went on. "You can see Neu Isenburg through a small window and you sit there often and stare. The room is so small that your single bed barely fits between the walls, and there's no space for furniture except a dresser and a little white desk by the window. I feel like you're scared to death, crying your eyes out."

Sonja's mouth was open in disbelief and her eyes were watering visibly. "I cried myself to sleep every night."

Scott reached out and caressed her forearm for a moment.

"But, what the *fuck*, Scott?!" Sonja jerked her arm away and stood erect. "That's exactly what it looked like, even seeing Neu Isenburg from the window!! How could you possibly know?! What *theeee* fuck?!"

"I don't know." Scott said quietly, looking at the bar's countertop. A few drops of sweat streaked down his chest and he scratched there.

"What's even weirder, or I don't actually know which one is weirder..." Sonja broke the silence. "But, I feel like I've always known you, like we grew up together, Scott!"

"I know." He thought about telling her it was visions and dreams, but fear suddenly overwhelmed him as he felt the agony of Maria's rejection.

This time let's NOT say how I know!! Fuck, I don't know...

"What's on tap?" Two young guys plopped their butts down clumsily onto bar stools nearby, causing the stools' legs to honk as they slid on the floor.

"Call me tomorrow, Scott!!" said Sonja with an intense half-smile walking away. "We have to talk!!"

* * *

"I needed to tell her about the visions, couldn't stop myself! I don't know... it was the same with Maria, I thought just maybe she would have a memory of me, and I had to find out!" Scott's chin quivered and tears filled his eyes. "It seems totally logical to me that if my heart and soul were deeply moved by them so many times when I was a kid, that they might have had visions or dreams of me too! Why not?! But, fuck no,

Sonja felt scared, violated, and even pissed that I claimed she was my imaginary friend back then!"

Laura came to sit next to him and lovingly caressed his shoulder and back. Now Scott lost it and began blubbering loudly.

"Why the *fuck*... does this keep... happening to me?!!" His speech was barely intelligible. He sobbed intensely.

"My heart is with you, my friend, I feel your pain." Scott believed her. Laura's hand warmed his back and his soul right now.

"I know your heart feels broken, and this too will be hard to hear," Laura went on. Scott snorted and continued bawling from the depths.

"Just like Maria, Sonja's purpose in your life is not to be your girlfriend. She and Maria both have a far higher purpose in your life. Really! Far higher!"

Laura did her best to sound comforting. "Your friendship with them all those years was on a spiritual plane and it was absolutely as real as it was beautiful. But their participation was only in the realm of spirits, before they were born, so they are truly not able to have conscious memories of you in the same way that you have of them."

Scott glared at Laura for a couple moments, and then bellowed from his wet twisted face.

"Girls just don't want to be with me!! I'm a worthless piece of shit! I've never been good enough!! My real family didn't want me, my adoptive parents were assholes to me, and I'm a complete fucking mess!!" He sobbed uncontrollably.

"Scott. I understand why you would see it like that," Laura said slowly and with love. "Your vulnerable young self felt that you were abandoned by your family - you had no other frame of reference. And, yes, of course your emotions were powerfully affected by that. And then, on top of that, your adoptive parents were not only assholes to you - they were abusive!! You were abused, Scott!!

"I was?" he asked. His face turned deep red from embarrassment. *People who were abused are fucked up!!*

"You bet your sweet buns you were abused!! Scott!! Not only did your adoptive parents smack you around and punch you on a regular basis, they also constantly degraded and humiliated and emotionally brutalized you - they even forced you to drink your own urine just because you wet the bed!! You were abused, Scott!!" Laura gazed into his eyes. She was dead serious. "Abused, Scott!!"

With all his being, Scott wanted her to be wrong!! Shame, disgust, revulsion filled his thoughts. He gagged from nausea.

"So... I'm one of those... I'm seriously fucked up?!" Scott's heart pounded furiously and his body buzzed from fear.

"We're going to fix you for sure!! You're really not that messed up, Scott! We will get you whole again!" Laura's voice was full of optimism and deep caring.

Scott was not feeling at all reassured.

"But, I've told you quite a few times, we have to change your perspectives and change how you responded to what happened, so you can take your power back. And that means reliving certain events. It's time! We can't wait any longer, Scott!!" Laura was being gentle but very persistent. "I know it scares you...

but we have to go back to your first day at the orphanage."

Aw, jeez, now?! He looked at the wall behind her to avoid eye contact. His heart was racing.

"But... I feel like I barely made it through when it actually happened!! What if I don't make it this time, what if I do go crazy and never come back?!" Scott's voice cracked.

"Sweet Scott. I get it," Laura said soothingly. "But, remember that you actually did make it through, that you had at least enough strength and intelligence to avoid going nuts back then. Today, because you are so much more wise and powerful, you'll come through those horrifying events with flying colors! I promise you!"

Scott wasn't ready to believe her. His heart pounded. His shirt was wet from sweat.

"I'll be right here with you, Scott!" Laura reached out and held both his hands affectionately. "I promise, you won't go crazy! I will guide you. I will keep you safe. I promise!"

His eyes widened with fear as Scott laid back on the mattress and tried unsuccessfully to relax.

Laura's voice was super calm now, radiating reassurance and power and love. "Breathe deeply... just a little faster than normal. That's it... Really deep... little faster... keep breathing... keep breathing... relax... keep breathing deeply..."

After a while Scott felt light-headed.

"That's it," Laura said slowly, very softly, when she saw his body go limp. "Now you're in a pre-hypnotic state. Totally aware and open... very relaxed... You remember everything... vividly... very clearly... you feel everything..."

"Scott, let's ease into reliving this day slowly... it will be less frightening that way..." she continued lovingly. "We'll start with one of the better events. It was at the end of your first day, and in your mind you flew through the open window, out into the universe. It was a vision, or maybe it was a dream, but let's go there." Laura paused and waited for him to process.

"Okay," Scott murmured faintly. He felt Laura's soft voice touching his heart.

"Relax completely, now... keep breathing deeply... What do you see, Scott?"

Scott's eyes were jerking back and forth under his closed eyelids. Laura observed him closely, waiting patiently for him to relay what was happening.

"Oh shit!!! He's by the window!!" Scott screamed!

"The man in black!! He's floating by the window... Opening it!" Scott's eyes opened briefly, bulging out of his face.

"Now I'm floating... too... He's pulling me towards him!! I'm flying through the window!!! Fuck!!!" Scott's whole being trembled.

"I'm here, Scott! I'm here for you." Laura whispered. "Where are you now?"

"Wow! Fast... Holy shit!! I'm in space... flying... past Jupiter... I feel like I'm... part of the universe... hear sparks, see flashes... intense energy... touching me, inside me... I feel huge... massively powerful... invincible..." Scott processed that for a few moments in silence.

"What else?" encouraged Laura.

"He's flying next to me... I'm scared... pull away!... won't let me... feel nauseous..."

"I'm here, Scott. You're safe. You're in a safe place," Laura reassured him.

"Wow!!... see his face... creepy smile... big chills... Who *are* you??!..." Scott murmured. His shirt was wet and he was shaking.

"I am the Universe... I hear myself repeating after him... *I am the Universe...*"

* * *

"I *AM* the Universe!!!" he yelled, and slammed the car door. He looked up to absorb the vast expanse of blue sky, and he actually did feel powerfully huge in his heart.

Laura said in our last session that this trip might be really hard emotionally. Feeling large is indeed a most fine place to start, thank you ever so much!! he thought, and grinned.

"Okay, this is it, fucker!! A new life!! New me!! Fucking Scott is dead! Scott is fucking dead!! Dead!!" He barked the words angrily, but then broke into a boisterous laugh because it felt so amazingly good to *finally* be allowing himself to take his power!!

Sticking his chest out, he stood majestically erect, lifted his head with bold self assurance, and took a very big breath. A sparking buzz ran through his body, and his deep voice resonated loudly.

"I am Wolfgang!! I've *always* been Wolfgang! I AM Wolfgang!! *Wolfgang!!!*"

He walked slowly past the vacant lot that was directly across the street from their apartment. The skin on his chest and face stung as he remembered being smacked by that tetherball. The rusty metal post was still standing and the lot was still vacant, even after 39 years!

Wolfgang was grinning from ear to ear, his heart racing feverishly as he walked. Suddenly he felt like he was floating as a familiar and deeply emotional connection came back to him, a blissful heart-moving oneness with the scene ahead! He was unable to speak, but his thoughts were screaming!

Feldstrasse 21. Home!!! Holy shit!! Home!!! This is where I'm from!!

A few joyful tears ran down his cheeks.

Wow!!! I forgot what home feels like!! I'm a part of this place! I come from here!! From HERE, fuckers!! I belong somewhere!!!

Now rivers of tears flowed as his heart was gripped by the agonizing loneliness of all these years of not belonging anywhere.

Wolfgang composed himself and was just about to press the outside buzzer for Apartment 1A when he noticed that the building's security door was not latched all the way. Gingerly, he pushed on the heavy green door. It creaked loudly like a blaring trombone as it gave way. He walked in cautiously. At the end of the short hall on the right, he stood paralyzed, his heart pounding, staring in awe at the glistening white door of 1A.

Home!! Wow! Maybe they'll let me look inside just because I was born in there!

He knocked twice. No one came.

Then he knocked three times, and harder. Anxiety charged every short breath, his heart thumping in his chest. Still no answer.

He turned to go, feeling disheartened and sad. But then he noticed that the cellar door stood slightly open.

I used to play doctor on the potato bin down there! I have to go look!

He remembered that Elke had always wanted it dark, but Wolfgang had to flip on the light switch this time. In his mind, he felt Elke's affectionate hand against his palm as he walked quietly down the stairs. The cellar didn't smell like raw potatoes, onions, and sooty coal any more, but the moldy pungent smell of decades-old dust was totally familiar. He smiled brightly. *It smells like home!*

He remembered how he loved the scent of sweet chamomile soap radiating from Elke's skin, how it blended beautifully with the marvelous sweet musty smell between her legs. His heart glowed once more with the happy feelings she always gave him. He wished the potato bin was still there just so he could touch it and remember.

I love you, Elke.

At the bottom he walked over to the part of the cellar that was right under 1A. One of the chicken-wire storage cages was unlocked and empty. He checked both directions to see if he was alone, and walked into the cage. With his back against the cinder-block wall, he sat down on the cold concrete floor and looked up at the ceiling, the other side of which was the floor of 1A. He stared, almost in disbelief that he was actually here!

Home!!!

Wolfgang was already breathing fast from intense emotions, so he shifted easily into Laura's accelerated deep breathing technique. He had planned on it. This was his pilgrimage, his homage to Wolfi, his chance to reconnect.

His breathing followed Laura's soothing calm voice as he heard it in his mind, radiating reassurance and love. *Breathe deeply... just a little faster than normal. Really deep... little faster... keep breathing... keep breathing... relax...*

After a few minutes his body felt big and light. He was buzzing brilliantly.

Ok... be there, vividly... remember everything... feel it all... reconnect with little Wolfgang!!

He smelled potato pancakes and pork schnitzel from somewhere upstairs and he felt very much at home.

Mama!!!

Wolfgang remembered Mama's delicious food. He felt the euphoria that was always there when she wrapped her arms around him!!

Mama!!!

Just like back then, as he perceived her love right now, she made him feel big, strong, safe, and light! Tears of joy, of recognition, of familiarity, streamed down his cheeks, and his chest retched. He was floating, yet he felt huge! Powerful!

As he leaned back and continued staring at the ceiling, in his mind he saw himself in the corroded metal bath tub which had sat on the worn planks of the kitchen floor on Saturdays. He felt the tub's cold rim under his pink hands, felt the lukewarm grungy water enveloping his lower body. Wolfgang smelled Mama's lilac perfume as she bent down close to him to wash him with a cloth.

I love you, Mama.

He remembered that day when Papa brought him home very late and very drunk. Papa had taken him to the bar after work again. He heard the loud pop as Mama smacked the white bag of dark-chocolate toffee wafers out of Papa's hands. Then Wolfgang recalled his own screams and the horror that he felt in his heart as Papa beat her to a pulp in the bedroom. Wolfgang could hear the booming thumps as he watched Papa's fists pounding Mama's breasts and face over and over and over!

Wolfgang felt the agonizing fear he had while he stood on the front steps and watched an ambulance take Mama to the hospital. His heart was racing now as he experienced the anxiety he had when he visited her in the hospital. He remembered how he glowed when she reached up from the white metal bed and handed him a wrinkled old red apple. He grinned as he again felt the ecstasy that his soul had experienced that other day when another ambulance brought Mama back home again! He had been happy beyond description!!

Mama!!!

Now in his mind he heard the loud knocking on the door the morning that stinky Frau Limburger's large frame darkened the outer hall. His being filled up with hatred again as he remembered the stench coming from that creature while she was dragging him aggressively up the hill to the orphanage. He recalled how fiercely angry he had been that she wasn't taking him back home to Mama.

Mama!!! You never said goodbye to me!!! Nobody explained!!! You never said goodbye!!

Wolfgang's gut wrenched with agony and he wailed loudly now.

I miss you!!!

Mama!!!

"I... MISS... you!!!" Now he was talking out loud, but he could barely form the words between sobbing and gasping for air. "I've been so fucking... alone and... lonely!!!! So... fucking... lonely... Mama!!!"

Suddenly Wolfgang was aware of distant voices from somewhere in the cellar!!

Oh fuck!!! I could get arrested just for being down here! Breaking and entering - without the breaking - just entering? I don't know! Fuck!!!

He stood up quickly and squeezed himself into the narrow corner past a square post along the wall! He held his breath. Some shuffling footsteps echoed down the hall and were getting louder!

Fuck!! Did somebody hear me crying, talking just now?!

He inhaled quickly a few times through his mouth and then held his breath again as long as he could...

The lights went off!

Now the cellar was pitch black. Somebody slammed the door at the top of the stairs.

Yes!!! Thank you!!! Wolfgang took a bunch of huge breaths, and held his hand over his heart in an effort to calm it.

Fuck!!! That was close, he thought. *I'm not ready to leave. I wasn't done, fuckers!!*

He stood silently in the dark corner for quite a few anxiety-filled minutes. His heart was pounding. He remembered cousin Manfred and how totally scared he said he was when they stood by the high cellar windows and watched the bombs exploding on Mannheim below.

The high cellar windows! He realized that his eyes had adjusted to the darkness and he could now see some faint light on the floor. It was coming from the far side of the cellar, from those windows.

Yes, that's it!! I'll keep the cellar lights off, do my connecting and remembering in semi-darkness. If someone turns the lights on to come downstairs, it's my warning signal, and I can hide. Perfect!

He sat down once more against the wall and relaxed into Laura's breathing technique. Soon the blissful floating sensation came back.

Damn!!! The lights came on!! Wolfgang stood up rapidly and hid behind the post.

Not far away, he heard the metallic clanking of a key in a lock, the squeaking of a cage door being opened and quickly closed again, more metallic clanking, and then lively footsteps running up the stairs. The cellar door slammed shut.

Fuck!!! They left the lights on!!

Wolfgang liked his warning-light security plan, so he hurried to the top of the stairs and flipped the lights off. Now it was totally black at the bottom of the staircase.

Oh shit!! He braced himself by running his hands along both sides of the stairway wall. Slowly and carefully he edged each foot into the darkness searching for the next step and the cellar floor.

The moment his feet hit the floor, he remembered his repetitive nightmare of the man in black! Now he felt the terror of that dream again!!

His heart thrashed fiercely as he remembered the feeling of being paralyzed and lifted into the air, then forced down into the buzzing blackness below, directly to him!

My God!!! I was scared SHITLESS in those dreams!!!!

He turned around in the dark and looked up to the cellar door. A hint of white light danced under it. Wolfgang remembered how he used to play in the hallway between 1A and 1B. Right now he visualized little Wolfi laying on the floor up there, and heard him making engine sounds as his hand guided his red toy car. Once again he saw that fantastic view from the driver's seat, where Wolfi's imagination always put him, and he giggled!

Damn!! I was cute, wasn't I? Wolfgang had never thought of himself as cute.

In most every session, Laura had encouraged adult Wolfgang to connect with little Wolfi. She had him hold little Wolfi on his lap with his arms around him, had him reassure little Wolfi that he would never be alone again and that adult Wolfgang would be with him from now on, and had him tell little Wolfi that everything was going to be okay, that Wolfi would survive!

Wolfgang imagined little Wolfi sitting on his lap again at this moment with his arms enfolding him, just like Laura had walked him through in sessions. He felt the beating of little Wolfi's heart as Wolfi leaned back into him. Wolfgang imagined lowering his head, smelling the sweet freshness of little Wolfi's hair, and feeling warmth and softness against Wolfgang's cheek. He pulled him close.

You'll never be alone again, Wolfi. I'll always be with you, Wolfi.

Wolfgang's heart overflowed with intense joy as he said the words once more to himself, to Wolfi, in his mind. He felt little Wolfi's beautiful precious innocence and his love radiating through Wolfgang's being.

I love him! I love you, Wolfi!

Suddenly, for the first time ever, he got it!! He finally believed what Laura said to him so often!

I was, and I am right now, really fucking beautiful!!

"Wolfgang!" he whispered lovingly.

He gazed through the blackness to the top of the stairs and softy said his name again.

"Wolfgang!"

He was overcome with deep emotion as he felt this vivid connection to fragile 5-year-old Wolfi, and felt the agonizing pain of what Wolfi went through. He wanted more than anything in life right now to help little Wolfi understand that he was going to be okay.

"Wolfgang!!"

A high-pitched whimper trumpeted out through Wolfgang's closed lips as he tried to muffle his sobbing. He was bawling from happiness, and simultaneously weeping for poor little Wolfi and what he had endured.

"Wolfgang!!"

His torso heaved from crying, which caused him to lose his balance. He stumbled backward into the area where a few rays of sunlight came through from the distant cellar windows.

As he looked at the pattern that the dim light was making on the floor, he noticed muted light rays dancing across his black socks, his black shoes, and up the legs of his black jeans.

I do like to dress in black, don't I? he mused. *Still going for the pop star image!*

He pulled his collar away from his neck to look - yup, black shirt. He glanced at his arms - black leather jacket. He touched the top of his head - yup, it's winter, black stocking cap. From head to toe, pop star, completely in black.

Wait!!! Holy fuck!!! I'm at the bottom of the stairs in the darkness dressed completely in black!! Calling Wolfgang's name.

Now he was bawling and sniffling loudly, snorting through his nose as he suddenly knew.

It's ME!! I AM the man in black!! Holy fuck!!!

He let out an intense primal groan and buckled with emotion.

I AM the man in black!!

For quite some time he stood there in the gloomy darkness, completely overwhelmed and in tears, processing this incredible realization, hoping to bring some logic and reason to all of this!! And then, piece by piece, it began to make sense.

Wow!! I get it!!! The thing that terrorized little Wolfi in the dreams was what the man in black knew was going to happen to him!!

I was imagining little Wolfi at the top of the stairs just now, saying his name, reaching out to him with reassurance, and love, and visualizing myself holding him, just like the man in black tried to do in the dreams!!

Holy fuck!!! I was always so petrified of him! Now, it makes sense!!! And, it's beautiful!! He, me, was always trying just to tell little Wolfi that he will be okay and that he's not alone!!!

And it was all happening across time, across the Universe, with future me appearing vividly to me back then, and now present time me vividly visualizing me of the past!

Right now Wolfgang felt stronger and more powerful than he ever imagined was possible! He was light as a feather.

Laura keeps saying it's about loving ME, and not about a girl! I get it now!! My life is NOT about being loved by Maria, or by Sonja, or Alexa, or by any girl on the planet, not even by Heidi from the orphanage!!

Wolfgang looked down at his body and marveled once more at the fact that everything he had on was black. *Except my underwear!* he thought to himself, and grinned!

Laura says it's about becoming whole again, about finding MY power, about coming back to ME, Wolfi, Wolfgang, the man in black, ME!! When we flew through space at the orphanage, the man in black, me, said I am the Universe. Laura says I am the Universe! That's some impressive power and wholeness!!

Suddenly he felt Mama's euphoric love again.

Mama!! I'm happy!!!

He saw her passionate brown eyes in front of his face and felt the deep connection to her precious soul. Then he heard her singing in that soothing angelic voice.

"Wolfi, wise and powerful, will always find his way."

"... wise and powerful, will always find his way."

His skin tingled! At this moment, he really did feel very powerful, and wise too! He glowed from the depths of his being, thoroughly in love with Mama, in love with little Wolfi, in love with adult Wolfgang, even with the man in black, and passionately in love with life!

In his heart he felt the love that Laura always gave him in their sessions, and he heard her enthusiastic words again now.

Wolfgang, you have no idea how powerful and beautiful and wise that you really are!! No idea!!

He always thought that probably Laura didn't mean it, that she was being nice, just doing her job. But now it wasn't about believing her any more. Today he knew with certainty that Laura was right.

I am the Universe.

~ End ~

About the Author

Walter Zajac is a highly-respected psychic medium, and NLP practitioner, who has brought insight to thousands of people in over 40 countries worldwide since 2002. He has spent many years studying the great teachers of spirituality, metaphysics, the Law of Attraction, psychology, and has a layman's knowledge of quantum physics.

His life has been filled with verified psychic phenomena, a verified shared near-death experience, and hundreds of dreams and visions that came true.

Walter believes we are here on earth to overcome challenges (that's when we're the happiest), to experience contrast in order to appreciate the true beauty of who we are, and that we are here to love, to be happy, and to have fun.

Walter was born in Germany five years after the end of World War Two, and has lived most of his life in the United States. He currently resides in Los Angeles, California.

https://www.walterzajac.com
https://psychicwalter.com

Made in the USA
Las Vegas, NV
04 November 2023

80241426R00177